Cats in the Churchyard

and other strange tales

Edwin Hird

i

Thanks to Alex for cover design and other technical help and advice, and to Joyce for putting up with me while I wrote this book.

Cats in the Churchyard

and other strange tales

Contents

Cats in the Churchyard

Chapter 1

Bang! Everyone in the factory looked around at each other. Everyone except Gary – he looked up because the sound had come from directly above him. Bang!

"Look out!" he shouted. "Get out! Be quick! Get out now!" The other workers looked at each other for a split second, then ran for whichever door was nearest. Mr Richardson followed them, grabbing the attendance list as he ran past.

"Fire assembly point!" he bellowed, his voice almost drowned out by the noise of the factory roof collapsing. They were all outside, and he followed them to the fire assembly point where they were all chattering anxiously. He glanced around then looked down at the list. Everyone seemed to be there, but he would call the register anyway. He got halfway down and realised two people were missing - the office staff. He looked around for another manager and saw Mr Thomas, the chief engineer. He beckoned him over. "Carl, can you continue with this?" he asked. "The girls in the office aren't here. I need to look for them."

"No, Norman, you do this, I'll look for them. I'm a bit younger than you."

"What's that got to do with it?"

"I'm stronger and more agile."

"Ok, but don't take any risks." Carl nodded his agreement and ran to the warehouse doors. He cautiously stepped inside and look up to the office. There was a big metal roof sheet jammed up against the office door. He called up to the women and they replied. They weren't hurt, but they were more than just a bit scared and couldn't get the door open more than about an inch. Carl went back outside and explained the situation to Norman.

"I'll get the big forklift and see if I can move those sheets," he said looking round the yard. He spotted the forklift which a few minutes earlier had been unloading a delivery of steel and jumped in. He hadn't driven one of these for quite a few years, but he was confident he could do it. He called out to one of the forklift drivers. "Neil, can you give me a hand? I need you to guide me in; I can't see the front of the forks from here because the lights have gone.

"Ok," Neil replied, and he stepped in and squinted into the darkness cupping his hands around his eyes to try to deflect the bright sunshine. Norman asked the other staff to be quiet while Carl and Neil did this delicate operation. Carl couldn't move the sheet very far, but he managed to get it far enough for the women to squeeze through the gap, and he carried them down one at a time on the forks because the stairs had collapsed. There was a big cheer from the workers when each one reached the ground and applause and shouts and whistles for Carl and Neil when the second one was safe. The women rushed into the outstretched arms of their colleagues and the safety officer came over with the First Aid Kit to make sure they were okay. Norman eventually managed to quiet them down.

"Look, as you can imagine, there'll be no more production today. I imagine there won't be any tomorrow. I'll get some structural bods in this afternoon, and I'd be grateful if the warehouse chaps" he was interrupted by a shout from the back.

"And chapesses!"

"Well, yes, but we don't have any female warehouse workers."

"That's beside the point. If we *did* they would be discriminated against."

"But if we *did* I wouldn't have said 'chaps', I'd have … never mind. Chapesses too. As I was saying, if warehouse *people*, and when I say people I mean people of *all* genders, would come in tomorrow at, say ten, to see what we can do to rescue any materials and finished goods because I think a good part of the factory might need to be totally rebuilt, and we might need specialist engineers to rescue the machines. The rest of you can have the rest of the week off. Come back at nine on Monday morning and we'll review the situation." A few senior people gathered around Norman and Carl to discuss things, and the others drifted away in groups of two and three. Martine and Louise walked off towards their street, followed by Gary, Barry and Simon who lived just around the corner from them. When they got home, Martine invited them in for a cup of tea, which they gratefully accepted. The five had been close friends from school days and visits for tea were a regular thing. Martine and Louise were a couple, although lots of the older neighbours didn't understand that; Gary and Barry were twin brothers, and the four of them had been in the same class at school from starting as four-year-olds to leaving at sixteen. Simon was the younger brother of the twins by about four years, and the three brothers had lived together in the family home ever since their parents had died in a car crash five years earlier. Simon was still at school at the time, and it caused a lot of fuss. As he was a child social services said he needed to live with a parent, and they tried to have him fostered or adopted.

"We'll adopt him," said Gary, but his offer was rejected because he was single. "But what about Barry?" he asked, but he was single too. They couldn't be classed as a couple because they were brothers, and it was all going downhill quickly until Simon's headmaster stepped in.

"The boy has just lost both his parents, you can't take away his brothers too, it'll be too much," he told them. "Simon's a sensitive lad, and it would push him over the edge." They didn't want to listen until he pointed out that his brother-in-law was a local magistrate and his cousin was an MP. That made everything okay but making him a ward of his brothers created a mountain of paperwork, as there had to be essays written on why Gary would be the senior brother when Barry was two minutes older. Gary was the more sensible one of the two, and more willing to accept responsibility. Eventually it was all settled with the help of a local councillor who turned out to be the headmaster's best friend from university.

"Do you guys want a sandwich or something for lunch?" Martine asked while she was making the tea, already knowing the answer.

"Yes, please!" came the chorus from the other room.

"My bait's in my locker," said Barry. "But Mr Richardson wouldn't let me in to get it. "Said it wasn't safe. How can it not be safe? He doesn't know what I put in it."

"Not the bait, you fool," answered Gary, rolling his eyes. "Going to get it wouldn't be safe." The others all chuckled at this.

"Oh, I see," said Barry sheepishly. After a while Louise brought in five mugs of tea followed by Martine with a tray of sandwiches and some small plates. Barry picked up a sandwich and examined it. "What on earth is this?" he asked, frowning at the sandwich. Martine and Louise laughed.

"Eat it up. It's good for you," answered Martine. "It's peanut butter and coleslaw." Barry grimaced. Simon tucked in enthusiastically.

"No, it's good. Get stuck in," he told his brother. Gary started at the other end.

"This is good," he said. "What's in it?"

"You mean you can't tell?" Martine looked at him disparagingly. "It's jam and cheese and pickled onion." He looked at her askance then carried on eating.

"No, I thought I could taste jam and cheese, but wouldn't have thought of putting them together, but it's excellent. I'll have a go at making these at home."

"Come on, Gary," said Louise. "It isn't difficult, even for you." They all laughed and carried on eating. "You know we are vegetarians, so we have to do something to make our food exciting." The tray was soon cleared, and Simon picked a book up from the floor while Gary helped Martine clear things away.

"What's this book?" he said. "Folk-Lore of the County?"

"Yes," answered Louise. "Mrs Wood next door inherited a load of stuff from her great grandmother who died last week, and she was going to throw it out, but gave it to us instead, because she knows we are into 'unusual things' as she put it. It's quite interesting." Simon flicked through the pages, stopping every now and again when something caught his attention.

"Now this sounds cool," he said, reading one section about yew trees thoroughly. "If you run round the yew tree in the churchyard three times anti-clockwise at midnight you will see the devil." He looked up and grinned. "Shall we have a go tonight? We don't have to be up for work tomorrow." Gary and Barry glanced at each other and smiled.

"Yes, said Barry," but what do we do when he appears?" Louise and Martine rolled their eyes.

"No, Barry, I don't think he will appear," said Louise. "Not even for you."

"Not even for me?" Barry looked puzzled. "What do you mean?"

"Those things are for weak minded folk, mate," answered Martine. "You aren't weak minded enough."

"Am I not? That's the nicest thing anyone's ever said about me. Most folk think I'm not very bright. Or is that different to being weak minded?" The others laughed.

"Don't take any notice, Barry," Martine smiled at him. "You're a very nice bloke, and we're all good at something." Barry thought for a moment.

"Yes, I'm good at pool," he said with a smile.

"Play you for a pint tonight in The Arms," Louise challenged him.

"Ok, you're on." The five friends watched TV for a while, then Gary got up to go.

"Thanks for the lunch, girls," he said. "It was lovely even if it was a bit unusual. I'm going to do the shopping today instead of Saturday, so I won't need to rush back for the match. Anyone coming with me?" Simon got up, picked his jacket up from the floor, and put it on.

10

"I'll come with you," he said. "Barry can do the washing up while we're out." They bade the others goodbye and left. Barry turned to Louise.

"So you don't think we'll see the devil?"

"No. If he appears what will you do?"

"Don't know. Might poo my pants." They all laughed.

"It's a question of belief," said Martine. "If people believed it would work, they wouldn't do it. If you do it, you obviously don't believe it will work." Barry thought about this for a while, then decided against thinking too hard. He helped Martine with the washing up then went home.

Chapter 2

Louise went upstairs and changed her clothes.

"Where are you going?" Martine asked.

"The Arms. Got a pint to win," Louise replied.

"Oh, don't be too hard at the poor lad. Please let him win. It's the only thing he's really good at, but he's a really nice bloke."

"Ok, I'll let him win the pint game, but after that it's no holds barred. He can tell people he won a pint off me if he wants."

"Good. I might join you later, but this book is too interesting at the moment. The young couple are in love but I think the ghost is about to get them."

The Kings Arms was the only pub at that end of the town. People from outside called it a village; it was too big to be a village but too small to be a town. It had one small supermarket, two pubs, one at each end of the high street which ran the full length of the town, a few shops, and the factory which was the main employer. Ashfield Components Ltd made metal components for the interiors of caravans, which it sold to Greenhampton Caravans Ltd in the next village about ten miles away. It bought its raw materials from Thorn Hill Metals Ltd, about ten miles away in the opposite direction. Every now and again the owners of the three companies got together to talk about forming one big company from the three, as they were so interdependent that if any one firm failed the others would go under shortly after, but talks always ended acrimoniously with failure to agree who would be the senior director. Almost everyone in the town had a close family member who worked there, and there was always a vacancy for a school leaver. There was little opportunity for career progression, but the pay was decent and conditions weren't unpleasant, so very few left before retiring age. The five friends all started there immediately after leaving school. Gary showed promise and was being trained to be a supervisor, and potentially management. Barry was a 'gopher', fetching and carrying, moving anything that could be moved without a forklift, and Simon was an apprentice engineer. Martine and Louise worked in the office, Louise looking after accounts, invoicing and payroll, and Martine being the receptionist and Mr Richardson's assistant, and taking care of HR. Most of the people in the pub were factory workers, and they had to queue up for the pool table. Barry won the first game to great applause, as Louise was regarded as the best player in the town, and she bought him a pint which he drank while they waited for their turn to come round again. An hour later the others joined them, and Barry was quick to relate his victory.

"Well done, Barry," said Martine with a wink to Louise. "There aren't many people round here can beat Louise."

"Did she let you win?" asked Gary with a grin, until Martine's elbow caught him in the ribs.

"No," replied Barry. "She said I had played well."

"Well, you are the second best player in town," butted in Simon, catching Louise's grin. "It's reasonable that you might beat her now and again." Barry and Louise's turn came round, and she beat him by a substantial margin, then they retired to a table in the corner. Barry looked disappointed.

"Don't be down hearted," said Louise. "You would have won if you'd played as well as you did in the first game. I think the beer went to your head." Barry thought about this then cheered up.

"Next time I'm playing against you I'm not going to drink beer," he said. They all laughed.

Closing time came and the friends left the pub. They were heading for home until Barry stopped them.

"Aren't we going to the churchyard?" he asked. "I thought we were going to run round the tree." Martine and Louise looked at each other then turned to face the boys who were behind them.

"*We* didn't agree to anything," said Martine. "But we'll come along to watch."

Louise giggled. "Yes, we'll come along to watch you make fools of yourselves. I wish I'd brought my camera to take photos, if anything happens."

"Good. Come on then." Barry set off at speed towards the church. Simon called him back.

"What's the hurry? It's only half eleven." Barry stopped and turned to wait for them.

"Oh, yes. That's right. Well we can sit on the seat until it's time." He walked more slowly until the others had caught up then led the way into the churchyard and sat down on the seat. The seat bore a small wooden plaque saying the seat had been given by someone no one could remember of in memory of someone else no one had heard of who had died more than a hundred years ago. The others joined him. Louise looked at her watch.

"Well this is fun," she said.

"It'll soon be twelve," said Martine. "At least it isn't raining and there's a full moon so we can see. You don't have to stay if you don't want to. Look, there's only a few minutes to go." The boys stood up and walked over to the tree. Gary was struggling to hold his laughter in but he was doing it for his twin brother, so he tried to look serious. Louise moved along the seat to sit next to Martine and put her arm round Martine's shoulders. Martine glanced at her watch. "Ok, it's midnight," she called out.

The brothers looked at each other then Simon said "Go!" and they set off. Running round the tree three times didn't take long, but nothing happened. Barry was obviously disappointed and came back to the seat.

"Perhaps we need to do it naked he announced and started to undress. Martine turned her head away and covered her eyes.

"I can't watch; tell me when it's all over," she muttered to Louise.

"Oh, I'm going to have a good look," Louise replied enthusiastically.

"What?"

"Just curious. There's no sexual interest. I say, he's got plenty of equipment. But no, you're my type, he isn't." Martine turned towards her and they kissed passionately.

"Thank goodness for that!" Martine said when they broke for air before starting another kiss. They were interrupted by Barry returning to the seat.

"I'm getting dressed. It's a bit chilly and there's too many thistles and stuff," he announced as he put his clothes back on. The girls laughed as he struggled with his laces in the dark before returning to the tree. They returned to their snogging and ignored what the boys were doing. Bang!

They broke off and looked around. The boys were nowhere to be seen.

"What was that? Where've they gone?" Martine asked.

"Probably think they're doing a practical joke. Never mind. Fancy an early night?"

"It can't be an early night – it's after midnight."

"You know what I mean."

"Come on then, let's get home. Oh! What's that?"

"What?" She followed Martine's outstretched arm to see two cats, one orange and one grey. "It's just cats. Never seen them here before. Then again, never spent much time here. Come on, let's go home."

Chapter 3

Next morning Martine and Louise got up late and had a leisurely breakfast before showering and getting dressed. They did the washing up and put some clothes into the washing machine and set it away before settling down in the sitting room with mugs of coffee. Martine went back to her book while Louise picked up the folk-lore book that Simon had been so interested in and flicked through it.

"Some of this is quite interesting," she murmured, "But some of it is utter crap."

"What sort of crap?"

"Well, it says it's unlucky to see a new moon through glass. For one thing when the moon is totally new you can't see it, and for another, how does this luck thing work? Does 'luck' come floating in on the breeze and see someone and think 'That person saw the moon through glass so I'm going to make bad things happen'? And here's another one – wearing a new item of clothing and being pooed on by a bird brings you good luck – what if you're wearing someone else's coat? Does the good luck go to the wearer or the owner? It's twaddle. But there are some things like observing plants and animals to forecast the weather which I suppose could hold water."

"Yes, my granddad always looked at the plants and animals before making decisions about planting his vegetables and they always grew well. He often won the leek show, but there was a rumour he achieved that by burying a dead dog at the bottom of the trench six weeks before planting the leeks."

"But what if he didn't have a dead dog to hand?"

"He had a shot gun, so he'd go out and 'create' one."

"That's nasty."

"Yes, but that's the way they did things in those days. Is that the washing machine finished? I'll go and put the washing out on the line. It should dry quickly on a nice day like today."

"As it's such a nice day shall we go out somewhere?"

"Can if you want. Any idea where? And shall we invite the boys to come along? They're always a laugh."

"Yes, let's. And if we stop at a pub for lunch I'll thrash Barry at pool just to remind him who's the best pool player in town."

"You've got a vicious streak, you. Poor Barry. He was delighted to beat you last night. He'll be talking about it for months." Martine went to the door and opened it. There on the doorstep sat the grey cat from the churchyard. "Oh, look who's here!" She bent down and picked it up. "She must have followed us home last night." Louise came to the door to see what she was talking about.

"How do you know it's a 'she'?" she asked. Martine turned it over.

"See? No bits."

"I thought male cats hid their bits anyway."

"Oh, I don't know. I'm assuming it's a 'she' until proven otherwise. I'm going to call her 'Lady Jane' because she's grey."

"I think that's the wrong spelling."

"But cats can't spell so it doesn't matter." Martine put Lady Jane down on the path and went around the corner to the boys' house and knocked on the door. There was no answer. She knocked again. And again, but to no avail, so she went back home. "They're not in," she said, disappointed. "So it's just the two of us. Where shall we go?"

"Let's just go for a random drive in the countryside, find a little teashop for lunch, then just sit and admire the view."

"Good idea." Off they went, keeping well away from the towns, up into the moors and admired the view until it was time for a late lunch then stopped at a teashop. Of course, they couldn't leave without buying some souvenirs, so Martine bought some biscuits and a teapot stand and Louise bought a book about the history of the area. They arrived home at about nine and had some of the biscuits before turning in.

Meanwhile, the boys found themselves in a strange place. They didn't have a clue where they were, but it was pitch black. They couldn't see anything, but they could see each other. The last think they remembered was running round the yew tree, then there was a bang, then there they were, sat on the floor, surrounded by nothing. Simon was the first one to speak.

"Where are we? Any idea?" The others shook their heads.

"Haven't a clue," answered Gary. Barry opened his mouth to speak but didn't say anything and shut it again. Gary rose to his feet. "I'm not sure we are anywhere," he said. He stretched out his arms, then raised one arm up as far as he could. He walked around with his arms outstretched but felt nothing. He bent down and touched the floor. It was firm but not hard, and he couldn't tell if it was natural or man-made. "I honestly haven't a clue, but I

suggest we don't go too far away from each other for now."
Barry looked at Simon then back to Gary.

"Don't worry, mate. I'm going nowhere without you two," he said with a bit of a tremble in his voice.

"Me too," said Simon. "Where do we go from here?" Gary shrugged his shoulders.

"Don't know that either. We can't go anywhere from 'here' until we know where 'here' is. I think we should stay together but move forward slowly."

"Good idea, but which way is forward?" asked Simon. Gary turned his back on them.

"Follow me," he told them. "This way is forward, for now anyway, until we decide it isn't." They walked on, always staying within touching distance of each other, for what seemed like hours.

"Can we stop for a bit now, please?" asked Simon. "My legs are starting to ache a bit."

"Ok," said Gary. "Let's sit down and rest." They sat in a triangle facing inward for about half an hour, saying nothing. Barry got up.

"Are we ready to move on?" he asked. "I don't like this place. I want to get out as soon as we can." The others nodded.

"Er, which way were we going?" asked Simon.

"That way," answered Gary and Barry together, pointing in different directions. They laughed briefly, until they realised it wasn't a laughing matter. They froze. They could hear footsteps coming towards them.

"Can you hear what I hear?" whispered Gary. The other two nodded. "Which way is it coming from?" Barry and Simon both pointed in different directions. "Stay together," whispered Gary. They waited in silence. The footsteps got closer. Suddenly someone appeared in the distance. It looked like a woman, but they weren't sure until she got closer. She was dressed in some sort of armour which looked a bit like tortoise shell, with sandals laced up her legs, and flowing yellow hair. Not blonde, but yellow, and it flowed as if in a stiff breeze even though there was no movement of air. Her face was neither pretty nor ugly, and expressionless, with steely blue eyes staring straight at them. In her left hand she carried a long stick which she used as a walking pole. As she approached them, they realised how big she was; at least twelve feet tall but proportioned like a normal woman and with muscles that wouldn't be out of place on a top strength athlete such as a weight-lifter. She stopped about two yards away and looked down on them. They didn't know whether to speak first or to wait until she spoke.

Chapter 4

The next day Louise and Martine got up at more or less their normal time. Lady Jane was on the doorstep, so Martine brought her in and gave her some water to drink, as the weather had been very dry and there were no puddles in the streets.

"What do cats eat?" she asked Louise.

"Meat, mainly," Louise answered with a sneer. "Something we haven't got."

"Yes, that's what I thought. Do we have anything she might like?"

"You could try cheese. It's an animal product even though it isn't actual meat. Apart from that, I haven't a clue." Martine took some cheese from the fridge and crumbled some onto a saucer and put it on the floor next to the water. Lady Jane sniffed it and looked a bit disgusted at first, but after a few more sniffs ate it voraciously. Martine smiled, pleased at her success. "I'll get some cat food from the corner shop. I'm going this morning; we're nearly out of milk." Louise volunteered.

"Thanks. I would have gone but I intend to take advantage of not being at work to get the ironing out of the way. On your way give the boys a knock, just to see if they're all right."

"No, they'll be ok. They might be asleep anyway."

"Not at this time of day, surely?"

"You didn't have any brothers; I had three, and yes, they'll stew in their beds if you let them."

"Ok, don't give them a knock. Is that someone at the door?" Louise got up and went to answer it.

"Gosh! Not another one!"

22

"What is it?"

"It's the other cat; the orange one." She came back into the room carrying the orange cat, which was bigger and heavier that the grey one. "What are we going to call this one?"

"Your choice; I named Lady Jane." Louise put the cat down beside the water bowl and gave it some crumbled cheese. She stood in thought for a few moments.

"Carrot," she announced.

"Carrot?" echoed Martine, pausing ironing, which she had only just started. "Carrot? What sort of name is that?"

"It's just as good a name as Lady Jane, and it is spelled correctly. I have a GCSE in English, you know. And it's better than Marmalade or Clementine. Carrots are generally orange, admittedly not always, but generally they are. I'd better get some cat meat pronto." She grabbed her purse and went out. The cats both seemed perfectly at home as though they'd lived there all their lives. Martine finished the ironing and sat down on the sofa. Lady Jane immediately jumped onto her lap and looked lovingly into her eyes. She smiled and stroked the cat gently. Carrot sat at her feet. When Louise returned both cats jumped up and ran into the kitchen. Louise and Martine glanced at each other and laughed. Louise opened the meat and gave them a small amount each on saucers, and they both tucked in. She came and sat next to Martine.

"I didn't give the boys a knock but I had a look through the window and there's no signs of life so either they've gone out or they're still in bed."

"I hope they're all right."

"You mother them too much. They're grown men. Leave them to themselves. If they need help they'll ask for it."

"Yes, I know, but …"

"But nothing. They are good friends, very good friends, but stop worrying about what is probably nothing."

"Okay."

The big woman frowned at them and moved a step closer, towering over them.

"Who are you? What are you doing in my home? Why don't you like my home?" she said in a big voice that echoed as though they were in a big cave.

"Well," said Gary. "I'm Gary and these are my brothers Barry and Simon. We're sorry, we didn't know this was your home, and we don't really know how we got here. And I'm sure it's a nice home from your point of view, but it isn't something we're used to." There was a silence and Gary didn't know whether to speak or not. Barry was trembling and stayed quiet. Simon was visually examining the woman and was about to speak but Gary gestured him to keep silent. Gary plucked up the courage to take the conversation further. "What's your name? What type of person are you? You're much bigger than us. Are you a giant?" The woman laughed, which echoed, although Gary's words hadn't. She put her hands on her hips and took a step back and bent forward to see the men a bit better.

"I am Sighildra. I live here. This is my home. I have lived here for ever and will go on living here for ever. I am not of your world. I am, well, in terms you can understand I am part demon and part troll. You are obviously stupid if

24

you don't know how you got here. Did you walk? Did you fly? Did you swim? Or were you put here by the Lord of Darkness?"

"We were in the churchyard," explained Gary. "Then there was a bang, then we were here. That's all we know."

"Ah! Have you been dabbling in things that don't concern you?"

"We ran three times round the yew tree in the churchyard," volunteered Barry. "Anticlockwise," he added, in case it made a difference. Sighildra put her hands over her ears and grimaced.

"Do not say the name of that accursed tree in this place," she shouted. She took her hands away and scowled at the men. "You have been sent here by the Lord of Darkness as punishment for your stupidity. Does he want me to punish you? I must ask him. But first I will tell you what happens here. You are my prisoners until the Lord tells me to let you go. If you want to return to your world and your time you must find the gate. There is a gate, but I must not show you where it is, or it will close and open somewhere else. But I will not stop you looking for it. That is part of The Game. If the Lord tells me to punish you before you find it, I will carry out his wishes and you will be here forever."

"Do you mean until we die?" asked Simon.

"No. Forever. While you are here you cannot die, unless someone, or something, kills you. I will not harm you without permission from the Lord of Darkness, but there are others here who might."

"Thank you for telling us that," said Simon, "but where are we? You have told us we are in your home, but where is this place? Are we deep underground? Are we on another planet?" Sighildra laughed.

"You are in none of those places. You are near the Gates of Hell. That is part of The Game. In your search for the way out you might discover The Gates, because all gates look the same. But if you go through the wrong gates, The Gates of Hell, you will be damned for eternity and never able to leave." She laughed heartily while the brothers looked at each other, worried.

"You said you cannot show us the exit," Simon was doing all the thinking at the moment. "But can you help us to find it?" Sighildra stopped laughing and sat down.

"No-one has ever asked me that before. I must make a decision. Will I help you? I will not show you the way, but will I help you? Others have been too stupid to ask that question. I must go now. I will return with the answer to your question. I suggest you start looking for the exit."

"Why is that?" asked Simon.

"What?"

"Why should we start looking now?"

"Oh. Because if the Lord of Darkness thinks you are stupid and useless he will let us play with you for our own entertainment, the way a big animal plays with a small animal before eating it. Then he will instruct us to punish you, which always ends in death. He might let us eat you afterwards." She rose to her feet. "I will be back." She walked away, chuckling gently. The brothers remained silent until she was out of sight.

"That doesn't sound good," said Barry, almost in tears.

"No, it certainly doesn't," replied Gary. "We need to find the exit.

"Us," said Simon. "She said 'us'. I wonder who or what the others are. And she said the others would harm us without waiting for permission from the Lord of Darkness."

"Well I don't want to find out," said Gary getting to his feet. "Let's look the exit." The others got up and waited for Gary to decide which way, then they followed him, staying close.

Chapter 5

Later that morning Louise went out to wash the car. It hadn't been washed for some weeks and although the weather had been quite dry their trips into the countryside had left mud splashed along both sides and the back. Carrot had gone out to watch Louise and Lady Jane slept on the sofa bedside Martine. Suddenly Lady Jane jumped up, leapt down onto the floor, and ran into the hall. She went almost to the kitchen but stopped short. She sat and stared at the blank wall, the other side of which bore a cupboard under the stairs with access from the kitchen. She had got up in such a hurry that Martine's curiosity was aroused, and she followed to investigate. The cat was staring intently at the blank wall as though she could see something. Martine could see nothing, other than the wall, until she stood directly behind the cat, and there it was. Lady Jane was staring at a door. Martine opened the door and looked down into the darkness. She couldn't see anything, but she could hear voices. She leant forward and listened carefully while Lady Jane slowly crept forward, almost into the doorway then suddenly stepped back, the hair along her spine bristling. The voices sounded familiar. They were very quiet, as though they were a long way off, but she recognised them. They sounded like the boys, but she couldn't quite hear what they were saying. She called out to them, but no reply came, so she went back to her book on the sofa. She read for another fifteen minutes or so then glanced at her watch. She went into the kitchen and made a pot of tea, then poured it out and took the two mugs out into the road. She handed one to Louise.

"Oh, by the way, I know where the boys are," she said.

"Have they phoned or something?" asked Louise.

"No. They're in our cellar." Louise stopped drinking.

"What? What cellar?"

"You know, like a basement thing. A room downstairs, beneath the floor."

"But we haven't got a cellar."

"Yes, we have, I've just seen it. Lady Jane found it." Martine was quite 'matter-of-fact' about it, as though it had always been there. Louise had a sip at her tea then stood with her hands on her hips.

"No. How long have we lived here? Five years? Nearly six. And I have never seen a cellar. If we had one, I think we would have spotted it before now. It isn't something you can easily hide or overlook. Where is it anyway?"

"Under the floor. That's how cellars work."

"No, I mean where abouts in the house. Where's the door?"

"Along the passage, just before the kitchen, under the stairs." Louise looked away and wiped her forehead, then turned back to Martine.

"Have you been drinking?"

"Of course not. It's only eleven o'clock. Come and see if you don't believe me." She turned and went back into the house. Louise gathered up the bucket and sponges and followed her. They both went along the hall and stopped just short of the kitchen door.

"Well, where is it? It's well hidden." said Louise in a sarcastic tone. Martine was puzzled.

"It was here," she said, pointing at the wall. "I'm sure it was. There was a white door with an old-fashioned handle, and I looked into it." Louise didn't speak, but continued into the kitchen, put the equipment away in the cupboard under the stairs, making a point of opening and closing the cupboard door with wide gestures, then washed her hands and went into the sitting room and sat down on the sofa. Carrot jumped up onto her lap.

"You didn't see any strange new doors, did you?" she said to Carrot, scratching the cat's head lovingly. Martine came in and sat beside her looking confused.

"I don't understand this," she said after a while. "It was there. Lady Jane found it and I opened the door and looked in. It was totally black, nothing to be seen, but I heard voices."

"Oh, voices in your head, is it? Don't worry; I still love you." Louise leant over and gave her a peck on the cheek. "Is it there now? No. Perhaps you imagined it. What are we having for lunch?"

Barry stopped and put his head on one side.

"Did you hear that?" he asked. The others stopped and shook their heads. "It was a voice calling to us. It sounded a bit like Martine." They all stood in silence and listened.

"No, I didn't hear anything," answered Gary. "Come on, let's find the exit, but we'll keep quiet in case someone is calling to us." They walked ahead, as much as they could work out where 'ahead' was, looking and listening all the time, but all around them was blackness, so they didn't see anything. After a while they heard footsteps coming from the side. The paused and strained their eyes to see. There was Sighildra walking purposefully towards them. They waited until she was in talking distance then backed away slowly while Gary addressed her.

"Hello, Sighildra," he began tentatively. "We haven't found the way out, but we haven't given up trying. Are you here to help us?" Sighildra stopped. She sat down and grinned at them.

"I've spoken to the Lord of Darkness and he says I can have my little game before I catch you and eat you." She threw her head back and laughed loudly. "But he says to make the game more interesting for me I can help you a little bit."

"That's very good of him," said Simon. "How are you going to help us?"

"I couldn't think of anything, but the Lord of Darkness suggested I might help you by not telling the others which way you went." She looked at them with a strange expression on her face then laughed again, louder and longer this time. The three men looked at each other.

"So when does the game begin?" asked Simon.

"Oh, it's already begun. The others know you are here somewhere, but they don't know where. And I'm not telling them, so that when I catch you, I can have you all to myself and don't have to share you with them." She rose to her feet and stepped forward. The men got up and set off at a jog. Simon looked round then called to the others to stop.

"Look, we've left her behind. She's just walking and starting to look out of breath. I think she can't run." The others stopped and peered back through the gloom.

"I think you're right, Simon," said Gary. "She looks exhausted already. She can't run. All we have to do is find the exit and avoid the others."

"*All* we have to do?" said Barry. "*All* we have to do? Yes, but where's the exit?"

"Which direction did you hear the voice from?" asked Simon. Barry looked around and pointed vaguely in several directions.

"Oh, I don't know," he said, frustrated. Eventually he settled on one direction and pointed. "Probably that way, but I'm not sure."

"Ok," said Gary. "That's good enough for me. Let's go, but not too fast. We don't want to wear ourselves out in case 'the others' are that way." They set off at a brisk walk, stopping every now and then to listen for footsteps or voices. They could see nothing other than each other, and sometimes wondered if they were making any progress, but glancing back Sighildra became smaller and smaller until she was just a bright speck. This gave them confidence or sorts but were still worried in case they encountered 'the others' as they didn't know if they would be like Sighildra or would have more energy, less patience, or different destructive skills.

Chapter 6

Martine stomped into the kitchen and set about making beans on toast, muttering to Lady Jane.

"You know it was there. You saw it. Why doesn't she believe us? After lunch we'll go and look for it. We'll show her. She thinks I'm seeing things. Well, I'm not. And you're not. You're not going soft in the head either. Look out! Don't get under my feet. You don't want beans on your head." She took the plates of food into the other room and put them on the table then returned for the mugs of tea. They sat at the table and Martine looked away.

"Come on, darling," said Louise. "It does sound a bit far-fetched that we should live in this house for more than five years and not see a door, isn't it? We'll look for it after lunch." After lunch Louise went into the hall and tapped the wall at various points and measured how far back the cupboard under the stairs went. Martine stood watching, arms folded, avoiding eye contact.

"I don't know why you're putting on this show. I know you still don't believe me." Louise wrapped her arms around Martine, who tried to push her away but wasn't strong enough.

"Let's go out for a ride and stop somewhere nice for tea, just like we did the other day." She stroked Martine's hair and planted a kiss on her cheek.

"Okay," Martine smiled. "But I want to try something before we go. And I want you to watch me do it too." She wriggled free and picked Lady Jane up from the sofa. She brought her into the hall and put her down on the floor in the hall and stood directly behind her. The door appeared in front of the cat. "See? There it is," she announced.

"Sorry, can't see it," said Louise, folding her arms.

"Come here," said Martine dragging Louise across so she was directly behind Lady Jane. Louise's mouth hung open.

"Yes," she said, incredulous. "I can see it now." She reached out and touched it, then grasped the handle and slowly pulled the door open. She looked inside but couldn't see anything. Blackness. "Hello?" she called. After a few seconds she thought she heard something. She turned to Martine, who had a satisfied smile on her face. "It's the boys. They're in there somewhere. I think. Come on, let's go in." But she didn't get there. At that moment Carrot came in flying through the air and crashed into Louise so hard that she was knocked over into Martine and they all fell to the floor. They picked themselves up only to notice the door had disappeared, as Lady Jane had run off into the sitting room.

"Do we have a cellar?" asked Martine with a satisfied smile.

"Well, sort of. Yes, I suppose we do, but it isn't what you might call a normal cellar. But yes, it's a cellar." They got to their feet and sat down on the sofa with the cats. "So if the boys are down there, what do we do next?"

Martine shrugged her shoulders. "Haven't a clue, but we need to do something."

Louise got to her feet. "I'm going to call to them and see if we get an answer." She picked Lady Jane up and went into the hall.

The boys pressed on towards where Barry thought the voice had come from, stopping every now and then to check that Sighildra wasn't gaining on them. Then it happened. They stopped, and Sighildra was still a tiny dot in the distance, but they heard footsteps approaching. The boys stood back to back looking in all directions but couldn't see anything, until Barry cried out.

"Look! Over there!" He pointed at what looked like empty blackness, but after a few seconds Gary and Simon could see some tiny specks. "It must be 'the others'. I hope they're no worse than Sighildra."

"Keep your voice down," said Gary. "They don't know which direction we are. We don't want to give our position away." But it was too late. They had been attracted by the sound of Barry's voice and changed direction to home in on the brothers. Barry was ready to run, but Gary and Simon held him back.

"Let's see what we are up against," said Simon. "If they're like Sighildra they'll not be quick enough to catch us." They waited until their pursuers were close enough to be seen clearly. They looked very much like Sighildra. There were five in total; three male and two female, all dressed in the same tortoise-shell armour and sandals strapped up their legs, all carrying big sticks, all with flowing yellow hair despite there being no wind, and all walking steadfastly forward with looks of determination.

"Are we still walking towards the voices, Barry?" Gary asked.

"I think so. But I have to admit I'm not certain."

"We'll assume we are, until we have an indication that we're not," Simon commented. The brothers pressed on hoping they were going in the right direction.

Louise plonked Lady Jane unceremoniously down on the floor in the hall by the spot where the door had appeared and stood directly behind her. The door appeared and she pulled it open. By now Martine had joined her, and they both leant in and listened. They heard nothing, and saw nothing, but Martine leant in a bit further and called out.

"Barry! Gary! Simon! It's me, Martine! Can you hear me?"

"It's me too! Louise! Can you hear me?" Louise's voice was deeper than Martine's, so she had shouted too, hoping one might carry better than the other. They listened in silence, then they heard something.

Barry stopped walking and the other two stopped behind him. "Listen! It's the girls!" They listened attentively. "Yes, we can hear you," he shouted at the top of his voice.

"I hope it is," whispered Simon. "Because if it isn't, he's just given our position away." Gary nodded.

"Can you see us?" shouted Martine. "We can hear you but can't see you. Do you have a torch? Can you shine a light?"

"No, we have nothing like that. I'm waving my arms. Can you see me now?"

"No. We'll get a torch and shine it. Louise, go and get the big torch." Louise returned with the torch and turned it on. She shone it into the cellar, but still couldn't see anything.

"Yes, we can see you now!" shouted Simon as he pointed to the light. "We'll follow the light, because we're being chased." Gary looked round and saw the five pursuers had got quite close.

"Come here," one of them shouted. "We want to eat you."

"Er, no, we don't want to be eaten," Gary replied and urged his brothers on. In about ten minutes they had put quite a distance between them and the chasing pack, but not enough for safety. Gary glanced round again and noticed that only three were following them. What had happened to the other two? He looked to both sides and saw the other two approaching from the right. "Come on," he said "We need to pick the pace up. They've split up and they're getting close." At this they raised their jog to a fast trot and managed to increase the gap.

The girls were still leaning into the cellar, and still couldn't see anything at all. Lady Jane suddenly snarled and arched her back.

"She can see something, even if we can't," said Martine.

"Yes, but I wonder what," answered Louise. Suddenly Lady Jane leapt forward into the darkness and slowly got smaller and smaller until she had disappeared altogether.

"Oh, dear," said Martine. "I hope she knows what she's doing." She took Louise's hand and held it tightly. "Do you think we should follow her?" At that Carrot appeared and sat in the entrance to the cellar, facing the girls, and snarled.

"I think Carrot doesn't want us to do that," said Louise.

Lady Jane landed on her feet not far from the brothers, which made them start. They stopped running and clung together in case it was hostile.

"There's a cat here!" shouted Barry.

"What colour?" asked Louise.

"Grey," Barry replied.

"That's okay," shouted Martine. "Her name is Lady Jane and she's friendly. Do whatever she tells you."

"Do whatever she tells you?" muttered Gary. "I've never taken instructions from a cat before."

"No, but this isn't a normal situation," said Simon. "Do as Martine says." Lady Jane sat down in front of them. "I think it wants us to sit. They sat. Lady Jane got up and went behind them and sat again. The group of three chasers was getting close, and the brothers readied themselves for flight. When they were about ten yards away Lady Jane jumped to her feet, arched her back, and snarled fiercely. The pursuing men stopped in their tracks and put their hands over their ears, grimacing, just as Sighildra had at the mention of the yew tree. The cat slowly stepped forward, and the men slowly stepped back. Lady Jane's snarl got louder and louder until it was nothing like the snarl of a little cat, but more like the roar of a lion or a tiger. The men turned and fled, as much as walking quickly can be described as fleeing. By this time the two women had crept up on the group from the other side, but Lady Jane quickly ran round and gave them the same treatment. They too fled with their hands over their ears. Barry got up and went to Lady Jane to pick her up, but she moved away a few paces then stopped. Every time he took a pace forward, she moved away then stopped. "Do you think it wants us to follow?" asked Simon.

"Good thought," said Gary. "Come on." He and Simon got up and they all followed Lady Jane, who set off at a canter, pausing every now and then to let them catch up. After a while she slowed down a little and started looking from side to side, sniffing the air, as though she were searching. Suddenly she set off again, going slightly to the left. During the pause Gary had looked behind and, seeing no signs of the demons, breathed a sigh of relief.

Chapter 7

Carrot continued to snarl every time the girls looked into the cellar, so they stood back. Carrot pushed the door with her nose and it slammed shut. As soon as she walked away the door disappeared.

"Well, that's that. What do we do now?" Louise asked.

"Good question. Ask the cat."

Louise picked Carrot up and sat on the sofa with the cat on her lap. "Carrot, dear cat, what do we do next?" She didn't really expect an answer, but Carrot jumped down onto the floor and went to the front door. She came back and tugged at the bottom of Louise's trouser leg and went back to the front door. Louise and Martine looked at each other.

"I think she wants us to go outside," said Martine slowly. Louise nodded, and they put their jackets on as the weather had turned a bit cooler. They followed Carrot out into the street and locked the front door. Carrot trotted along the path, obviously not in a hurry, but equally obviously knowing where she was headed. The pace was gentle but steady. After a while they ended up at the churchyard. Carrot sat at the gate, so Louise opened it and they went in. Carrot stopped and looked around, sniffing the air, then set off for the far corner.

Meanwhile Lady Jane had led the brothers to what looked like a wall. They couldn't see it clearly, because everything was dark apart from themselves and the cat, but they could see enough to know it was a wall. There was a doorway in the wall, with a metal barred gate over it, which looked as though it hadn't been opened for a very long time, and Lady Jane stood pawing at it.

"Come on, she wants us to open it," said Simon, trying unsuccessfully to pull it open.. "I think it's seized up."

Barry stepped forward. "I'll do that. I'm the strongest," he said, and with a big pull detached the gave from its hinges, falling over backwards, to be caught by his brothers. He flung the gate to the side and they all followed the cat who by now had disappeared into the gloom through the opening. "Don't let her get out of sight!" shouted Barry.

"Don't worry," said Simon. "I can still see her." They followed for about half an hour until they saw light up ahead. It wasn't bright light. It wasn't like daylight, but after the hours they had spent in the darkness it was welcome. They realised there were side walls, which drew in so that they were walking along a corridor, the light brightening as they went. As they approached the end of the corridor, they could see another metal gate, much the same as the one in the wall. They all smiled as they hurried towards it. When they got there the cat was sitting facing them. Barry stroked her head and thanked her for her help. She got up and moved to the side then sat again.

"Over to you, Barry. Give it a go and see if you need help." Barry stepped forward and grasped the metal bars firmly with both hands. He gave it a bit if a shake then turned to face the others.

"It's a bit tougher than the other one. I think I might need a bit of help. Come on, Gary, there's room enough for two here." They pulled and pushed the gate, gradually loosening it, and it eventually gave way and they were able to put it to one side.

41

Carrot led the girls slowly across the churchyard to the dry tangled grass in the far corner where there was a bit of a depression in the ground. Louise stepped into it and it gave way. Martine grabbed her arm to stop her from falling, and they both got down on their knees to see what was beneath the grass. Pulling it away, they saw about six or seven stone steps leading to a metal barred gate. They heard noises and stepped back in case it was whatever had been chasing the boys. There were sounds of metal grating on stone, and a big bang followed shortly after by Barry's head appearing through the grass.

"Barry!" Martine shouted, waving as she ran forward. "Are you okay? Are the others there? Is Lady Jane with you?" Barry waved back with a wide grin.

"Yes, we're all here, we're all okay. And yes, your little cat is here. She's a hero. We wouldn't have escaped without her." Lady Jane bounded out and Martine tried to catch her, but she ran straight to Carrot and they touched noses.

"Come on out," shouted Louise. "It's great to see you again. We hadn't a clue what had happened to you. Carrot was a hero too." The boys climbed up the stone steps and all five gave hugs and kisses.

Martine looked round. "Where have the cats gone? They were both heroes here." They all looked round but the cats were nowhere to be seen.

"Don't worry, they'll turn up," said Louise. "Let's go back to our place for a cup of tea."

"Good idea, meow," said Martine.

"What?" said Gary.

"Good idea, meow," said Martine again. "Did I just say 'meow'?" The others burst out laughing.

"Yes, you did, meow," replied Louise, then paused before asking "Did I just say 'meow' too?" The boys thought this was hilarious, until they saw the girls' worried faces.

"What's happening?" asked Simon.

"I don't meow know," Martine answered. She looked at Louise and burst into tears. Louise put her arm round Martine's shoulders.

"Let's get you two home," said Gary. "We'll see what's what when you've had a cup of tea." He put his arm round Louise's waist, as she was crying now too, and Barry supported Martine while they walked the short distance to the girls' house. Every time Louise spoke there was at least one 'meow' in the sentence, sometimes two. Simon was walking in front but when he turned round to speak to them, he froze. They froze too.

"What's up?" asked Gary. Simon spoke slowly and deliberately.

"I'm not trying to be funny," he said. "But what's that on your faces? It looks like hair." Martine put her hand up to her cheek. She turned to face Louise, and her legs gave way.

"Louise, you've got hair on meow your meow face," she said, trying not to cry.

Louise touched her own cheek. "That's not meow hair," she said, with a quiver in her voice. "That's fur meow." The girls were struggling to walk now so Gary and Barry picked them up and carried them. Simon fished around in Louise's jacket pocket and found the house key and ran on ahead to open the door. They went inside and the twins gently put the girls down on the sofa. Simon was already in the kitchen making tea. Gary took Barry to one side.

"Did you notice Martine getting lighter?" he asked under his breath.

"Yes, but I just thought it was me getting used to her. She isn't very heavy and I'm strong."

"Louise is a bit heavier than Martine, but by the time we got here she was much lighter." They turned to the girls who were climbing out of their clothes which were now much too big for them. Simon appeared at the door with mugs of tea on a tray, but almost dropped them, and only just managed to get the tray to the table.

"Look what's happened," he said. "Martine, Louise, can you hear me?"

"Meow yes, of course meow," Louise answered.

"Meow yes," said Martine. They looked at each other. Martine's face, now much smaller, was covered in grey fur; Louise's in orange fur. They were both very much smaller and their faces began to change shape, as did their arms and legs. They were now much too small for their clothes and climbed out of them and jumped down onto the floor. They had become cats. There were no signs of the original Lady Jane and Carrot.

Chapter 8

Charles and Theresa Watson arrived at Mr Johnson's house and rang the doorbell. Mrs Johnson let them in and showed them through to the office. Mr Johnson was a stout man of about fifty with short dark hair. He sat in a wheelchair behind a desk. Mrs Johnson brought two chairs and indicated to the Watsons to sit; she brought another to the end of the desk, where she, too, sat. Mr Johnson extended his hand.

"Excuse me for not getting up," he said, tapping the armrest of the wheelchair. "Feel free to call me Gavin. This is my wife, Maggie." They shook hands.

"I will," said Charles. "I'm not used to too much formality; I'm Charles, this is my daughter, Theresa." They settled into their seats. "Pray tell me what this is about. Your phone call sounded a bit vague."

"Yes, sorry about that. I feared if I said too much you might think I was some sort of nutter or timewaster. The whole business is a bit difficult to believe, but we've sort of promised one of our tenants we'll try to help. It's about two young ladies who appear to have gone missing."

"Well, I'm sorry, Gavin, but we are psychic investigators; we are not Hercule Poirot." He made to get up, but Gavin held up a restraining hand.

"Don't be too hasty, Charles. This isn't a straightforward case of missing persons. There is a psychic element to it, which I struggled to come to terms with at first. If it weren't for Maggie's insistence that we take the man seriously I would have dismissed it as the rantings of someone with too much beer inside him. The two young ladies are tenants, as is the young man who asked for help.

We are landlords of a number of houses, and the ladies are, er, just want to make sure I get the names right – don't want you hunting down someone else." He scanned the papers on his desk. Maggie pointed to the correct sheet. "Ah, yes, thanks. They are Miss Martine Baker and Miss Louise Greenford. They live in a village called Lower Ashfield, about twenty miles from here. Do you know it?"

Charles shook his head. "Never been there, but I've passed signs for it."

"Well, it's only a little place; you can't get lost. They live in Bedford Terrace, and the young man, Barry Wheatley, lives in Buckingham Terrace, which is just around the corner, literally less than two minutes away on foot. Maggie visited them for the annual inspection, and Barry told her the ladies wouldn't be in, but he had a key and could let her in. Do you want to take up the story from here, dear?"

Maggie nodded. "This was quite normal for these two households. I visit on an annual basis just to make sure they aren't trashing the place and to catch up on any repairs to be done, you know, usual landlord-tenant stuff. Both houses were always all in order. The girls' house was always immaculately clean and tidy; the boys' house less so, but always acceptable. Barry shares the house with his two brothers ever since their parents died. Apparently, the five of them were old school friends, they work at the same factory, and spend a lot of their spare time together. Well, I did the inspection on Barry's house first, then we walked round to the girls' house and he let me in. He followed me in and while I did the inspection, he fed the cats. I'm trying to remember what he said next." She referred to her notebook. "Er, I think that's when he mentioned the girls'

46

disappearance. He started to get a bit agitated and said something about not knowing when they would be back, then told me something about them being 'trapped inside the cats'. The cats were all over him, they are obviously very fond of him, and I began to wonder what he meant. He's been a tenant for many years, both as part of the family when his parents were alive and in his own right, jointly with his brothers, of course, and while he definitely isn't the sharpest knife in the box, he is generally quite sensible and responsible, and this seemed a bit out of character for him. I tried to coax it out of him, and at first he didn't want to say much in case I thought he was mad, but eventually he told the tale, and what a strange tale it is!" She paused to clear her throat and Gavin passed a glass of water to her. "The long and the short of it is that one evening on the way home from the pub they had gone into the churchyard to try out some ancient folklore ritual, and it had gone wrong. They somehow ended up trapped in the cellar of the girls' house, and the girls rescued them, with the help of the cats. However, the girls somehow got trapped inside the cats. At least that's what I could gather from what he was saying. He was getting very upset at this point, as the girls were very close friends with the boys, him in particular. He wanted me to say we would do something to bring them back. I couldn't promise to do that, but I said we would try to find someone to help. And that's why we contacted you. My sister had a friend with noises in her house, and you made them go away, so word of mouth being the best advert, here you are."

Charles stroked his chin and stared into space for a moment. "Yes, we're willing to have a look, yes. Interesting. Very interesting."

"Just a minute," said Gavin. "How much is this going to cost? We want to help our tenants, but we are a business, and can't fork out an arm and a leg on the rantings of someone to whom we have no contractual obligation. And what qualifications do you have?"

"Theresa has a degree in chemistry from Cambridge as well as a keen interest in physics, electronics and psychic disturbances. I have a PhD but I tend not to use my title for fear I wouldn't be taken seriously." Gavin smiled and Maggie tried to hide a giggle.

Theresa looked confused. "Sorry, I don't understand," she said.

"I'll explain later, darling. As for cost, nothing. I only charge people who waste my time, and this sounds exactly what I'm looking for. This could be an important part of my research. I lecture at the university, where I'm a professor, and that gives me a decent income. This would form part of my research and could become a chapter in my next book. Names changed to protect the innocent, of course, but it sounds very interesting."

Gavin smiled. "That's a relief. You'll need this, then." He pushed a few papers across the desk. "Plans of the house," he explained. "Oh, and these. Contact details for Mr Wheatley, and, er, Miss Baker and Miss Greenford, not that *they're* likely to be of much use." He passed a sheet of paper across.

Charles picked up the plans and gave them straight to Theresa without looking at them. "Here, darling, see what you make of this." She unfolded the sheet and examined it.

"Daddy," she said after a moment. "There's no cellar here." She looked up at Gavin.

Gavin smiled. "Exactly. I was hoping you would notice that."

"Yes," said Maggie. "But he was most insistent on that. That's the strange thing. The cellar is only there at certain times, which seem to depend on where the cats are and what they're doing."

"The cats that he claims the girls are trapped in?"

"Yes. The cats are key, in his mind."

"This gets more interesting by the minute! I would like to start immediately, if that's okay with you. I don't have any lectures for the rest of this week, nor next week. Let's get onto this Theresa. The sooner the better."

"Don't we need to have a document of engagement?" asked Gavin.

Charles shook his head and smiled. "No need for that. You're not engaging us. You're permitting us to do research on your premises."

"But what about insurance?" asked Maggie. "And we need to speak to Barry, Mr Wheatley."

"I very much doubt that psychic phenomena will be mentioned as an inclusion or an exclusion in your insurance policy," Charles said with a grin. "And we have plenty of insurance anyway, or at least the university has. As for Mr Wheatley, it isn't his house we're investigating, and I'm sure, from what you've said, he'll welcome us with open arms. But feel free to come along to introduce us if you think it'll make him any happier. I would like to start tomorrow at nine.

"Well, yes, that will be fine," said Gavin as Charles and Theresa gathered the papers together and prepared to leave.

"I'll be there tomorrow at nine," said Maggie. "I'll ring him now to let him know." The Watsons shook hands with the Johnsons and left. Gavin and Maggie exchanged glances. "Well, they seem keen," she said as soon as they'd gone. "I hope they can do something for poor Barry. He is really upset about this."

"It isn't our problem, dear, as long as they keep paying the rent. I don't want to sound heartless, but they might have just run off to avoid some unpleasant situation or other."

"I've met them, many times, and you haven't. I don't think they're the sort to do that."

"Well, good luck to Dr Watson and his daughter."

Chapter 9

A small van rolled up and stopped outside number three Buckingham Terrace. They waited until Maggie arrived, as agreed, and she unlocked the house and showed them in.

"I'll just pop round the corner and get Barry. Won't be long." She returned in less than five minutes and introduced them to Barry.

"Mr Wheatley," began Charles, holding out his hand.

"Mr Wheatley!" exclaimed Barry, shaking hands firmly with Charles. "I'm not used to that. I'm Barry."

"Good. I'm Charles and this is Theresa." She shook hands, too. "I would like to get the full story from you, in your own words, if that's okay. Maggie has told us a lot but there's always the possibility you might have some vital piece of info that you haven't disclosed, or that she considered unimportant."

"Are you okay with this, Barry?" asked Maggie. Barry nodded. "In that case I'll go. I have lots of work to do. Feel free to telephone if you need me for anything. I think I gave you my mobile number. I'll be in this area for the rest of today, then back at the office tomorrow." They bade farewell and she left. Barry and Charles made themselves comfortable on the sofa and the cats immediately joined them.

"Shall I start getting stuff in, Daddy?" asked Theresa.

"Yes. Bring all three laptops and the magnetic and sonic detectors and the big oscilloscope. We'll decide what else we need later. Set the laptops and the oscilloscope up on that table in the corner and see if there's a good bit of floor for the detectors."

"Good bit of floor?" asked Barry.

"Yes," answered Theresa. "Preferably a bit without carpet."

"Oh, I see. The hall and the kitchen don't have carpets."

"Excellent," she said, and started bringing equipment in.

Barry picked a book up from a little table. "This is Martine's diary, and it has all the story in it. I only know part of it, because we were stuck in the strange place when the business with the cats first started."

Charles read through the pages for the last week and made notes as he read. After about twenty minutes he looked up. "This cat here," he said, pointing at Lady Jane, the grey one, "this is Lady Jane, the one that first found the mystery door. Is that correct?" Barry nodded. "And the other one," he pointed at Carrot, the orange one, "This is Carrot, the one that stopped them going through the door?" Barry nodded again. He continued through the diary, making copious notes and occasionally asking for clarification. After a while he lifted his head and looked Barry in the eye. "Tell me about the 'strange place'," he said.

"Well," said Barry, obviously uneasy. "It's difficult to say what it was. Everything was black. The floor was black, and it was sort of rubber but it wasn't. It was sort of stone but it wasn't. I've never seen anything like it before. Everything was black all around. There was nothing to see, but we could see each other. Me and my brothers, that is, we could see each other even though there wasn't any light."

"How did you get there?"

"I don't know. We were just messing about 'cos Simon had been reading Louise's book about ancient folklore they'd been given by a neighbour." He paused to find the book, which he handed to Charles, open at the correct page. "It said if we ran round the yew tree in the churchyard three times anticlockwise at midnight we would see the devil. We had been to the pub, I had won a pint off Louise playing pool, and because there was no work the next day we decided to go to the churchyard and try it out. The girls weren't interested so they just sat on the seat and watched, but we gave it a go and nothing happened. Then we tried again and there was a bang and we ended up in a heap on the floor in the other place. Then we met the big woman."

"Big woman?"

"Yes. She was huge. About twelve feet tall and dressed in armour which looked like tortoise shell pieces, and old-fashioned sandals like the Romans, and yellow hair blowing in the breeze, except there wasn't any breeze. She scared me, she did." Charles indicated him to stop while he retrieved one of the laptops from the table. He called up an image and showed it to Barry. "Yes, that's what she looked like. Not exactly, but very close. She scares me just looking at that. Said her name was Sighildra."

"Ah!" exclaimed Charles. He tapped away on the laptop for a moment, then he smiled broadly. "Yes. Sighildra. Ancient Norse demon. Nasty piece of work. But there are worse. Please continue."

"Yes, she said the others might be worse."

"What others?"

"The others that came after us. They were just like her. There were five – six including her. But the cat scared them away."

"This wasn't mentioned in the diary. Which cat? And how did it scare them away?"

"That's 'cos Martine wasn't there to see it. After we heard Martine's voice, she sent Lady Jane down, and she got between us and them and roared like a tiger. That scared me as well. A little cat like that roaring like a great big fierce tiger. They covered their ears and turned and ran. Well, actually no, they didn't run, but they walked away as fast as they could."

"Good. Do you mind if we have a break now? I've some questions to ask but I haven't decided what they are yet."

"That's okay. I was getting a bit worked up. Telling you reminded me of how scared I was and how much I miss the girls. Would you like a cup of tea?"

"Tea would be excellent, Barry. Thank you. I'm sure Theresa would like one too."

Barry went to the kitchen where Theresa was sat on the floor connecting wires to boxes. "Don't touch anything!" she shouted. Barry jumped. "Sorry, didn't mean to startle you, but I have all this in the right place and haven't got it fastened down yet."

"Oh, sorry. Would you like a cup of tea?"

Theresa looked up at him and smiled sweetly. "Oh, yes, please. That would be lovely. But keep away from this end of the kitchen until I'm done."

In twenty minutes Theresa had finished and the three of them were sat in the other room drinking tea.

"You're obviously very fond of the girls, especially Martine. Is she your girlfriend?" asked Charles. Barry laughed and shook his head.

"No, wish she was," he replied. "She's on the other bus."

"On the other bus?" Charles was puzzled.

"She's gay, Daddy. Try to keep up."

"Oh, I see," he said, embarrassed.

"Are you gay too?" asked Theresa.

"You can't ask him that!" said Charles, even more embarrassed now.

"No, I'm not," Barry answered with a smile. "Don't worry, Charles. Just as well to get the facts straight."

"Anyway," said Charles, wanting to change the subject. "How are you doing?" This to Theresa.

"All secure. Just about to turn it on." She drained her cup and went into the kitchen, pressed a few buttons then returned and sat at the table with two laptops in front of her. She picked up the plans and glanced across at the oscilloscope.

"Do we have a void?" asked Charles.

Theresa sighed. "Yes, we do, but only about 500mm, just like on the plans."

"Never mind. We'll spend the rest of the day getting some baseline measurements, then tomorrow, well, Barry, will you be here tomorrow?" Barry nodded. "If you're available to help us, we can start working with the cats. Got to admit I haven't had a great deal of experience with animals, but you seem totally at home with them."

"That's because they aren't normal cats. They're Martine and Louise." He smiled and Charles and Theresa glanced at each other with raised eyebrows. Barry didn't seem to notice.

"I hope you're right," said Charles, scratching his head. "Because that might give us a potential solution to your plight, for one thing, and open up a whole new avenue of research for me for another, but I can't guarantee that's the case."

"Oh, I know the girls are in these cats. I can tell from the way they look at me. Don't you worry about that. I've known the girls since we were four. Went right through school together and worked together since the day we left. And Louise is the best pool player in town, and I'm the second best." He grinned and stroked the cats.

Charles and Theresa glanced at each other. "Okay, so you know them probably better than anyone else around here," said Charles. "I'm looking forward to working with you on this tomorrow."

"Well, if you don't need me now, I'll be off home to have some lunch. I just live round the corner." He scribbled on a piece of paper. "Here's my number of you need me. I'm at number five Bedford Terrace." He smiled at Theresa, who smiled back, then he scratched the cats' heads and left.

About two hours later they sat back with another cup of tea to review their findings. "Nothing in the way of voids, Daddy," said Theresa, disappointedly, "Other than what's shown on the plans. No electromags either, apart from a strange hum from the cupboard under the stairs, which I can't identify. I've set up all the normal cages etc. to make sure it isn't picking anything up from the distribution board or smart meters or anything. They don't have anything out of the ordinary here. There's the TV, digibox, laptops, radios, alarm clocks, and microwave, and I've turned all the kitchen equipment off but it makes no difference. It isn't a strong signal, but it doesn't seem to have a source that I can pin down."

Charles got up and inspected the equipment on the table. "Yes," he said slowly. "I see what you mean." He tapped a few keys on one of the laptops. "Yes, it is rather weak, isn't it." He picked up a hand-held device from one of the boxes of equipment and took it into the kitchen. He wandered round for a while. "No, exactly as you said. No obvious source. Hm. Is it permanent?"

"Yes, never goes away. If you go outside it disappears immediately. It's only in the house, but I can't work out where. I tried going upstairs but it disappears about three stairs up."

"Well, I've got all the base readings I need for now, so if you're finished, we'll call it a day. We can leave the kit here. We won't need it any more today."

"I've got a couple of hand-helds in the van, and there's a laptop and a couple of detectors in the workshop if we need them." They turned things off, apart from three machines which they wanted to record overnight, packed up, and went home.

"I'm curious to see what we discover tomorrow with the cats," commented Charles.

"You and me both," replied Theresa.

Chapter 10

The next morning Charles and Theresa arrived shortly after nine o'clock to find Barry was already there feeding the cats. He made a pot of tea and brought the drinks through to the sitting room.

"Hello," he said. "Cats today?"

They nodded. "We'll give them time to finish their breakfast first, then I would like to start with Lady Jane," said Charles. They sat and chatted about how Lady Jane had scared off the giants, until the cats came in, licking their lips, and settled on the sofa next to Barry. He picked Lady Jane up and held her in front of himself and looked her in the eyes.

"We're going to work with you today, Lady Jane," he said. "We need you to show Charles and Theresa how to make the door appear, so they can do their work. Don't worry, they won't hurt you. I'll see to that. Just do as we ask and it'll be okay." He put her down on the floor. Charles and Theresa glanced at each other, not knowing what to say. Theresa tried not to laugh. Barry got to his feet and went into the hall. Lady Jane followed him. She sat looking at the blank wall, and Barry squatted behind her. Charles and Theresa couldn't see anything. "No, you'll not see from there. You have to come here," Barry said. Theresa cautiously walked over to him, and when she was almost touching him her mouth dropped open.

"Come here, Daddy!" she exclaimed. "It's true. It's there, the door. Come and see" She stepped over Lady Jane to stand at the other side so that Charles could see.

"Good Lord!" he exclaimed. "I've never seen anything like this before. Where's my notebook?" He dashed back

58

into the sitting room and returned already scribbling notes. Just as Barry reached over the cat to grasp the handle and pull the door open, they were interrupted by a beep from the kitchen. Theresa dash through and knelt beside one of the boxes on the floor.

"Daddy! It's there! There's a void!" Charles dashed to the table in the sitting room and tapped a few keys on one of the laptops.

"Upon my word! It's a substantial void. In fact," he paused while he did more keying. "In fact, according to this, it's bottomless!"

"No, it can't be," called Theresa, quickly stepping over the cat to get to the sitting room. This surprised Lady Jane, who escaped into the kitchen. The door disappeared, and with it any detection of the void by the devices.

"Damn!" Charles muttered under his breath.

"You shouldn't have jumped over her like that. You frightened the poor little thing," said Barry as he went to the kitchen and gathered the cat into his arms and sat down on a stool. He spoke to her gently while he stroked her to try to calm her down.

"Sorry, everyone. My fault," apologised Theresa. She went to stroke Lady Jane who shied away from her at first, but soon came round. "Sorry, little cat, I didn't mean to startle you. It's just I was so excited. I've never seen anything like that before. Can we try again? I promise not to make any sudden movements." She knelt beside Barry and looked the cat in the face and smiled. "Are we friends again?" She gently scratched the top of the cat's head, who purred at this attention. "I think that means yes."

"Can we try again?" called Charles from the other room.

"Yes, but can we give her time to recover first?" answered Barry. "About fifteen minutes?"

"That'll give me time to make a cup of tea," said Theresa as she put the kettle on then gathered the mugs from the sitting room. Barry returned to the sofa with Lady Jane and sat down. Carrot joined them.

"I think we'll leave Carrot until tomorrow," said Charles while he drank his tea. "She didn't make the door appear, if I remember rightly. Is that so, Barry?"

"I didn't see the door at all until this morning," he replied. "I was in the other place at the time. I've only got Martine's diary to go on."

"Ah, yes. We'll try Carrot tomorrow. We'll concentrate on Lady Jane today, as she seems to be the main protagonist."

"Protagonist? What's that mean? She's just a cat as far as I know."

"Sorry, Barry. What I mean is she's the one that makes things happen."

"Oh. I see." He looked at Lady Jane. "You're a protagonist." He scratched her head a bit more. When they had finished their tea they went back into the hall. Lady Jane sat looking at the blank wall, as though she knew what was expected of her. Barry stood behind her, and the door appeared. Charles reached across to the handle and gently pulled it open. The machine in the kitchen bleeped again, and Theresa went in to look at it.

"Yes, it's there," she said. "Exactly like before."

"Yes, this is the same," said Charles, examining the laptop on the table. "This is amazing."

Theresa stepped over Lady Jane very carefully and stood next to Charles, leaning forward to see the screen.

"That's absolutely amazing!" she said. Charles scribbled in his notebook. "Are we going in?" she asked.

Charles shook his head. "Certainly not. Not until we know the extent of the void, anyway. This needs a lot of safety kit. Supposing you fall in – what then?"

"Good point, but I wasn't intending falling in for one thing, and for another, according to Martine's diary, Lady Jane jumped in and came out the other end. I would like to do a few little experiments, like does it only work with Barry, or would it work with me. Would it work with Carrot, or does it only work with Lady Jane?"

"Yes, no problem with that. Go ahead but be careful. I want to record more measurements while the void is open. Are you able to stay a while and help Theresa, Barry?"

Barry nodded. "Oh, yes. We haven't got work at the moment. The roof came in and we've been sent home on full pay until it's fixed. We don't expect to go back until a week Monday at the earliest. I can be here all day if you want, apart from going home for lunch. And if you want me here tomorrow, I'll bring sandwiches, if you let me know today."

"Good man! Yes, we might need you all day tomorrow, depending on what we do with Carrot, and on what Theresa achieves today, so we might need you later today too."

"Okay. I'll just pop home and put some bait up. I'll be back in ten minutes." Barry left.

"He's a good chap, Barry," said Charles.

"Yes. Looking forward to working with him. I think we might need him here all week," said Theresa, with a smile. Barry returned twenty minutes later with a Tupperware box, which he put in the fridge. "Right," he said. "What do you want me to do?"

"Well, let's see," said Theresa, as though she hadn't thought it through. "I would like to shine a torch into the void to see if there's anything to be seen, for one thing, and I'd like to try opening it myself, with Lady Jane, of course, to see, well, to see if I can. I might need you to help with her if she isn't comfortable with me. Let's try that first, shall we?" They went out into the hall and Theresa squatted in the hall. Barry picked the cat up and gently placed her in front of Theresa, and the door appeared. Barry opened it, and it all looked just like the previous time. He shut it, and Theresa got up, and it disappeared. "Excellent. Now can we try it without you? Go outside and I'll pick her up and see if she settles." Barry went out through the front door. Theresa picked Lady Jane up and tried to squat in the hall. She nearly lost her balance but managed by transferring Lady Jane into one hand, so she had a free hand to steady herself against the wall. She put the cat down on the floor, and the door appeared. She reached up and opened it, and the cat remained unmoved. "That's good. Good cat!" She stroked it then got up and the door disappeared as soon as she moved away. She let Barry back in and related the facts. He looked disappointed.

"So you might not need me, then?"

"Oh, no. I think we'd better have you here, just in case. And I will definitely need you for the next thing. I want you and Lady Jane to stay here, to keep it open, so I can have a look inside." She went to the van and returned with a big torch. "Okay, let's have a go." Barry got into position and held Lady Jane in front of him. The door appeared and Theresa gently pulled it open, then she got down on her knees and shone the torch inside. "I can't see anything," she said. "Nothing at all." She transferred the torch into the other hand and felt under the doorway with her free hand. There was nothing there. It was as though the house were floating with no physical means of support. Theresa leant further in to try to get a better view. Suddenly there was a noise at the front door. It was just the postman pushing a couple of letters through the letterbox, but Lady Jane was startled and ran off into the kitchen. The door disappeared immediately, leaving Theresa trapped in the wall. It went from her left shoulder to her right hip, entirely closed around her. She struggled to move but couldn't. Barry sprang up and grabbed Lady Jane and brought her back. He sat on the floor in front of Theresa's flailing legs and put the cat down in front of him. The door immediately reappeared, and Theresa could move again. He reached forward and pulled her back by the belt of her jeans; she sat on the floor gasping for a moment. Barry released the cat and the door disappeared again as soon as Lady Jane ran away.

"Are you alright?" he asked, touching her arm, and getting up and helping her to her feet. She gasped, trying to get her breath back, and he led her into the sitting room and gently settled her onto the sofa, then he disappeared and returned with a glass of water in one hand and the cat in the other. Charles had been concentrating on one of the laptops and hadn't noticed the commotion out in the hall. He looked up and came across when he saw Theresa being helped in.

"What on earth happened? Are you okay?" he said, kneeling down beside her and taking her hand. She burst into tears.

"Oh, Daddy, I thought I was going to die," she sobbed. "And I think I would, if it hadn't been for Barry." She explained what had happened. "I couldn't breathe, and it was getting tighter and tighter and I thought my boobs were being ripped off. And I dropped the big torch."

Charles looked up at Barry. "Thank you, young man. It sounds as though you've saved my little girl's life." Barry blushed, not knowing what to say. "I think you need to rest a little," he said to Theresa. "I might be able to take some more measurements, with Barry's help, while you are recovering. And if I remember we'll pop by the university tomorrow and pick up another torch."

"No, I'm alright now, Daddy. I'll make us a cup of tea and have a little rest then I'll be back to work."

"Are you sure?"

"Yes. Tea?" Barry and Charles nodded and smiled. She went into the kitchen and put the kettle on.

"She's made of stern stuff," Charles whispered to Barry. "Best keep an eye on her for the rest of today, but if she thinks we're making a fuss she'll get cross." Barry grinned and gave a thumbs up.

At about four thirty they started packing up. Charles decided to leave most of the equipment where it was, but as they were leaving Theresa turned to Barry. "Er, would you like to go out for a drink tonight?"

"Oh, er, yes, that would be lovely. You mean like on a date?" he replied sheepishly.

"Exactly," she replied. "And not because you saved my life, but because I think you're really nice."

"Well, that's kind of you to say. Why don't you just stay here now? I can run you home after."

She smiled and shook her head. "No, I need to get changed and sort my hair out. I can't go on a date looking like this, with scruffy jeans and trainers and my hair in a mess."

"But you look fine," said Barry.

"You're sweet, but no, you deserve better. Pick you up at about half seven?"

"Yes, that's great." She gave him a peck on the cheek then got into the van and drove off.

Chapter 11

The next day Charles and Theresa turned up at nine. Barry was already there, feeding the cats. They repeated many of the previous day's experiments, but with Theresa and Carrot instead of Barry and Lady Jane, but with the same results. Charles went out to the van and returned a little while later carrying a metal bar with plates on the ends. Theresa set up a video camera, pointing at where the door would appear. Charles asked Barry to reveal the door, with Lady Jane's help, and put the bar across it. "Stand up, please, Barry, and pick the cat up." Barry did as requested. "Now walk away slowly." Barry took two slow steps to the side, and the door disappeared. The metal bar stopped the bottom from closing, but only for a while. After a minute or so the bar started to bend, and eventually bent in half and sprang out of the doorway. They all ducked as it shot along the hall.

"Wow! That was a near miss!" exclaimed Barry.

"Yes," replied Charles. "That bar can take ten tonnes, and it bent like a cheap household spoon. And it just goes to show what a close call Theresa had yesterday. There's power in that door. Or wall. Or whatever it is."

"Have you ever seen anything like this before, Charles?" asked Barry.

Charles shook his head. "No, never. We are dealing with forces I've never experienced before, and I've quite a long history of psychic investigation." He wrote a few notes in his book then returned to the laptop on the table. An hour later he looked at his watch. "Nearly lunch time, folks. Shall we take a look at the churchyard this afternoon while the weather's fine?"

"You're the boss, Daddy. I'll make the tea and you can tell us what you want to do while we eat." He nodded. "Barry, do you think you can take one of the cats up there?"

"I'll give it a go. They tend to do what they want, but Lady Jane is a bit easier to handle than Carrot."

They sat down and ate their sandwiches while Charles explained the action plan and discussed with Theresa which equipment they might need.

An hour later Charles and Theresa drove up to the churchyard. Barry followed on foot with Lady Jane in his arms, making sure she didn't escape. When he arrived, the Watsons had already unloaded some equipment and carried it up to the far corner of the churchyard where the steps were.

"Barry, can you and Lady Jane sit on that seat over there until we get some base line readings, please?" Charles called out. "We want to see if introducing the cat to the area makes a difference."

Barry nodded his agreement and sat talking to the cat while Charles and Theresa did their measurements and made copious notes. Theresa ran down the few steps and found a wall of rough stone blocks at the bottom. She tapped a few keys on the hand-held device, and moved it about, changing its orientation.

"This wall's about 200mm thick, solid stone, and just has soil behind it, pretty much for ever," she said after consulting the device for about twenty minutes. Charles walked over to the flat directly above the bottom of the steps. "No, Daddy, no difference," she called after about ten minutes.

67

"Barry," Charles called. "Can you and Lady Jane come over here and stand where I'm standing, please?" They walked across and Charles moved away.

"Daddy, it's here!" Theresa called after about a minute. "Come and see this – it's amazing!" Charles hurried down the steps and looked over her shoulder at the device. "The wall isn't stone. I don't know what it is, but it isn't stone. And it's only about 50mm thick, and there's a void behind it which seems to go on for ever!"

"By George!" Charles exclaimed after studying the readings. "This is absolutely remarkable. We must find out what's causing this. Now then, do you think we could try to break through the wall?"

"I could help with that!" called Barry, taking a few paces to the side to come round to the steps. "I'm very strong."

"Well, yes, thanks for the offer, Barry, but we need you to stay up there to maintain the wall's constitution. Now that you've moved away the wall has suddenly become much thicker." Barry apologised and resumed his former position. "That's it. That's exactly it. Stay right there. Don't move, and don't let the cat escape." Lady Jane was trying to wriggle free, but Barry tightened his grip on her and talked to her gently, which calmed her down. Charles went to the van and returned with a cold chisel and a hammer. He started hammering at the blocks but didn't seem to be making much of an impression.

"Daddy," said Theresa, who had been looking on and was starting to get bored, as Charles had been hammering away for a good half hour with no discernible success. "Daddy, suppose you or I hold Lady Jane and Barry does the hammering. He does have some quite chunky muscles."

Charles stopped work and wiped his brow on the sleeve of his jacket. "Good idea, darling. Why didn't I think of that? I think you might have more success with our cat friend than I would. Pass me that hand-held and go and change places with Barry." She gave him the device and went up to where Barry was standing. He gently, and very carefully, passed Lady Jane to her. "That looks fine so far, darling. Barry, can you walk away very slowly, please?" Barry took three big but slow steps to the right, then walked forward and came down the steps to join Charles. "That's splendid. You're maintaining the integrity of the void, darling," he called up with a big smile.

Barry looked up at her and smiled. He gave a thumbs up then turned to Charles. "Okay, Charles, let's see how I get on with this." He took the hammer and chisel and struck a few big blows near the middle of the wall. Lady Jane was disturbed by the noise, which was quite considerable, and seemed to be echoing on the other side, but Theresa managed to hang on to her. After ten minutes Barry managed to knock one of the blocks free, so he stopped for a rest while Charles shone a torch through the hole.

"Well done, young fellow," Charles said after looking through the hole with what looked like a small telescope. "I can see absolutely nothing."

Barry was disappointed. "You mean I've done all that work for nothing?"

Charles shook his head and grinned. "On the contrary, Barry. Because of your work I can see nothing. That's a good result. It would have been disappointing if we could see soil or rocks. But no, there's nothing there behind this wall. It's amazing what's holding the ground up. By now Theresa and the cat should have plunged down into the

69

abyss, but they haven't. When you get your breath back can you shift a few more bricks?"

Barry set to work again, and in about ten minutes had managed to remove three more bricks. Just then it started to rain.

"I think we need to call it a day," said Charles. "I don't like working in the rain. It can distort some of the readings, and the physical work can be dangerous. If it's fine tomorrow I would like us all to come back here, and I'll bring a laptop and remote camera. If that's okay with you, Barry. You made short work of those bricks."

"Oh, yes," said Barry. "I'll be back tomorrow. I'll feed the cats first thing and wait there until you arrive, then I'll show those bricks who's boss." He grinned at Theresa, who smiled back and handed the cat to him.

Chapter 12

The next day the Watsons met Barry at the house and had a cup of tea while they waited for the cats to finish their breakfast, then Charles drove up to the churchyard while Barry and Theresa walked there, carrying Lady Jane. When they arrived Charles had already set up his laptop and camera and was peering through the hole in the stone blocks, but all he could see was soil. Barry took the cat up to the ground above the steps, and Charles let out an exclamation.

"Well done!" he shouted. "I can see in!" After a few minutes he called Barry down. "Barry, I would like you to remove some more bricks, but Lady Jane needs to stay up there." Barry passed the cat to Theresa, who took her up to the top. This made Barry's work much easier, and he had cleared a hole big enough to climb through in less than half an hour. Charles leant through, but not too far as he didn't want to suffer the same disaster that had befallen Theresa. He shone the torch and the camera around making methodical sweeps, then repeated the process with two of the hand-held detectors. "Hmph," he said, seeming quite disgruntled. "Nothing. Other than everlasting emptiness."

"Like I said yesterday, have I done all that for nothing?" asked Barry.

"Not at all, Barry. It's an unusual situation, in that the void appears to go on for ever, but I had hoped to detect something. I wonder ... Yes, we'll give that a try." He attached a stout rope to one of the detectors and placed it on the floor just inside the hole. "Theresa, darling, can you bring the cat down here, please?"

"Okay, Daddy. I think she wants Barry. She's getting more and more difficult to hang on to."

The hole immediately filled up with soil and the bricks turned into stone blocks. Charles seemed pleased. He consulted his laptop, but it showed no readings. He tugged at the rope and it came away at the point where it entered the soil. "Damn!" he exclaimed. "Barry, can you take Lady Jane back to the top, please? I want to see if that detector is still there and isn't damaged." Barry did as asked, and the soil disappeared, and there on the floor lay the detector, covered in soil, but otherwise undamaged. Charles retrieved it and called Barry down. "I think I've got all I can from here. For now, anyway. Let's go back to the house for a cup of tea, and perhaps an early lunch." The others agreed and Theresa held the cat while Barry helped carry the equipment back to the van.

Back at the house Barry and Theresa made tea and coffee while Charles sat on the sofa, scowling at an empty page in his notebook. Carrot jumped up and sat beside him. He looked down at her and scratched the top of her head while he munched on a sandwich. "I think you know something, young Carrot. If only you could talk." Barry and Theresa were just about to enter the room with drinks and biscuits, but Theresa signalled to Barry to stop.

"He's talking to the cat," she whispered. "This isn't like him. He generally doesn't get on with animals."

"That's because these cats aren't ordinary cats," answered Barry, as quietly as he could, but Charles looked up.

"Tea, Daddy. It might help you think."

"Yes, thanks. I need some inspiration. Despite this being a very interesting case, I am running into a brick wall with every idea I have. When you have a minute can you check to see if that background noise is still there?"

A few minutes later Theresa came back into the room. "Yes, Daddy, just the same as before. If you don't mind, I would like to take another look into the cellar, now that we've got a more powerful torch."

"Yes, that's fine by me. Having the void open will give me a chance to check some readings, and perhaps we could experiment with some sounds."

Theresa positioned Barry and Lady Jane, and the door appeared, as expected. She opened it and shone the torch in, being careful to stay back this time. "Look, Barry, can you see it? There's something there!" Barry came as far forward as he could without losing the position needed to keep it open.

"Yes, I can see something, but I can't make out what it is," he replied after a few seconds of peering in. Theresa went out to the van and returned with a pair of binoculars.

"It looks like a person!" she said to Barry. "Hello!" she shouted and passed him the binoculars. Barry had a good look and his expression turned to one of horror.

"No! Be quiet! It's her!" he said. Theresa looked at him, puzzled.

"Who is it?"

"It's Sighildra! She's the one who chased us. She wants to eat us. Don't attract her attention." But his warning came too late. Sighildra had been alerted by the sound and turned to face them. She walked slowly forward, and after a few minutes she was close enough for them to see her clearly without the binoculars. "We need to close the door!"

"No, this is interesting. Daddy! Come and see this!"

Charles came into the hall and peered over Theresa's shoulder. "By George!" he exclaimed and dashed out to the van returning with a camera. "This is absolutely fascinating." He stepped forward to get a better shot.

"Daddy! You're almost pushing me over!" shouted Theresa.

"Sorry, darling," he replied. He tried to take a step back but lost his balance and fell against his daughter's back, pushing her into the doorway. She fell in, tumbling through the air, screaming as she fell. Barry and Charles looked at each other, horrified. Lady Jane struggled free from Barry and leapt in after her, followed by Carrot who jumped over the two men. The door disappeared immediately.

After falling for what seemed like forever, Theresa landed on the floor. She got up slowly, checking her limbs and body, and decided she wasn't hurt. She felt the floor and decided she didn't know what it was. Looking round, she saw Sighildra approaching. "Who are you?" she called.

Sighildra stopped. "I am Sighildra. Who are you? And what are you doing here?"

"I'm Theresa. I fell through the doorway. Up there somewhere." She pointed up, vaguely. "I don't want to be here, really. Could you show me the way out, please?"

Sighildra stood with her hands on her hips, threw back her head, and laughed heartily. "Of course I could," she answered. "But I don't want to. You're mine now, and I'll play with you until I get bored, then I'll eat you."

"That's not very nice," said Theresa. "And when you say 'play with me', what do you mean?"

"It's a game. You look for the exit and I follow you. I might help you, or I might mislead you, and when you are worn out I'll get bored and eat you. If the others don't get you first."

"Others? What others?"

"Oh, there are others like me. If they get you first they'll eat you, and they get bored more quickly than I do." She laughed again and stepped forward. Theresa turned and ran. "Where are you going?"

"I'm looking for the exit. I'm not going to sit about and wait to be eaten." She ran, not knowing which way to go, but definitely running away from Sighildra. After a while she stopped and looked back. Sighildra was still there, and walking towards her, but *walking*, not running. She stood and watched, and came to the conclusion that Sighildra couldn't run, but was still a menace. Theresa turned back to continue her search for the way out, then stopped dead in her tracks. In front of her were five more people, just like Sighildra, walking towards her. She glanced to both sides, then chose one at random and ran to her right. The giant people changed direction to follow her, then there seemed to be some sort of argument between them, but they carried on walking in their plodding fashion. Theresa decided running wasn't necessary, but kept up a quick walking pace, ever increasing the gap between her and her pursuers, until she saw a grey flash about fifty yards ahead. Should she stop? Was this another of the strange people? No. The grey streak up ahead turned to meet her – it was Lady Jane. She called to the cat, who came immediately and rubbed her face against Theresa's leg. Then an orange streak, and Carrot was beside her too. Suddenly she heard a voice, a woman's voice, which she didn't recognise, and she couldn't tell which direction it came from.

"Come this way," said the voice. "Follow me." Theresa looked around then realised Lady Jane had taken a dozen or so steps away from her. The little cat stopped and turned to look at her, then turned away and took a few more steps. She followed, feeling that at the moment she had nothing to lose. Carrot followed on a few steps behind.

Chapter 13

Meanwhile Charles and Barry had made their way to the churchyard in the van. When they got there Barry jumped out and set off for the steps in the corner, until Charles called him back.

"Here, take this. We might need it," he said, handing Barry a large blue plastic box from the back of the van. He himself picked up a rucksack and two orange bags. When they reached the corner, Charles was out of breath, and couldn't give Barry meaningful instructions, but Barry didn't need to be told. He ran down the steps and, seeing the hole was full of soil, took a small spade from the blue box and began to shovel the soil away. He didn't seem to be making much progress, when suddenly the soil disappeared, as did the stone blocks. The black bricks were there, with nothing behind them. Barry made to go through but Charles stopped him. From one of the bags he took a stout leather belt, about six inches wide with metal rings, and handed it to Barry. "Put this on, and make sure it's tight," he said while he got a blue nylon rope from the other bag. He attached this to one of the rings and fastened the other end securely to a nearby beech tree. "Right, in you go."

Barry stepped forward to go in through the hole when it disappeared. He turned to Charles with a puzzled look on his face. "What do we do now?"

Charles indicated to him to wait. A moment later the hole appeared, only to disappear shortly afterwards. "Don't worry," he said. "One of the cats must be close to us, but not close enough. Go in, but if the rope goes taut, stand still and wait for it to slacken." Barry indicated thumbs up and went in.

Theresa and the cats walked steadily forward, stopping every now and again for Lady Jane to sniff the air. She seemed to know what she was doing, but every stop gave the giant people time to catch up a bit. At one point Theresa decided they were getting too close, and tried to urge Lady Jane on. Carrot turned to face the giants and began to snarl. Her size increased to that of a large dog, and her snarl increased in volume and tone until she sounded at first like a wolf, then like a tiger. The giants stopped and covered their ears. Some fell to the ground; others turned and walked away as quickly as they could. Theresa smiled and scratched Carrot's head, then turned back and followed Lady Jane who by this time had set off again. Eventually they came to a place where they could see the side walls, and it narrowed into a corridor. Lady Jane led the way and the others followed, but it became obvious to Theresa that the little cat was tiring. When she thought about it, she realised she was tiring too, as was Carrot. They slowed down considerably, but up ahead Theresa saw light. And then she saw Barry, stumbling towards them. When they met he collapsed against the side wall.

"Are you okay?" asked Theresa, going down on one knee to wipe the sweat from his face.

"Yes, of course I am," he answered with a broad grin. "Just getting my breath back. Are you?" She nodded, but realised she wasn't. She helped Barry up to his feet, and almost collapsed herself. He picked her up and put her over his shoulder, fireman's lift fashion, and stumbled along the corridor which got narrower. As they neared the end Barry saw Charles' anxious face, and tried to shout to reassure him, but couldn't. The two cats passed them and went on ahead, walking, but struggling. As they got closer Barry's legs gave way, but he gamely crawled along with Theresa on his back. He spoke to her but got no answer, so he stopped and lowered her to the ground. Realising she was unconscious he picked her up with one arm and staggered along, putting her back into the fireman's lift position when the corridor got too narrow for anything else.

Outside Charles saw the cats approaching and gathered Carrot into his arms. He sat at the entrance, making sure there was enough cat inside to keep the portal open, then he hauled away at the rope the best he could with one hand, bracing his feet against the entrance. Eventually Barry and Theresa emerged, and collapsed at the bottom of the steps. Charles let go of the cat and both cats crawled slowly up the steps. The portal closed, returning to its original soil and stone blocks, but all four adventurers were clear. They sat while Barry removed the belt, and Theresa started to come round. When she saw Charles she burst into tears and threw her arms round his neck. By now the cats had reached the top of the steps and they lay on the grass, panting. Lady Jane started to get bigger too, and Charles followed them, leaving Barry and Theresa hugging at the bottom of the steps. Charles went over to thank the cats, but realised they were no longer cats. Their fur began to fall out, and they transformed into young women, totally naked. Charles put his jacket over the one that had been Carrot, then pulled off his jumper and put it over the other. He turned back to give the news to Barry, only to see him and Theresa crawling up the steps on all fours, getting smaller as they came. When their clothes were too big, they just walked out of them. That's when Charles noticed that one had a fine covering of orange fur, the other grey. By the time they got to the top they were both covered in thick fur and had become cats.

"Now I know why Barry was so sure," said Charles, sitting down on the grass and letting the cats climb over him.

Fear in the Workplace

Chapter 1

"Why is it always cold around my desk?" exclaimed Victoria, pulling her cardigan around her shoulders.

"It's just your imagination," laughed Lisa.

"Think warm thoughts. Imagine having a bath in a giant mug of Horlicks," offered Eric, ever the practical one. Victoria was embarrassed. She hadn't intended the others to hear. This was her first week in the job, and she didn't want anyone to think she was a complainer. Keith raised an eyebrow without lifting his head, then carried on with his work as though he hadn't heard. The telephone brought her out of her thoughts with a start. It was Eric.

"We need to go over some costing figures together. Shall we do it at your desk or mine?"

"Yours is probably warmer than mine. Do you want to start now?"

"Fine. Pull up a chair."

She trundled her chair across the office, laden with papers and files, to Eric's desk and made herself at home.

"It's much warmer here," she commented, removing her cardigan.

"I don't believe you. And don't get carried away, taking clothes off like that, I'm a married man," Eric replied with a smile. They worked quietly together for an hour, then Victoria returned to her desk. She opened her mouth to speak but thought better of it. Pulling her cardigan on quickly she sat down and got on with some work. Keith glanced out of the window then sprang to his feet.

"Is that the time? I've an appointment in the conference room. See you guys later." He grabbed a handful of papers, pen, and calculator, and disappeared through the door.

"I'm too warm but I daren't turn the heating down for fear of upsetting the ice-maiden over there," said Eric with an exaggerated wipe of the forehead.

"Actually, I feel warmer now," said Victoria. "The coldness seems to have disappeared suddenly."

"It's me," said Eric, "I radiate warmth."

"I think it's Keith," laughed Lisa, "He radiates cold."

"Actually, you can't radiate cold," Eric corrected her. "Cold can only travel by conduction or convection, because cold is heat travelling backwards, which radiation can't do."

"Okay, professor, you've made your point," said Victoria, "but Lisa has something. The room got warmer when Keith left."

"There is a simple explanation. Observe." Eric pointed out of the window. "The sun has risen over the artificial horizon of office blocks. We have effectively just experienced dawn, hence the rise in temperature." He sat down and carried on with his work. Lisa and Victoria looked at each other and giggled.

"I suppose he's right," Victoria whispered.

"He usually is," Lisa replied.

"Usually? What do you mean?" Eric asked with indignation.

"Okay, almost always."

"You're getting closer. What's this 'almost' bit about?"

"Come on, Victoria, let's get some lunch and leave Mr Perfect to enjoy the sun-drenched office." They left together.

The two women walked along the high street side by side and turned into a sandwich bar.

"Keith has a strange name. Is he foreign?" asked Victoria.

"Yes. East European," replied Lisa. "He's from Romania or somewhere like that, apparently, but he hasn't said a word himself. I've picked up bits and pieces from the others. They say the villagers chopped his father's head off and that's why he came here."

"Do they still do that sort of thing?"

"It doesn't happen in Hammersmith, or not very often, anyway, but over there it's a regular occurrence."

"Why did they do it?"

"I haven't a clue. But you know what men are like – probably for handling the ball in the penalty area or something or cheating at dominos."

They returned to the office armed with sandwiches and chocolate bars.

"Here, I'll show you the rear entrance," said Lisa, dragging Victoria into an alleyway. "This is quicker than using the front door, but it's a bit dodgy after dark." They entered through a small door and ascended a flight of stairs. "This is the other end of our corridor, and that's the conference room." Lisa pointed to the half-open door of a darkened room. Victoria glanced in but could see nothing. "There aren't any windows," Lisa explained, "because it's in the middle of the building." They returned to their desks and ate their sandwiches.

Keith returned sometime after three o'clock. He got on with his work without a word to anyone. Victoria eyed him suspiciously. Where had he been? She instinctively knew that there was more to the tall lean man but was afraid to dig too deeply. At the end of the day she gathered her

85

belongings and bade her new colleagues goodnight. Keith alone didn't answer.

The next day nothing much had changed. The area around Victoria's desk was still cold, until Keith disappeared into the conference room, which coincided with the sun peeping over the top of the unemployment office, so it didn't prove anything. The week continued, each day being just like the last, until on Friday, spurred on by the need to know more in order to sleep at the weekend, Victoria plucked up the courage to act. She waited until a few minutes after Keith had left for his daily visit to the conference room, then followed the corridor, making sure she wasn't seen. The conference room door was half open, just as on Monday, and the room was in darkness. She crept up to the door and edged one eye past the frame to look in but could see nothing. Suddenly, she detected movement in the room. She fled along the corridor and burst into the office. Lisa and Eric looked up in surprise.

"Goodness Victoria," exclaimed Lisa, stepping across to her. "Are you alright? You look as if you've seen a ghost!" She settled Victoria into a chair and turned to Eric. "I think she could do with a cup of coffee." Eric was already on his feet.

"On its way," he called as he left the room.

"What's happened? You're trembling. Tell me what's wrong," said Lisa, looking into Victoria's wide eyes. Victoria burst into tears.

"I'm sorry," she sobbed, "I feel so stupid. Nothing has happened, but I had an overwhelming feeling of evil. I'm not easily frightened, but I'm scared now, and I don't know why." Victoria told Lisa about the unlit conference room

86

with something in it. Lisa said nothing but looked into Victoria's eyes and saw genuine fear. Victoria had stopped crying now and was calmer. "Lisa," she said, quietly, "what about Eric? What are we going to tell him? He'll think I'm stupid." Lisa thought for a moment.

"We'll tell him you've seen a ghost. Just for now anyway. He can be quite understanding so don't worry about him." She had just finished speaking when Eric entered bearing a tray of drinks.

"There you are, m'dear," he said, handing over a steaming mug, "get that down your neck. Wonderful thing, caffeine, can't get enough of it. I wish they made coffee with extra caffeine. Now, what's the problem?"

"She thinks she saw a ghost or something. In the conference room," Lisa volunteered. "Don't laugh, she's badly shaken."

"I wasn't going to laugh," Eric replied curtly, "I keep an open mind about anything that can't be disproved, providing it's feasible. Just because we don't understand something doesn't mean it doesn't exist. Why don't you take her outside for a breath of fresh air? I'll cover the phones." Victoria shook her head.

"No, I'll be alright in a minute," she replied, trying to hold the coffee without spilling it.

"When you think you're up to it," said Eric after a short silence, "I'd like to hear more about what happened. I'm interested from a scientific point of view."

"I don't feel like it at the moment," she replied, "but perhaps next week, if you don't mind." Eric held up his hands.

"No problem. You've had a shock. Take it easy for now." He rose to his feet. "Anyway, I'm off for a spot of lunch." He left the room.

Lunch wasn't really on his mind. He was concerned at the state Victoria had been in and wanted to see the room for himself. He hadn't been in the conference room for several weeks but didn't remember it as being particularly unpleasant. He made his way along the corridor quickly and quietly and found the room just as Victoria had left it a short while ago. The light was off, and the door was half open. He paused at the door to listen, and heard a sound, but he couldn't quite work out what it was. He turned on the light and strode in confidently. There were no signs of life. Perhaps the noise had been an insect, or a mouse. Both options seemed unlikely, as the whole building had been recently cleansed of an infestation of mice, and the ratcatchers had insisted the chemicals would keep all rodents and insects out for at least six months. All cracks had been sealed, and there were no windows; the room was effectively air-tight except for the air-conditioning vent and the door. He wandered round the room, touching the furniture as he passed, then, happy that everything was as it should be, set off in search of a bag of chips.

Victoria spent a restless weekend in her flat and returned to work on Monday morning looking absolutely worn out. She was the first to arrive, and sat at her desk, motionless, waiting for the others. Keith silently entered the room and greeted her with a weak smile.

"Oh! Hello. I didn't hear you come in," she said. Keith shook his head.

"I don't believe in unnecessary noise." He grinned, then sat down and got on with his work. Victoria felt cold but tried to tell herself it was all in the mind. She wanted to say something to Keith, to challenge him about the darkened room on Friday, but she daren't. Not when she was alone with him. But she would feel silly if she said anything when the others were here. What could she do? She had no-one to turn to. Lisa had given her support on Friday, but she got the impression that at half past five she had suddenly ceased to be Lisa's problem. Eric had seemed genuinely concerned at first, but when he returned from lunch he was distant, aloof, as though he didn't even know about her problem. Victoria felt very alone. Suddenly the room came alive as Lisa and Eric bustled in, talking and laughing.

"Are you alright? You look awful!" Lisa said after exchanging greetings.

"I'm just a little tired," Victoria answered, "I didn't get much sleep over the weekend."

"We'll have a chat later." Victoria felt greatly relieved. She did, after all, have someone she could rely on. She pressed on with her work and decided to do something positive about the problem. At half past ten she got up and left the room. If last week was anything to go by, Keith would be getting ready to disappear in a few minutes, and she was going to be prepared. She made her way along the corridor, past the unlit conference room, and on to the back staircase. From her vantage point she could see the conference room door quite clearly, but no-one would see her unless they were deliberately looking for her. Sure enough, a few minutes later, Keith came along the corridor, armed with papers, pens, and calculator. He paused at the open door, and looked both ways along the empty corridor, as though he didn't want to be seen, then went in. Pleased with her success, Victoria suddenly realised she didn't know what to do next. She hadn't planned this far ahead. What should she do? She could leave it at that, with him in the room, but what would that prove? Perhaps he had a headache and wanted to be in the dark. So what? She had done the same herself before. No, this was the opportunity for action. Clenching her teeth, she strode forward into the room and turned the light on. Her mouth opened to address him, but no sound came out. He wasn't there. His papers were on a chair in the corner of the room, but he was nowhere to be seen. Statues have been guilty of more movement than Victoria was for a short while, then something touched her arm and she passed out.

Chapter 2

Steve answered the ringing telephone. It was Jenny, asking him – no, telling him – to call in to her office. Another job, probably. Steve didn't like this. When he first got involved he was desperate for the money, and now he couldn't get out of it. His record of petty crime, his father in prison for GBH, wouldn't stand up against her completely clean slate, degree from Oxford, and several professional qualifications. If he told the police what was going on no one would believe him, and she knew it. He made his way up the back stairs to her office, tapped on the door, and went in. Jenny and Keith immediately halted their whisperings and turned to smile at him. Steve didn't like Jenny, but he liked Keith even less. There was something unpleasant about this tall, lean, good-looking young man. Jenny spoke and confirmed Steve's fears.

"We've a little job to do," she said, quietly. "Be at my flat at seven tonight, and we'll tell you more."

"Er, can we make it eight? Or eight thirty would be better," Keith butted in.

"Alright, eight thirty," Jenny agreed, "but be on time, I've got other things to do. This is an important job, and Mr Konopinski is paying well, because this is personal."

"Personal? In what way?" Steve asked.

"Some bloke has been messing about with his daughter," Jenny answered. "Mr K isn't happy about it, especially when he discovered the man was already married."

"I see," Steve muttered, "right then, I'll see you tonight." He left the room quickly. He couldn't wait to get away from Keith. He made his back to his office, shaking

91

his head slowly. Why had he ever got involved with these two? He wasn't a real criminal, just a petty crook trying to go straight. If it weren't for his stupid gambling debts he wouldn't be in this pickle. Anyway, he couldn't see a way out, so he may as well do the job as well as he was able. After all, if this is personal, Mr K might take a bit more interest in it, and he wouldn't be pleased if it went wrong.

Steve arrived at Jenny's flat a few minutes early. It was summer, and still light. Jenny let him in and made him a cup of coffee.

"Where's Keith?" she asked him unpleasantly, as though he were to blame for Keith's late arrival. "I told him to be on time. I've got a social life even if he hasn't."

Steve sat in silence. His social life had been disrupted by these jobs, but that didn't seem to matter. Then again, when he got the money his wife was happy, and didn't ask any difficult questions. He sipped his coffee, ignoring Jenny's escalating anger. Eventually Keith arrived. Steve didn't move. He heard Jenny complaining vociferously, but by the time she had ushered Keith into the room she was calm and business-like. They all sat round a small table and Jenny produced a large envelope which she emptied onto it. She pulled a photograph from amongst the papers.

"This is our target," she began, but Steve interrupted.

"I know him – that's Andy Anderson. He's a lift engineer, but he's pretty rubbish. Who's the bit of skirt? She's gorgeous!" Jenny glared over the top of her glasses at him.

"The 'bit of skirt' is Elisabet Konopinski, Mr K's daughter. She is pregnant. Mr K is not happy about that, and wants his revenge on Anderson, who has refused to marry the girl, on the grounds that he is already married, although I understand he is separated from his wife. This could be easier than we thought. As I said this morning, Mr K is paying well for this one. What do you know about Anderson?"

"Well, he's a lift engineer," Steve began slowly, wondering how much he should tell them. "He lives somewhere close to the office, but I don't know exactly where. He's useless, and last time he came Stan told the lift company that if he's the only engineer available not to bother sending him, because the lift would have a better chance of healing itself. He's a pretty miserable sort, too. Nobody likes him, and some of the other engineers refuse to work with him. Getting rid of him would be doing the world a favour." Steve sat back and folded his arms.

"Good," said Jenny. "So if he disappeared no-one would complain. Keith! Pay attention! I'm talking!" She spoke sharply, but Keith didn't seem to notice. He was holding the photograph and staring at it.

"This," he said, "is the most beautiful woman I have ever met." He held the photograph for the others to see. Jenny wasn't amused.

"You haven't met her," she snapped.

"Not yet," Keith replied, his eyes fixed on the photograph, "not yet, but I will. I will soon."

"Don't you go getting mixed up with her," Jenny rasped. "You know what Mr K is like when he gets angry." She shuddered. Steve had never met Mr K, but if Jenny was worried, well, he had to be quite fearsome to frighten Jenny. She snatched the photograph from Keith and said

"Come on. We've work to do and I haven't much time left tonight."

Half an hour later Steve and Keith were on their way home.

"It's near here, isn't it?" Keith asked as they walked.

"Yes," Steve replied. "Just round here." He indicated a side road with a twitch of his head, keeping his hands in his pockets on such a cold night. "Come on, I'll show you." He took a couple of corners, with Keith following, then stopped abruptly. He flattened himself against the wall and indicated a door opening further along the street. "That's him coming out of that house." They waited in silence. Anderson came out followed by a woman and closed the door. The couple strolled along the street, arm in arm, away from Steve and Keith. "That's probably her," Steve whispered. Keith nodded.

"It is. It's her."

"You can't be certain from here."

"I can. I recognised her from the photograph."

"Pull the other one. It's dark and they're too far off. You can't possibly see."

"Yes, I can. It's her. Come on."

They followed at a distance, until Anderson and his companion turned into a pub. Keith was going to follow, but Steve grasped his arm. "What do you think you're doing?" he asked. Keith looked puzzled at Steve's caution.

"I'm following them. Find out about their habits, like usual." He pulled his arm free and made as if to go in. He turned to Steve. "Come on, I'll buy you a pint." Steve protested.

"He'll recognise me. Then what?"

"So what? You've done nothing wrong. You live round here, so why shouldn't you be in this pub? This is an opportunity to get his trust. That'll make it easier. Come on." Steve hesitated. "Would you like me to tell Jenny you passed up an opportunity like this?" Keith grinned as Steve reluctantly stepped into the pub. Keith bought the drinks while Steve sought the man out. He tapped him on the shoulder.

"Hello, Andy," he said with a smile. "Didn't know you came in here. This is my pal, Keith. Mind if we join you?" Anderson gesticulated to the empty chairs. They sat and chatted with him for a while, mainly about football and beer. Elisabet sat in silence. Then they finished their drinks and left. Half an hour later the couple came out. Anderson paused to light a cigarette. They jumped on him, pushing the woman to the ground, and Steve struck Anderson a violent blow to the solar plexus. The man dropped to the floor in a heap, unconscious. Steve stepped back. Elisabet slowly got to her feet, then ran off.

"That's enough. He's out; he might be dead. I hit him hard and in the right place. Stuff I learnt in the army," said Steve.

"No, that's not good enough," said Keith. "Jenny said Mr K wanted him dead. Mr K gets what he wants."

"Well I'm doing no more. I'm out of here." Steve turned and walked away very quickly.

"Never mind," said Keith. "I'll get rid of the body. I know just the place." Keith picked up the silent Anderson and slung him over his shoulder as though he were a sack of potatoes and strode off into the night.

Chapter 3

"I can't believe it. I simply can't!" Stan paced the floor impatiently while Steve leant against the wall staring at his half-smoked cigarette. "How on earth did we keep a dead body in the basement for three weeks without anyone noticing? Three weeks! I can't believe it." Steve shrugged his shoulders and gesticulated vaguely.

"Haven't a clue." Steve continued the contemplation of his cigarette. There was a knock at the door. Steve opened it and two men entered. "Come in, have a seat," he said, indicating chairs.

"What are you doing here, Ray?" Stan asked as he sat behind the desk.

"Brother Gibson is allowed representation at a disciplinary meeting, and he asked me to attend in my capacity as his Official Friend," Ray replied smugly, as he sat back in the chair and folded his arms.

"But this isn't a disciplinary meeting," Stan replied, "Jimmy is here to give me some facts. I wouldn't dream of sacking him anyway. He's our best cleaner."

"You can't say that, Mr Atkinson," said Ray, "it could cause offence to the other cleaners."

"But the other cleaners don't know I've said it."

"They will, Mr Atkinson," Ray said, being smug again, "they will when I tell them."

"I must remind you, Ray, that a disciplinary meeting is confidential." It was Stan's turn to be smug, until Ray deflated him.

"But you just said it wasn't a disciplinary meeting."

"Okay, but ... so why are you here then?" Stan suddenly brightened, as Ray looked flustered.

"I think I should stay in case disciplinary matters arise, if brother Gibson agrees, as his Official Friend." Jimmy, confused by all this, decided to agree, although he wasn't really sure what he was agreeing to. Stan was clearly annoyed.

"Official Friend indeed! You hate his guts!"

"That's just personal. In my official capacity I am his Friend." Ray smiled. Stan and Steve, seeing the funny side, tried not to laugh. Jimmy remained passive, not understanding the irony.

"Anyway," Stan suddenly became more business-like, "let's get on with it. I've got to speak to the police tomorrow. Tell me, Jimmy, when was the last time you cleaned that cubicle?"

"Well, I'm not sure, Mr Atkinson," Jimmy spoke slowly, trying to count on his fingers, "I think it was about four weeks ago."

"I thought all toilets were cleaned at least once a day," said Stan, looking at Steve.

"That's right," Steve replied. "Why haven't you cleaned it since then, Jimmy?"

"There was a man in it. We're told not to go in a cubicle if there's somebody using it."

"So you cleaned the rest of the toilet block every day, but not that cubicle?"

"That's right. I like it down there. It's nice and quiet. You don't get people being in the way."

"Except for that one cubicle, eh, Jimmy?" Stan asked.

"Well, yes, but he was no bother. He wasn't making a noise or a fuss or anything like that."

"Jimmy, how did you know there was someone in there?" Steve asked.

"I looked under the door and saw his feet, like it says in the book."

"Does it say that, Steve?" Stan asked, trying to remain calm.

"It does. We introduced that about ten years ago when the salesmen bolted the doors and climbed over the top and no one could go until they realised. We only had one gents' toilet in the old building. Remember?" Stan nodded.

"Yes. So how did you know it was a man, Jimmy?"

"It was the gents' toilet. Women aren't allowed in the gents' toilets. It says so in the book." Stan felt he was fighting a losing battle.

"But didn't it smell?" he asked.

"Yes, but toilets are like that, smelly, especially if they haven't been cleaned properly."

"But Jimmy, didn't you think it a bit odd that this one cubicle was always in use?"

"No, Mr Atkinson, there's usually somebody in when I go to clean them."

"So does this mean you often leave a cubicle uncleaned?"

"I must advise brother Gibson not to answer that question," Ray butted in. He was pleased to be able to justify his presence. "He might end up being disciplined."

"No, Ray, it's alright," Jimmy answered, firmly but calmly, "I usually wait a few minutes for them to come out, then a few more minutes for the smell to go, then I go in and clean."

"So when you waited and he didn't come out, what then?"

"Well, I went and did other things, then came back later, but the door was still shut."

"Didn't you think it strange when he stayed in there a long time?"

"No, he might have been reading the paper."

"But he wasn't making a noise, you said."

"Yes, some people are clever like that." Stan and Steve looked at each other, puzzled. Jimmy realised he needed to explain. "Some people can read without making a noise. Their lips move but they don't make a noise. That's clever, that is."

"So you didn't think to investigate when this cubicle was occupied for three or four weeks? It obviously needed cleaning, judging by the smell."

"I must remind you," Ray butted in, "that brother Gibson is an operative. He is not management. You are suggesting that he should have made a management decision. This is not within the scope of his duties." Stan held up his hands in submission.

"Okay, Ray, point taken, but he could have asked Steve for advice."

"Deciding that advice was needed...." but he didn't finish the sentence. Stan's hands were in the air again.

"Can we forget that I said that last bit please? I have to get my facts together for the police and haven't time to worry about what is or isn't a decision at present. Steve, I need you to explain this to me, but let's leave it for a week or so." He turned back to Jimmy and smiled. "Well, Jimmy, thank you for your help. I don't think I need to ask you any more about this for now, but the police might want to talk to you tomorrow, or perhaps later in the week. You can both go back to your work now." He stood and shook hands with them both, then Steve opened the door and they left. As they walked away Ray's voice could be heard.

"Well done, Jimmy, between us we managed to get you off Scot free. I think you owe me a pint."

Stan sat at his desk with his head in his hands. Steve lit another cigarette and smiled. Stan was clearly not amused.

"Cheer up," Steve said, "we got Ray in and out of here in less than half an hour, and without him calling a strike."

"Yes, there is that," Stan admitted, "but what am I going to tell the police? Jimmy thought the dead man was reading a newspaper?"

"Do you want me in to help?"

"No, I think they want to talk to you independently. Who was the dead man anyway?"

"A lift engineer. They'd been in all week trying to fix number two."

"Didn't anyone notice him missing?"

"Obviously not."

"Well, our main priority at the moment is to keep it out of the papers. It doesn't do for a PR company to have its offices full of dead bodies."

"Hardly full! Just one corpse isn't exactly an epidemic!" Steve replied scornfully. Stan grinned wryly.

"That's not how the tabloids would see it. They would have a field day."

The next day saw a sombre-looking police officer arrive at reception. Stan came down to greet him, and took him up to his office, calling at the coffee machine on the way. DCI Hodges looked grim.

"It is important, Mr Atkinson," he said in a low voice, "that we are not disturbed or overheard. Is that likely here?"

"Well," Stan was a little taken aback, "I didn't think it would be necessary, but if you wish we can go to one of the meeting rooms. If we stay here the phone will be ringing and people will be popping in and out."

"Yes," DCI Hodges replied, "privacy is essential." Stan led the way up two floors and along corridors to a small room overlooking the shopping centre. He placed a 'Meeting in Progress – Do Not Disturb' sign on the door, then the two men sat down at opposite sides of the table.

"We're always willing to co-operate with the police, but I didn't quite expect this level of secrecy," Stan said, trying to lighten the mood a little. DCI Hodges failed to be lightened.

"We don't send chief inspectors to routine death cases," he replied, looking Stan in the eye in a way that made Stan's flesh creep. "What I'm about to tell you must not go any further at present." Stan nodded. "Mr Anderson, the late Mr Jonathon Anderson, that is, well, there's no evidence he died of natural causes or committed suicide. There's a possibility he was murdered."

Chapter 4

Victoria opened her eyes. She realised she wasn't standing up, but wasn't sure why, nor why her eyes had been closed. It took a few moments to adjust to the bright lights shining down, but when she was able to focus, she saw Keith standing over her. She screamed and tried to get up but was held down. Her flailing arms were grabbed by unseen hands, then she heard a woman's voice.

"Don't struggle, you'll be all right in a few minutes." It was Lisa. Victoria felt relieved for a moment, then panic returned as she considered that Lisa might be in league with Keith. The hands relaxed their grip as she slowly tried to sit up. She looked around to find herself on the floor of the conference room. Keith and Lisa were at either side, looking concerned. Were they concerned for her welfare, or that she had survived their attack?

"Are you able to stand?" Keith asked. She nodded and rose clumsily. Lisa gripped her arm.

"Come back to the office," she said firmly but quietly," and I'll send Eric to make some tea." Victoria meekly allowed herself to be led away by Lisa. Keith didn't follow.

Back at her desk with a mug of Eric's excellent tea Victoria was feeling much better, to the point where she could laugh about the incident.

"All I did," Lisa explained to Eric, "was to touch her arm, and she just slumped to the ground, like a rag doll."

"I thought you were Keith," Victoria giggled.

"Keith was nowhere to be seen. He appeared while I was trying to pick you up. You've got this thing about Keith." Lisa turned to Eric again. "She thinks he's some form of demon." Eric laughed. Victoria stopped giggling.

"There's something evil about him, and I'm going to prove it." She was clearly annoyed, so the others didn't say any more. She left the room quickly.

"I think she's got a mental problem," Eric commented.

Lisa sighed. "I think you could be right." They pressed on with their work in contemplative silence.

It was lunchtime, so Victoria took off to the municipal library to research the powers of evil. The brisk walk helped to burn off some of her anger. She knew now that they didn't take her concerns seriously, but she knew she was right. The problem now was how to prove it. She selected three books and took them to a corner where she could work undisturbed. Zombies didn't say much, and had bits falling off all the time, so that was out. Werewolves only caused problems at night at the time of the full moon, so that was out too. Several other strange beings which Victoria hadn't heard of were also quickly discounted, because of wailing, or strange appearance, or inability to speak. She turned the page and shuddered as she saw a drawing of a tall man dressed in black with his arms raised menacingly. Unlike the figure, she had never seen Keith wearing a cloak, but she found it very easy to visualise Keith's face on the dark form. Too easy. She looked at the words beneath the drawing and her blood turned to ice – 'The Vampire'. She slammed the book shut. Sprang to her feet, and walked away hurriedly, but stopped a few feet from the table. She was drawn to the book, even though she was desperately trying to put it all out of her mind. Opening her bag with trembling fingers, she took out paper and a pen and began to write. Vampires' weaknesses were her main interest, so she found them and scribbled them down quickly. Unable to cross running water; fear of the Holy Crucifix, fear of garlic, she turned the page and froze. Fear of direct sunlight – was this why Keith spent so much time in the conference room? She hurriedly wrote it down and scanned the rest of the page. Vampires don't have reflections – that should be easy to test. They can only be destroyed by a wooden stake through the heart – difficult to arrange in Hammersmith – or by decapitation. Decapitation – that wrang a bell. She looked up from the book for a moment and went over the events of the last week. Of course! Lisa had said that the local people had cut off Keith's father's head. That was why Keith came to England – to avoid a similar fate! She looked at her watch and packed her things away. Hurrying back to the office, she resolved to visit the library again after work. Meanwhile, how easy would it be to test the reflection theory?

Back in the office she waited for the others to return from lunch. Lisa and Eric arrived and set to work, after commenting on her looking better. It was after three o'clock when Keith returned. The sun had dropped behind the offices across the road a few minutes earlier. He sat at his desk. Victoria studied his face. He looked tired, as she did after a night of interrupted sleep. Had he just woken up? She slipped a small mirror from her bag onto the desk and hid it with papers. Next time he left the room she would look for him in it. He had to pass her desk, so there was no way he could avoid it, no way she could miss him. She would know before the day was out. He glanced up at her, then carried on with his work. Did he know she suspected? He glanced up again about half an hour later. It was as though he wanted to leave the room, but not while she was watching. At five thirty he still hadn't moved from his desk. Victoria went home convinced she was right, but worried that her investigation was no longer a secret. What if he followed her? How far would he go to ensure her silence? Vampires weren't renowned for their philanthropy, or their support for freedom of speech. She hurried through the darkening streets, hesitating at every junction. Should she aim for the safety of her flat, or would the solitude provide Keith with the opportunity he wanted? Should she stick to the main streets where he could see her easily, or should she try to escape along alleyways where there was nobody to help? Eventually she arrived home, short of breath, her mind in turmoil, but home, among familiar things. She bolted the door and waited, not daring to sleep, for the dawn.

The next morning, she woke in the chair, her neck aching, her limbs stiff, a cup of cold coffee on the table. She had survived the night. Either Keith hadn't been able to follow her, or else he didn't see her as a threat. Perhaps her suspicions were unfounded. Not about him being a vampire, of course, there was no doubt about that, but about him realising she knew. She smiled. Today was the day. He couldn't avoid her mirror without risking the rising sun. Today her suspicions would become hard facts. Today she would have evidence. Today she could silence the sceptics. Lisa and Eric would be in awe of her courage and cunning. An hour later, washed and breakfasted, she strode along the street with confidence and determination never experienced before. At the office her bravery began to waver. She opened the door to find Keith already at his desk. She paused in the doorway, then, confident of his need to avoid the sun, she smiled a greeting and sat down.

As sunrise approached, she prepared her pocket mirror on the desk. He wouldn't be able to see it, but she could with a barely perceptible head movement. Suddenly Keith rose. Victoria clenched her teeth and waited. He dashed past while she stared into the little mirror. She didn't see him. Proof. A few hours later Keith returned. Victoria was ready with test number two.

"Would you like a sandwich?" she asked, offering him part of her meagre lunch. "There's nothing wrong with it, I just think I've got too much. It's garlic sausage." Keith backed away toward his desk. "It's very nice," she said, rising to her feet and holding it out to him. He held up his hands in protest and shrank back. A look of panic spread across his face as he realised he was cornered.

"No, sorry," he stammered. "Can't eat things like that." He looked terrified, confused, how was he going to get out of this? "Can't even touch it – religious reasons, you know." Victoria's face fell. She looked down at the sandwich, dejectedly.

"Sorry, didn't realise." After staring at it for a moment she threw the food onto her desk and dashed out. She fled to the toilet block, tears streaming down her face. He had foiled her plan. Still, she had her proof from the mirror test. She pulled herself together, made some minor repairs to her make-up, and returned, calm again, to her desk. The next day Victoria went to visit the personnel officer. She knocked on the door and went in. The personnel officer smiled warmly. Victoria closed the door.

"Ms Grover," she began, but didn't get very far.

"Don't call me Ms." The older woman replied sharply, "you sound like a wasp in a jam jar."

"What should I call you then? Are you Mrs or Miss?"

"Call me what you like. You've a fifty-fifty chance of being right. Or of being wrong, but don't call me Ms." Her expression was a mixture of fun and anger.

"Okay then, Mrs Grover," Victoria tried again.

"Wrong!" Miss Grover laughed hysterically. Victoria was wondering if there was any point in continuing, when Miss Grover became serious, as though a switch had been thrown. "Sorry. Sit down. You can call me Jenny." She beamed a huge smile at Victoria, who opened her mouth to speak, then waited for another interruption. "Come on, girl," she said, "I haven't got all day."

"I need to speak to you about a confidential matter. I need your assurance that you won't tell anyone until you are ready to take action."

"Yes, of course. Go on." She looked solemnly at Victoria's agitated face.

"It's about Keith."

Jenny threw herself back in the chair. "God, not again! I suppose he's been, er, how shall we put it, fondling you in places you'd rather not be fondled. Has he?"

"Oh, no! Nothing like that."

Jenny was taken aback. "Oh! Well, I don't see why not. You're pretty enough. Just his type, I would have thought. Moreso than the others, I would have said. Anyway, what's the problem then?" Victoria leant forward and lowered her voice.

"You've got to get rid of him," she said, earnestly, "because he's a vampire!"

"Vampire you say?" Jenny grabbed a notebook and began writing furiously. "Well, firstly, what makes you think he's a vampire, and secondly, what makes you think I can get rid of him? There's nothing in the staff handbook to

107

say that people aren't permitted to be vampires. Heavens, we even employ Young Conservatives here! I'd get rid of them if I it was up to me, but they won't let me." Victoria was shocked at Jenny's matter-of-fact approach to the situation.

"Surely he's a danger to other staff!" she said.

"Well, you could have a point there, but he's been here for quite some time and, frankly, you're the first person to complain about anything, apart from a few girls who complained about sexual advances."

"Could he be lying about his age? Vampires live for hundreds of years."

"No. He has a legitimate birth certificate. Tell you what. You obviously know more about vampires than I do. Why don't you run along and try to dream up an excuse that will stand up in court, eh?" Victoria reluctantly agreed and left the room. Jenny picked up the phone and pressed a few buttons. "Hello, Katie? Jenny here. Do you remember last week we got a brochure from a company that does things for stressed out employees? Well dig it out. We've got a live one. The new girl, Veronica, or whatever her name is."

Chapter 5

"Murdered!" Stan was shocked

"That's right, murdered." DCI Hodges watched Stan's face, looking for any hint that Stan wasn't completely taken by surprise, but found none.

"Are you sure? Are you saying that one of our employees killed him?"

"At present we are keeping all options open, which means yes, we are considering that as a possibility." The policeman looked grim, all the while studying Stan's face intently.

Stan looked worried. "But with one or two exceptions the present staff has been here for more than five years. This means I could've been working with a murderer for years – laughing with him at the Christmas party, perhaps even given him a lift home."

"That's right. It's possible."

Stan looked at DCI Hodges and leant forward. "How was he murdered?" he asked, almost in a whisper.

Hodges sat back. "I, er, can't say. Not at the moment," he said, averting his eyes from Stan's gaze.

Stan became agitated. "What? How can you expect us to help if keep us in the dark? Tell me how he was murdered and I might be able to throw some light on it."

"Well, er, it's not quite that simple," DCI Hodges was clearly embarrassed, "you see, we're not sure. Well, not yet anyway."

Stan's eyes opened wide in disbelief. "Not sure? Are you sure he was murdered?"

"Well, almost certain about that. Look, I'd appreciate you keeping this quiet. If word got out, well, you can imagine…." Stan now had the upper hand.

"I'll keep quiet if you'll level with me. I've the safety of our people to consider, but I'm not going to have you making a fool of me. Now then! What's this all about?"

Hodges leaned forward and put his head in his hands. He shook his head slowly before looking up into Stan's face. "As you can appreciate, Mr Atkinson, people sometimes die sitting on the toilet. Usually it is a simple case of natural causes. Heart attack, asthma, diabetes, something that they have pills for, but don't think to carry them to the toilet. We tend to treat these cases with, shall we say, discretion, as there is the potential for embarrassment for the bereaved family. Well, when the call came in we assumed this would be a routine case, but when the doctor examined the body he sent for the two men who brought the corpse in and questioned them for over an hour. They told me what they told him – that the victim was still wearing his trousers. Uncommon, I admit, but not exceptionally so. They also said he wasn't sitting down, which goes along with the trousers bit, but he was leaning against the door. Almost as though he had been put there. My interview with the doctor was something of a waste of time. He insisted the man had been murdered but refused to say how. Just kept shaking his head and saying he couldn't believe it. Worse still, he refused to complete the death certificate. Until he does that I can't finish my paper work, which means we can't release the body for burial."

Stan had calmed down a bit now and was more willing to cooperate. "What is it that he doesn't believe? The way he was murdered?"

Hodges nodded. "That seems to be the crux of the matter. The lads that brought him in said there wasn't a mark on him. I haven't a single clue. The only thing we have to go on is that he was probably murdered elsewhere, then hidden in the toilet. But that's not much."

"Can't you examine the body yourself? When the doctor is out, perhaps."

"We've tried that. The doctor left instructions that no-one was to be let in. He has the authority to do that in cases of infectious disease. Until he tells me the cause of death, I have no proof that it wasn't infectious disease, so my superior won't go against the doctor."

Stan looked at Hodges and smiled. "I see the problem. You have my full cooperation, and you have my word that what you've told me won't go beyond this room. What do you need from me?"

"Thank-you, Mr Atkinson," Hodges smiled.

"Please, call me Stan." Stan interrupted.

"All right then, er, Stan. First we need a list of names and addresses of all employees and contractors who have habitually visited this building in the last six weeks."

"Okay. I'll speak to the personnel manager. We'll see how quickly we can get if for you. Your name is….?"

"Hodges. Detective Chief Inspector Hodges. I thought you already knew that." The two men rose to their feet and left the room.

Back at the police station DCI Hodges went upstairs to visit Dr Smith. The doctor was leaning back in his chair, gazing up at the ceiling. He looked round as he heard the door close.

111

"Doc, I need to speak to you about the Anderson case," Hodges said as he took a seat.

"Oh, Les, do we have to go into that again?" replied the doctor.

"Indeed, we do. I need something concrete to go on. I want to get this one wrapped up quickly. I'm under pressure to investigate it and I don't know what I'm actually investigating. I'm in danger of losing my reputation because you won't put pen to paper."

"It's not like that, Les, and you know it. I can't complete the paperwork until I'm sure what killed him. You've got to respect my professional obligations." He turned away and pretended to sort some papers.

"Doc, I've got to do something, and if you won't help me, I'll have no alternative but to ask the super to give this to one of the other doctors. Don't get me wrong, I don't want to be difficult, but you're forcing my hand." The doctor turned to face him and thumped the desk angrily.

"You don't understand, Les. Another doctor would behave exactly as I have done." He turned away again. They sat in silence for a short while. Les shuffled uneasily in his chair.

"Doc, will you tell me what you think might have killed Anderson? I won't hold you to it, and I won't make it public, if it is so important to you, but I need to know what sort of killer I'm after." The doctor stared hard at the floor, then slowly sat up and looked the policeman straight in the eye.

"The problem is," he said after a pause, "I'm not sure I believe what I've found. If I'm right no-one will believe me, regardless of what evidence I can show. If I'm wrong, well, I'll be the laughing stock of the constabulary. Either way, I'll have to resign, and I'll never be able to work in forensics again." Tears welled up into his eyes. Les looked away, partly in disbelief, partly to preserve the doctor's dignity. After a few moments he rose and left the room. He returned a couple of minutes later with two mugs of tea. Dr Smith was more composed. He smiled weakly as he accepted the tea.

"Look, doc, you're a good doctor. I don't want to hear any more about you resigning. The force needs people like you. Now sit here and think about it. I'm going back to my desk, but I'll be back in about an hour. Give it some thought and see if you feel able to tell me later on. Like I said, if you want, it can be just between the two of us for now. Sooner or later it will have to be made public, but I'm willing to give you as much time as I can to come up with an acceptable answer. See you later." Hodges closed the door quietly as he left the room.

An hour later DCI Hodges returned to Dr Smith's vacant office. There was an envelope on the desk bearing his name. He took the piece of paper it contained and read it.

"Les, by the time you read this I will be dead. There's no point trying to revive me – what I took would kill an elephant in a matter of minutes. I'm sorry to have to do this, but it's the only way out for me. I haven't slept since I examined Anderson's body. It's too much for me to bear. I haven't been able to do anything else since they brought him in. I'm doing myself and everybody else a big favour by taking my own life. I have nothing to fear now. The paperwork is completed and is in for typing. Anderson died

113

from having his blood removed through two holes in his neck. He was killed by a vampire."

Chapter 6

Victoria returned to her desk, a little worn out from her encounter with Jenny. Keith was watching her. She felt sure that he knew she suspected and wondered what he might do. Lisa and Eric behaved as though everything were normal, unaware of the fiend they had worked with for all those years. Perhaps they were in league with him. Perhaps he had somehow managed to hypnotise them, so that they didn't notice anything unusual about him. At least she had got the point across to Jenny, who seemed the type that wouldn't stand for any nonsense. All she had to do now was to find a reason why vampires weren't allowed in the workplace, and she was home and dry. Tonight, she could visit the library and do more research. She might be able to find something quickly. This time tomorrow Keith might have been escorted off the premises, or, better still, taken away by the police. The minutes dragged by, but eventually, after what seemed like an eternity, it was time to leave. She picked up her things and bade goodnight. Halfway to the door Keith's voice stopped her.

"Victoria, I was wondering if you could stay an extra half hour tonight. I've a couple of little things I must finish today, and with your help I'll get them done much more quickly. Can you stay?" She froze. She turned to face him. He was smiling at her. He knew. There was no doubt about it. He knew.

"I'm sorry, Keith," she replied, "I have something important to do tonight. If you'd said earlier, I could have worked through my lunch break. Sorry I can't help. Goodnight." She looked sad, but as soon as she turned away from him, she grinned. Her remark about the lunch break made her feel good. She strode out, down the stairs, past the security men, and on towards the library. Just before she reached the library entrance someone spoke her name from behind. She stopped suddenly. Her heart missed a beat as she recognised Keith's voice. She tried to look calm as she turned to face him. "Why hello, Keith. I thought you had lots of work to do," she said. Try as she might, she couldn't stop her voice from wavering.

Keith grinned as he slowly approached her. "I have, dear girl, but it can wait. There are more important things than work," he paused, "you, for instance." She turned and fled into the library and ran up the stairs. Halfway up she found herself facing Keith again.

"Why are you doing this? Just leave me alone!" she shouted.

"We'll have none of that in here!" called an attendant, "Keep the noise down. This is a library, you know."

"Can you help me? This man is bothering me," she answered, pointing to where Keith was, except that he was no longer there. The attendant wasn't interested and walked away. Victoria was relieved and carried on up the stairs. Suddenly, there he was at the top of the stairs, leaning against the wall in a casual manner, and grinning. He winked at her. She turned and ran down the stairs and back out into the street. She could hear his footsteps getting closer and closer. A policeman was approaching them on foot.

Victoria grabbed him. "Help me! Please help me! That man is chasing me!" she cried, but Keith had disappeared. Without waiting for a reply, she ran on along the street. She could hear Keith's footsteps again, but she daren't slow down to look. Should she try to lose him in the side streets?

116

Should she keep to the main street where there were people to help her? Either option seemed futile, as he disappeared and reappeared at will, and covered distances in no time at all. If only she were in her flat. She had some garlic powder there. It might not be as good as fresh garlic, but it might give her the chance to do something. But what? She didn't have a stake to plunge through his heart; she didn't have the means to cut off his head. The sun had dropped behind the shopping centre some hours ago. The flat was definitely the best option. Even if all she could do was to sprinkle the garlic powder over herself, that might be sufficient to ensure her safety. She pressed on to her flat, the footsteps getting ever closer. Why didn't he pounce? Was he unwilling, or unable, to make his move in public? Or was he enjoying the thrill of the chase too much to end it too soon? She ran on, her heart pounding, her eyes wide with fear, flecks of foam escaping from the corners of her mouth, until she rounded the bend and her flat hove into view. A haven! All she had to do was get inside and find that garlic powder. She struggled to extract the key from her bag as she ran, not wanting to drop the pace. With the key clutched firmly in her hand she threw herself into the hall, took the stairs two at a time, and forced the key into the lock. Entering, she slammed the door behind her, then stopped dead. Keith was sitting on the edge of her bed, arms folded, legs crossed, showing no signs of having ran almost a mile. His clothes and hair were neat and tidy, and he looked calm and composed.

He grinned. "Hello, Victoria," he said, rising.

"What are you doing here? How did you get in? Touch me and I'll scream!" she gasped, her face florid from the exertion.

"You won't scream," he said, moving slowly towards her. "You're worn out. You can't do anything. Can you?"

A few days later Keith came into the office followed by a young lady.

"Victoria isn't coming back. This is Mary. She's taking over from her." Lisa and Eric introduced themselves. Later that morning Mary looked around and pulled her cardigan around her shoulders.

"It seems very cold near my desk," she said, to no one in particular.

"Victoria used to say that," Eric commented.

"I liked Victoria," said Lisa. "She was nice."

"She was!" Keith muttered, turning away from the others. "Very nice!"

Fog Over the Pennines

Chapter 1

It was an unusually cold day in March. Snow lay on the
ground, the wind was strong and gusting, and the
passengers stood in a long slow-moving queue waiting to
get onto the coaches. The first coach filled quite quickly, as
did the second and third. The fourth coach was late to
arrive and the stairs were narrow. The passengers were
disgruntled before they even got on. The train had to be
cancelled because of fallen trees on the line and the bus
replacement service had been difficult to organise as lines
were closed all over the region. This was the last of the four
coaches replacing what earlier in the day was the commuter
service, but at eleven in the morning most commuters were
well on their way. These were shoppers and sightseers,
with the occasional businessperson, but the rail company
had cancelled so many trains in recent weeks it was in
danger of losing the franchise, so the replacement bus
service was essential. It didn't cost them anything because
the insurance company stumped up, but it was the hassle of
doing it, and past experience showed that it caused more
complaints than an outright cancellation. The driver and his
assistant counted the people on and decided there were two
missing.

"We'll give them another five minutes, Ron, then we'll
be off and it's their fault if they're late," said the driver.

"Righto, Bill," replied Ron. Just then they appeared. A
middle-aged woman gesticulating with her umbrella with
one hand and dragging an elderly lady along with the other.
Bill didn't mind waiting for the elderly, as his mother was
getting on a bit and he knew the grief she caused with
unexpected toilet stops and the 'wrong sort of mints' when

121

they took her away anywhere. Ron helped them up the steps and into their seats and made sure they were comfortable before signalling to Bill that all was ready. He pulled out of the railway station and headed off after the other three coaches. The snow got worse and they soon fell behind, as the other coaches were more modern and better looked after, but that didn't matter. This fourth coach had a straight through journey to the other end, so they would catch up a bit when the others stopped to pick people up or drop them off along the way. The journey was quite circuitous, because some of the roads were blocked by snow and fallen trees too, so what should have taken less than an hour and a half was going to take more than two hours. Ron and Bill didn't mind. They were both nearing retirement, so career opportunities were long gone, and they just got on with doing their jobs to the best of their ability, looking after their customers in ways some of the younger drivers didn't. After about half an hour the snow stopped and the wind dropped, which was just as well, as the old coach was struggling up the steep hill. Suddenly they were in thick fog which had just appeared from nowhere. Bill stopped and cleaned the lights, which by now had a frozen covering of snow, but visibility was still very poor.

"If it gets much worse we'll have to stop, Ron," he said as they set off again.

"I'm surprised you haven't stopped already, Bill," replied Ron. "I know you're a stickler for passenger safety."

"Yes, but I don't like to disappoint them either." The fog did get worse, a lot worse, and Ron made an announcement to the passengers, most of whom just accepted it as one of those things. Three or four made a bit of a fuss, only to be shouted down by the others, but they calmed down when Bill said he was stopping at a little hotel he knew where they would be able to get tea and coffee while they waited for conditions to improve. He wasn't supposed to do this without prior arrangement, but the owner was a personal friend who was happy to do the paperwork afterwards, and didn't complain about the extra revenue, and it kept the passengers happy. He eased the coach into the Pennine View Hotel car park, which was deserted apart from two cars belonging to staff. The people got off and filed into the hotel foyer, to be shown through to the restaurant by the smiling host. The staff were efficient and smiling and soon everyone had a hot drink and biscuits or cake. Bill and Ron sat down with Roger, the hotelier, and chatted about the weather. Being from a farming family Roger had opinions on the weather and declared he would be surprised if it cleared up in the next two hours. About fifteen minutes later one of the passengers, a smartly dressed man in a business suit, stopped by the driver's table on his way back from the toilet.

"Hey, driver!" he said, interrupting Ron and Bill's conversation. "When we gettin' this show back on the road?" His accent was American, probably from the New York area. Bill gesticulated toward the nearby window.

"Not just yet, sir," he said. "The fog is worse now than it was when we stopped."

"I ain't blind, but I got a meetin' in Carlisle later on today that's worth a lot of bucks an' I ain't gonna miss it."

"Well, we'll set off as soon as it's safe. We didn't stop here just for a cup of tea."

"Well, y'know, I figured you Brits stop for tea at every opportunity. You get us movin' as soon as you can and not a moment later. I got a lot ridin' on this meetin'."

"Yes, I want to set off as soon as it's safe. We don't want to delay any more than necessary either."

"Good. We got an understandin'." The American was just returning to his table when there was a scream from somewhere at the back of the room and a woman came running out of the Ladies' Toilet with her hands to her face, obviously distressed. One of the other passengers took her arm and helped her to a chair. One of the waitresses came over.

"What is it, madam?" she asked politely. "Is something wrong? Are you alright?" The distressed woman pointed to the back corner.

"In the toilet," she gasped between sobs. "The woman in there, I think she's dead." The room had gone silent but was now filled with gasps. Another woman got to her feet.

"I'll have a look," she said calmly. "I used to be a nurse."

"Thanks," said Roger. He called to the waitress. "Beth, you go in with her." Beth nodded her agreement and followed the woman. When they came out their faces were white. "What is it?" asked Roger.

"She's definitely dead," said the woman. "But her throat's been torn out. It must be an animal attack. Unless it's a vicious murder." Beth's legs went from under her and the other waitress helped her to a chair and brought her a glass of water.

Chapter 2

The room went silent. The American was the first to speak.

"If it's murder somebody better call the cops." He took his mobile phone from his pocket and pressed a few keys. "Goddammit! There's no cell phone signal. What is it with this country? Anybody else got a signal?" Some of the other passengers tried, but with the same result. Roger had gone into the office but returned shaking his head.

"The line was down this morning, but it looks like it's still down. We've got no land line. The mobile signal is always a bit patchy round here, but it's often non-existent when the weather's like this." He called to the other waitress. "Sharon, do you think you can give me a hand to move the body?" Sharon got to her feet and nodded.

"I'll get a trolley from upstairs." She disappeared through a door at the back of the room. The American was getting agitated.

"What is it with you Brits? We got a dead body in the john and a killer on the loose and no phones that work and we can't get away and you all just sit there like it's a typical Thursday. We need to do somethin'. We ought to be takin' action in case the killer gets some other woman who gets caught short and winds up dead."

"Calm down, or you'll give yourself a heart attack," said a middle-aged man. "There's nothing we can do for now."

"Nothin' we can do? We can see what weapons we got. We can make an action plan. We can make sure the doors are locked. You folk just sit around bein' calm and we'll all be killed." Roger stood up and addressed the room.

125

"Just a minute," he said. "This is my hotel so I'm in charge. We *are* going to do something. I have an action plan. This is what we do. When anyone needs to go to the toilet they do not go alone. Someone goes with them and someone else stands guard outside the door. Every five minutes we try our mobiles and the land line to see if we can get through to the police. When the fog clears a bit, we *all* get on the bus and go to the nearest town. If we lock all the doors we could be locking the killer in with us, so I'm not sure about that. We all stay calm and carry on, and we all co-operate with each other. Now then, we know we have a nurse. Does anyone else have any specialist skills that might prove useful?" Three people came to Roger, who wrote things in a little notebook. Meanwhile Sharon had returned with a trolley. Ron and Bill went across to her.

"We'll give you a hand," said Bill. "Roger's a bit busy. Where are we going to put the body?" Sharon stopped and put her hand to her mouth.

"Oh, I hadn't thought about that. I assumed Roger knew what he was going to do with it."

"Is there an empty room we could put it in? A storeroom or something? Obviously not a room with food. Perhaps a garage?" asked Ron. Sharon thought for a moment.

"Yes, there's an empty barn round the back. I know it locks because the handyman keeps tools and paint and stuff in it. And there's no windows and not much in the way of vermin."

"Good. We'll put the poor woman in there for now. And we need to know who she is, so I want you to witness that I look in her handbag but don't steal anything."

"Yes, I can do that. Never thought about stealing anything from dead people. That's disgusting," said Sharon.

"Yes, but you'd be surprised at what some people would do." Sharon shook her head in disbelief and held the trolley still while Ron and Bill lifted the body onto it. They pushed it to the back of the hotel, through the warehouse and out into the yard. Sharon got the key and opened the barn. There was a wooden workbench on one side so they moved the tools and gently laid the body there and put a dust sheet over it. Ron took the woman's driving license from her handbag, showed it to the others, and put it back. He took the handbag. "I'll ask Roger to put this in the safe," he said. The others agreed. They went back into the warehouse where Sharon parked the trolley, then they went to join the others. Ron gave the handbag to Roger who went into the office and locked it away. He tried the phone but there was still no dialling tone. Back in the restaurant some of the people were getting restless.

"If you go into the snug," Roger said pointing to a door in the corner of the room. "There's a pack of cards and Scrabble and stuff like that, but don't go alone." Three or four people went in to try to relieve the boredom.

"I suppose you won't let me smoke in here," said the American.

"That's right," answered Roger. "But if you go outside and to the right there's a smoking shelter."

"Goddam stupid rules!" Off he went. The snow had started again, but the shelter was positioned to keep the weather out. Two women went into the Ladies' Toilet while another stood guard at the door. After a while she looked at her watch and beckoned to Roger.

"I'm sorry to disturb you," she said, "but those two ladies went in there twenty minutes ago and they haven't come out yet. Do you think that's a long time?"

"Yes, I do. Beth! Can you go in here with this lady and make sure those other two are ok? I don't want to go in in case they're not properly dressed." Beth came over from where she had been pouring teas and coffees. She was used to doing this when they had corporate parties and people would pass out in the cubicles, but today was her first dead body.

"Okay," she said, "But I could do without another dead body. I haven't recovered from the last one yet."

"Don't worry," said the lady on guard. "No one's been in or out and I've been stood here twenty minutes." Reassured they opened the door and went in, only to come running out.

"What is it?" asked Roger. "Not another one?" Beth shook her head, almost in tears.

"No, another two. They're just like the other one. I need to sit down." Two of the passengers helped her to a chair, and another helped the other lady who was on the verge of passing out.

Chapter 3

Bill and Ron looked at each other while Roger went to investigate.

"Susan," he called to the retired nurse. "Can you come and make sure these ladies are dead please?" Susan followed him in. They came out together a minute later. "I don't understand it," Roger said shaking his head. "No one went in or out, but they've been killed, and wounds like that couldn't possibly be suicide." He went over to Ron and Bill. "Can you give me and Sharon a hand moving them out? I don't want to ask Beth."

"No probs," said Ron. "D'you want to get the trolley, Sharon?" Sharon nodded and disappeared.

"Hey, should we let her go round the back alone?" asked Bill. Roger realised what he meant and went off after her. They came back with the trolley, smiling.

"I nearly wet myself, him coming running after me like that," she said.

"Better safe than sorry," said Bill. They lifted the dead ladies onto the trolley and took them to the barn, one at a time.

"That's all the benches full now," said Roger. "If there's any more they'll have to go on the floor."

"Hope it doesn't come to that," said Ron as they returned to the restaurant.

"Anyway, it proves one thing. It isn't one of our passengers," said Bill. "Have you got any other guests at the moment, Roger?"

"Yes, two young men, but they went out early and didn't come back. They said not to expect them until about six. They took packed lunches and went to do some wildlife survey or other for some bird trust. Counting merlins, I think they said.

"Merlin?" queried Ron. "Wasn't he the wizard in the King Arthur stories?"

"No," chided Roger. "They're like falcons but much smaller. You see them up here now and again, mainly in the summer, but they said the mild winters might bring them out early. Some mild winter!"

"Coming back to the case in hand," said Bill. "What about that American bloke? I can't see him in here."

"No, he went outside to have a smoke," Roger pointed out.

"So he doesn't have an alibi," said Bill stroking his chin.

"Are you Hercule Poirot?" asked Ron.

"If I am, you must be Captain Hastings," replied Bill, and they all laughed briefly.

"No, but seriously," said Roger, "He is the only one that wasn't here, and when the first one died, he came back from the toilet just before the alarm was raised."

"Yes, but he would have been in the Gents, wouldn't he?"

"We've no witnesses to which one he was in, actually."

"Good point. Let's keep an eye on him when he comes back. I'm not going to let him out of my sight until the little grey cells have done their work," said Bill, twiddling an imaginary moustache. They laughed again, then stopped abruptly as the American came in.

"Say, give me a coffee," he said. "It's mighty cold out there." They eyed him suspiciously. He realised something was wrong. "Hey, what's up? I'm cold and I need a coffee. Do I have to get it myself? What kind of hotel is this?"

"Where have you been, sir?" asked Roger.

"I've been outside for a smoke and I'm goddam freezin'. Now get me a coffee, will you?"

"While you've been out, where no-one could see you, another two people have died." The American went pale.

"Just a minute, just a goddam minute, you let two people die and you're blamin' me? I want my attorney to hear this before I say another word. You had an action plan. Don't go to the john alone, you said. Stay together you said. I'll tell ya who's to blame, and it ain't me. It's you. Two people died on your watch. You can't blame me an' you're not gonna. I was out the front havin' a smoke. How could I get back in to murder two people without bein' seen? Answer me that!"

"You could have gone round the back," volunteered Ron.

"Round the back? I don't even know where round the back is. No, you got the wrong guy."

"Ok, calm down. We're not saying it's you," said Ron.

"Dead right you're not!"

"No, but everyone else was in here or in the lounge. You're the only person here that doesn't have an alibi." The man sat down in an armchair and folded his arms.

"Well, I'm staying put right here. An' yous guys is staying here watchin' me. I ain't movin' for nothin' an' nobody. If I need to go to the john one of you is coming with me. No! Two of you is comin' with me. I ain't bein' accused of nothin' I ain't done. Now where's that goddam coffee?" Roger brought the man a cup of coffee.

"We don't have any evidence against you, nor against anyone else," he said. "But you are the only one without an alibi for the time of the deaths. I don't see how you could

131

have done it without getting blood all over your clothes anyway."

"That's a very valid point," said Bill. "So if it isn't one of the staff, isn't one of the passengers, isn't one of your guests, assuming they're miles away, who did it?"

"I don't see how it could be a wild animal either. It would have made a noise for one thing, and left marks on the floor for another," said Ron.

"There's no wild animals round here anyway," said Roger. "We don't see foxes, and sheep aren't exactly wild. The nearest we have to wild animals are birds of prey, and not many of them."

"No," said Ron. "They would definitely make a noise." Roger looked at his watch. He walked to the middle of the restaurant and spoke to the people.

"Ladies and Gentlemen, our kitchen staff haven't turned up, probably because of the fog, and the food delivery hasn't arrived either, probably for the same reason, but me and the girls can do a basic cooked breakfast if anyone wants one, or there's cereals and toast. How do you feel about that?" There was a general murmur of agreement. "Can you two go round and see who wants what while I put the stove on?" he said to the waitresses. They nodded and went round with their notebooks.

"I'll come into the kitchen," said Ron, "so you're not alone until the girls come through."

"Thanks, hadn't thought of that." A few minutes later Beth and Sharon appeared and set about putting the cereal dishes and cutlery on the sideboard and helping with eggs and bacon. "Oh, forgot about the folk in the snug. I'll go and see what they want. He went away, only to return a few minutes later, ashen faced.

"What's up?" asked Bill.

"The people in the snug – they're all dead. Just like the others, throats torn out." Bill and Ron looked at each other.

"Shall we go and have a look?" asked Ron.

"Can if you want, but I'm pretty certain." They returned a few moments later.

"Four at once," said Bill, shaking his head. Is there any other way in or out, apart from the door from here?"

"Well, there's the fire exit, but that hasn't been opened, 'cos if it had it would have set the alarm off. And it can't be opened or closed from outside, only from inside." Back in the kitchen Beth and Sharon had made good progress with the meal. Those having cereal were already eating and Sharon was delivering bacon and eggs to the others while Beth cooked the toast. She looked up as Roger came in.

"What's up Dad?" she asked. He shook his head.

"Another four dead," he said gravely. "Those in the snug." Beth burst into tears and Roger put his arms round her. She wiped her tears and looked up into his face.

"Are we all going to die, Dad?"

"Don't know, sweetheart, don't know. Hope not. We all need to stick together. Always go round in groups of three or four at least."

"But the people in the snug were together, four of them."

"I know, that's what worries me. I'll speak to the people when they've finished eating. Don't want to put them off their food." The American man had overheard Roger's conversation with Ron and Bill and came over to their table to eat his meal.

"Can't pin this one on me," he said. "You were both watching me all the time." Ron and Bill nodded in agreement.

"Yes, you're right," said Bill. "But the important question is who did it? If it was an outsider how did they get in without us noticing?"

"You tell me." After the meal Sharon and Beth brought teas and coffees round. The American tapped Bill's arm.

"Say, driver, any chance of leavin' here soon? I wanna get outta this hell hole before we all get killed an' I have an important meetin' in Carlisle in a few hours." Bill looked out of the window and shook his head.

"Come this way and I'll show you the problem. Visibility's down to less than three yards."

"How d'you know that without goin' out?"

"I know there's a little fence about three yards from the door and I can't see it."

"No. You reckon?"

"Yes, you stand there in the doorway and I'll take three steps and you'll not see me." They both went to the doorway and Bill went further out.

"I can just about see your shape, but yeah, I see what you mean," said the American. He turned to return to the table, but Bill didn't follow. When he realised, he went back to the door. "Driver? Driver? You there?" There was no reply. And he couldn't see Bill's outline. He ran to fetch Ron. "Say, your pal's disappeared into the fog." He related what had happened, and Bill and Roger came with him to the door. They called Bill's name. He didn't reply.

Chapter 4

The three men looked at each other in disbelief. Ron stepped forward to venture out but Roger grabbed his arm and held him back.

"Don't go out there, mate," he said anxiously. "We don't know what's out there."

"He's my pal," said Ron, shaking his arm free. "We've worked together for more than fifteen years. I'm not leaving him out there to face whatever it is."

"I understand," said Roger. "But we need to be sensible. Let's hold on to each other. If he isn't within five or six yards of the door, he's gone." Ron saw the sense in this, and the three men formed a chain, Ron outermost, the American hanging on to the door frame and Roger in the middle. Ron went out as far as he could without leaving go, to the point where the American couldn't see him. He swept back and forth a few times before coming back inside. He spoke to the others with tears in his eyes.

"No, he's gone. My pal Bill. He only had a few months to go to retirement. Let's go and sit down." They sat at the table and Roger indicated to Beth that they wanted coffee. Suddenly there was a shout from the kitchen. Beth came running out.

"It's Sharon! It's killed her! Killed her while I was stood here on the other side of the door." She broke down in tears and Roger and one of the women went over to comfort her. Ron and the American went into the kitchen to investigate, and there was Sharon, laid on the floor, with her throat torn out, just like the others. They went to the warehouse and brought the trolley back. They gently lowered Sharon's lifeless body onto it and pushed it out to the barn. They cleared a space on the floor and laid her down, covered by a dust sheet.

"That reminds me," said Ron. "There's three or four bodies in the snug. Roger didn't want to bring them through until everyone had finished eating." The American nodded.

"Ain't the best way to spend your Thursday afternoon, but let's do it." The two women in the restaurant gasped as they brought the four bodies through. One woman stood up and counted on her fingers.

"There's you three men, the nurse, the waitress, and me. That's six. Where's the driver?" she said, looking pale. The American told her about Bill's brief demonstration of the thickness of the fog. She covered her mouth and sat down quickly. "Does that mean we're stuck here?"

"Well, I think Ron can drive the coach, but setting off would be dangerous while the fog's still like this. I ain't never seen fog like this before, and we get some mighty thick fog in the states when the weather's wrong. But if we stay put, well, that could be dangerous too. I think if we all stick together we might have somethin' of a chance. But I'd sure be happier if I had my trusty Colt 45 by my side."

"I'm not generally in favour of guns, but I agree with you on this occasion."

"That's it. You don't never know when somethin' might turn up and you need to defend yourself."

"Well, today we don't have guns, so we need to make the best we can out of what we have. I think we should all stay in this room, and if we need to go to another, to make tea, for instance, we should all go."

"That might be a mighty good idea," said the American, getting to his feet. "I'll tell the others. You

136

ladies want a coffee?" he said. He had turned his back on them to make his way to the reception area, but turned to face them when they didn't answer. They lay slumped in their chairs, their throats torn out. He fled to join the others, panic on his face. How had that happened? The ladies were about three yards apart, perhaps four, and whatever had killed them had done them both at the same time, and while he was in the room, but without making a sound. He arrived in the foyer area, which wasn't separate from the restaurant, only to find Ron dead too, murdered in the same way. He made his way to the kitchen, which was just through a door by the reception desk. There on the floor were Roger and Beth, dead on the floor, just like the others. He froze for a moment, then went further in and searched some of the drawers, emerging with two big kitchen knives. He made himself a cup of coffee, then carried it and the knives back to the reception area. He sat down in the big armchair with a knife in each hand and the coffee on the table beside him. "Whatever it is, it ain't gonna get me. Not while I got these two knives. Wish I had my Colt 45. Still, I got these two knives. And the coffee will keep me awake. And these knives will protect me." He raised his voice to a shout. "Come an' get me. I got a knife an' I know how to use it. I killed folk in the war. I ain't scared to fight." He looked out of the window. The fog was thicker than ever. He glanced across to the main door which was ajar. The fog was starting to roll in and slowly spread out across the carpet. "Holy shit! How am I gonna fight this?" He looked around before settling himself in the chair, half alert, half comfortable. "Still, I got my coffee an' my two knives. I'm ready for it, whatever it is. I'm ready."

The Bike Ride

Chapter 1

It was a Sunday morning in September; a cloudy sky, but neither hot nor cold; neither dull nor bright. Three cyclists made their way northward along the A68 through the Durham countryside, as they often did on Sundays. Or sometimes Saturdays. They had started some ten years ago as a group of about twelve, friends and neighbours and work mates, all with an interest in cycling. Over the years people had dropped out. Some went away to university or college and never came back. Some took jobs with weekend commitments. Some dropped out to look after their children. One or two new people came along, but now the regular group which met *every* weekend was down to three, Rod, Maurice and Nigel. Each had an expensive bike, which they could afford because they didn't spend much money on anything else, really. And the bikes were cared for with attention to detail. As soon as they got home the bike would be cleaned and inspected for anything needing attention, so that it was ready for the next journey next weekend, and this was done religiously before food or drink or rest were considered, no matter how much they were needed; the condition of the bike always came first.

This was a typical Sunday, and each rider was dressed in colourful cycling clothes, with fluorescent strips, and each had a small backpack with a few sandwiches, a couple of bottles of water, a bag of crisps and an apple or a banana. Nigel also had a small first aid kit, a map and a compass. He was the cautious one, always ready for the unexpected. Traffic had been light, they had an early start, and all three seemed full of energy, so when they were nearing their usual lunch place Rod pulled into a lay-by and

141

said to the others, "Don't know about you, but I'm not hungry at the moment, and I'm not tired either. Let's go on a bit further, eh?"

Yes," replied Maurice. "But I've been up that road before. It's not really interesting. The countryside up there is a bit boring. We passed a side road a few minutes back pointing to Middleton and Alston. Shall we go along there? See what there is? And we can pick up the Staindrop Road for going home."

"Okay," said Nigel. "I've got my map and compass if we get lost." The other two laughed.

"Why do you always expect the worst, Nigel?" asked Rod.

"Expect the worst and you'll not be disappointed," Nigel replied with a grin as he remounted his bike.

They turned round and took the little road on the right. The surface wasn't brilliant, and it was very up and down, but there was plenty to see in the way of trees and flowers, and a bit of wildlife. An hour later Rod, who had been leading, pulled up near a derelict farmhouse. The others stopped alongside.

"Ready for lunch yet, chaps?" he asked. The others nodded in agreement.

"Let's have a look at this old house while we have a break. Any idea where we are, Nigel?" said Maurice.

"Haven't a clue, mate," said Nigel. "But I'll have a look at the map while we have lunch." They pulled off the road, such as it was, and leant their bikes against the side wall of the house. The front of the house faced south, so they sat in the weak sun and tucked into their sandwiches. Nigel got the map out and studied it for a while.

"Have we crossed a stream yet?" he asked. The other two shook their heads.

"Don't remember one," said Maurice through a mouthful of food.

"In that case," said Nigel looking up. "In that case I haven't a clue where we are. This house isn't on the map. There's another building about five miles past the stream, but I'm sure we haven't got there yet, and if we haven't crossed the stream we're definitely not there."

"Never mind," said Rod. "There's no hurry. We'll definitely be home for about six or seven. Do either of you need to be back before then? Going out or anything?" They shook their heads.

"I'm having a pint with Smithy but that's not 'til after he finishes work at eight," said Maurice.

"Might join you for that," said Nigel. "Haven't seen him for weeks. Is he okay?"

"Yes, been doing a lot of overtime to pay for repairs to his car."

"Anyway," said Rod. "I'm going to have a look at this old house before we set off again." He went inside followed by Maurice. The walls were of stone, in the style of a drystone wall, and the floor was of beaten earth, totally flat and smooth. There was a fireplace on one wall set into a primitive chimney breast. The only window looked out over where they had sat for lunch and onto what might have been a kitchen garden, sloping away from the house. At the bottom of the garden was a hedge made up of assorted bushes, and beyond that a paddock with a gorse hedge at the far side, which obscured whatever was beyond. This appeared to be the only ground floor room, but there was a wooden staircase in the back corner going up over the doorway.

"That's strange, Maurice, isn't it?" said Rod, looking at the staircase.

"Strange?" queried Maurice. "In what way is it strange?"

"Well, ignore that and look at the rest of the room. The house must be at least two hundred years old, perhaps three. Yes?"

Maurice looked round and stroked his chin. "Yes, s'pose so. Your point being?"

"Well, look at the craftmanship of the staircase. You would find that sort workmanship in a stately home or something at that time. Not a farmhouse in the middle of nowhere, surely."

"Yes, you could be right."

"And if a farmhouse of that time had a staircase at all I would expect it to be stone."

"Yes. See what you mean. So why do you think it's like this?"

"Don't know. I'm going upstairs for a look around."

By this time Nigel had joined them. "I wouldn't if I were you. If it's as old as the house it's probably riddled with woodworm or dry rot or something."

"Don't be so negative, Nigel. It's probably perfectly safe," said Maurice with a laugh. "I'm going up too. Might find some interesting antiques."

"Well you wait 'til I get to the top, in case two of us is too much weight for it," said Rod.

"See, you're beginning to think I might be right already."

Rod got to the top and indicated to Maurice it was okay to follow. Maurice went up, and they stood in the middle of the room looking round. There was a single window which overlooked the garden and the paddock, and a wooden bench by the window which they sat on to look out, after first testing its sturdiness. Maurice had brought his drink and fruit up with him and ate as he sat gazing out into the paddock.

"Look," he said, pointing out of the window. "Look, there's some sheep over there." In the right-hand side of the field he could see a few sheep which hadn't been visible from downstairs. "And one of them's coming this way. Almost as though it wants to give us a good view, see if we know what type it is." They laughed at this idea, then suddenly stopped laughing, because the sheep had fallen over, and its throat had been torn out.

Chapter 2

Rod and Maurice looked at each other in total silence. Even the birds had stopped singing.

"Nigel!" yelled Maurice. "Nigel! Come up here. Be quick!"

"I'm not risking those dodgy stairs," replied Nigel, laughing.

"No, Nigel, this isn't funny," called Rod. "Get your but up here pronto." Nigel came up and they pointed at the dead sheep.

"Five minutes ago that sheep was alive," said Maurice. "It was stood there eating grass, then it just keeled over, and then it's throat just, well, I'm not sure what it did, but there it is with its throat on the grass. It's dead now, but we were sat here watching, and we didn't see what killed it." As they watched another sheep wandered across, munching on the grass as it went. The three men stood in the window watching. Suddenly it fell over, and its throat was torn out, just like the first.

"Shit!" exclaimed Rod. "I'm getting out of here while I can."

"Calm down, mate," said Maurice. "Perhaps it's some sheep disease. You know, like foot and mouth or blue tongue or something."

"No," said Nigel. "The falling over I can understand being some sort of medical ailment, but the throat – well, I don't know of any disease, sheep or human or anything, that makes that happen. They must have been attacked by something."

"But we were stood watching them and we didn't see anything!" said Rod. "What attacked them?"

"Good question," replied Maurice. "I'm going downstairs to get a closer look. If it happens again, that is."

"Do you think that's wise?" warned Nigel. "If it can attack sheep, can it attack people?"

"Another good question, but if we just sit here we'll never find out."

"No, don't go, mate. You could be going to your death. I know you're bigger than a sheep, but whatever it is made short work of those two. If you go and end up like the sheep, how will we explain that to your family?"

"Yes, but if we stay here, well, we can't see whatever it is, so how will we know if it's gone? How long do we sit here staring at nothing happening? If we sit here for absolutely ever and never go home, what will our families think?" Maurice shrugged his shoulders and went down the stairs and the other two sat and watched him go, then glanced at each other.

"What do you think, Rod?" asked Nigel. "I know he's got a point, sort of, but do you think he's being stupid? It's not as though there's anything up here we could use as a weapon, and if he gets as far as the bikes, there's nothing there he could use either."

"No, but if he gets that far he could get away and bring help."

"Look, if you're PC Plod and some bloke comes into the Police Station and says, 'My pals are trapped in a derelict farmhouse by some monster that none of us can see but it's highly skilled at killing sheep' what are you going to think?"

"Yes, see what you mean. PC Plod's going to search him for substances."

Just then Maurice appeared, coming up the stairs. "I can hear every word you're saying, you know," he said. "And you've got a point. We need a strategy, just in case it *can* kill humans, but we need to get out of here. Or at least one of us does. Let's sit and think about this. What do we know? Come on, Nigel, you're usually the ideas man."

"I didn't see it the first time," said Nigel. "Well, I know you didn't see it either, but we all saw it the second time, or didn't see it, but there was nothing to see. The sheep fell over, then more or less at the same time, its throat burst open and bits of sheep fell onto the grass. But there didn't seem to be much blood, just sheep's parts. Did the thing leave any footprints?" They all leaned out of the window, but couldn't see any marks, as the grass was quite short and dry.

"No, I can't see anything to give us a clue," said Rod. "And the sheep seemed to die instantly. It didn't make any noise."

"So where do we go from here?" said Maurice. "Let's look at our options; option one – stay here. That's no good because we won't know when it's gone. Option two – one of us makes a break for it and tries to get away on a bike and brings help. Problem there is that whoever makes the dash might not get as far as the bikes, and if he does, what sort of help does he bring? And who would believe him?"

"Well, my dad would believe me, but I doubt the police would, or the fire service," said Nigel.

"Fire service?" said Rod. "But there isn't a fire!"

"Fire and Rescue service," said Nigel. "But Maurice has a point. What sort of help would they bring? And would they be walking to their deaths too?"

148

"So option two is a non-starter too," Maurice resumed. "Option three – we all make a run for it together. That gives us the chance that at least one of us would get away, probably two, perhaps all three if we're quick enough."

"Unless there's more than one monster," interjected Nigel.

"Unless there's more than one monster, Nigel, yes. It's good to be positive isn't it." said Maurice.

"Or realistic," Nigel pointed out. "We've had no indication that there's only one, or that there's fifty of the blighters."

"Okay, realistic. So option three might be our best bet, or it could be a non-starter – we won't know until we've tried it and it's either succeeded or failed, by which time it's too late. Option four – we try to fight it. The first problem there being that we don't know what we're fighting, the second being that we don't know how to fight it, the third being we've got no weapons, either up here, or back at the bikes, the fourth being that we can't see it so if we *had* weapons, we wouldn't know which direction to attack. So option four is a non-starter too. Option three, poor though it is, seems our best bet."

"Yes," said Nigel. "All the options are a bit pants, but option three is less pants than the others."

"Before we go doing something hasty, let's spy out the land a bit and see if we can spot anything," said Rod.

"We aren't being hasty," said Maurice. "We've thought about the options, but yes, there's no harm in having a good look, see if there's anything to make it a bit easier."

They sat on the bench and concentrated on the paddock, until they saw another sheep wandering across. Rod jumped up and leant out of the window. "Go away, sheep! Go away! They'll kill you! Get back to the other end of the field!" he shouted. The others pulled him back.

"Be quiet!" said Maurice in a loud whisper. "If the monster gets the sheep, we'll know it's still about and might get a clue. If it doesn't, we'll know it's gone, and we can make a break for it."

"Sorry, guys," apologised Rod. "Just trying to save the poor sheep."

"Hey, look over there!" whispered Nigel, pointing to the extreme left corner of the field. There was a cloud of mist, almost thick enough to qualify as fog. It was on the far side, up against the gorse hedge, and it was swirling slowly. The sheep moved slowly towards it, eating as it went, then there seemed to be a bit of agitation in the mist, and the sheep fell over, its throat torn out.

Chapter 3

The three friends watched, open mouthed. A few moments later the mist settled into a cloud in the corner of the field again and remained motionless.

"Well, that's one thing for certain," said Maurice. The others sighed and nodded. "But that gives us a new option."

"What's that?" asked Rod.

"We can sit tight and wait until the foggy thing goes away."

"But I don't remember seeing it when the first two sheep died," said Rod.

"Well, I don't either," replied Maurice. "But I wasn't looking that way at the time." They sat watching the cloud. It didn't move at all and seemed perfectly still. "This could be our way out. Stay here. I'm going downstairs. Watch to see if it moves." He got up gingerly and very slowly went down the stairs, making no sound. At the bottom he took a step outside, looking across into the paddock, but the hedge was too high, and he couldn't see the cloud. He walked forward, only to be stopped by his friends shouting.

"Get back up here! It's moving! It's coming for you!" shouted Rod from the window. Maurice ran into the house and up the stairs.

"Good plan," said Nigel. "Pity it didn't work. Perhaps we can try it again later."

"The problem is," said Maurice, "when you're down there you can't see the cloud because of that little hedge."

"So what sparked it off?" asked Rod. "Was it going downstairs, or was it going outside? If it was going downstairs that alerted it, we could go down then stay motionless until it forgets about us, then make a dash when it's off guard."

"Good idea," said Maurice," but how will we know?"

"Good point. I hadn't thought that far," said Nigel. They sat in silence looking at the cloud. "I think it's trying to rain," he commented, holding his hand out of the window. A few raindrops fell. Not enough to be called proper rain, but enough to wet the ground in places.

"Will the rain show any footprints or anything?" said Rod, leaning out of the window.

"Good thought," said Maurice, joining him. The rain gradually got heavier until it was proper rain, but not heavy, but it didn't show any marks on the grass in the paddock. A sheep came wandering along from the other end of the field. "There's another one coming to its death," said Maurice. The cloud began to stir. As the sheep got closer, something appeared from the cloud. It was a grey animal, similar to a wolf, but very scrawny with an uneven coat. It sprang out and grabbed the sheep by the throat. The sheep fell over, and the wolf thing stood there, drinking the sheep's blood, then limped back to the cloud. They looked on in silence and disbelief.

"Well, we know what it is now," said Rod after a long silence.

"Do we?" asked Nigel. "Tell me what it is then."

"It's, er, well, it's a sort of, kind of wolf thing. Or a kind of vampire thing that looks a bit like a wolf. I don't bloody know!"

"So we don't really know what it is, but we *do* know what it looks like. Do you think the rain made it visible?" said Nigel.

"That's the only difference, as far as I can see," said Maurice, "but I'm not sure that helps us."

"Actually, it might," said Rod. "I'm going downstairs, like Maurice did earlier. Keep an eye on it to see if it comes out of the cloud when I go down."

"And this could tie in with your question about whether going downstairs or going outside sparked it off," said Maurice.

"That's right. I'm going down now but I'll wait a bit before I go out. Watch to see what happens." Rod went downstairs and stood in the doorway. Nothing happened. He waited. Still nothing happened. Nigel tiptoed to the top of the stairs and whispered loudly, "No movement. Step outside." Rod took a single step and the cloud started to swirl immediately. Rod couldn't see this, but from the upstairs window they could see the wolf-like thing leave the cloud and it was over the hedge and into the garden in a fraction of a second.

"Get in here! Get upstairs! Quick!" shouted Maurice. Rod turned and ran up the stairs. The animal had disappeared. "Where is it? Is it in the house?"

"Hope it doesn't come up here!" said Nigel, nervously.

"No, it won't," said a voice from behind them. They froze, not knowing what to do.

Maurice slowly looked round. In the corner sat an old man on a rickety chair. "Who are you?" he asked.

"More to the point, who are you? What are you doing in my house?" Rod and Nigel turned to face him.

"Sorry," said Nigel. We didn't know this was your house. Or anybody's house. It didn't look lived in, and we just came in for a bit of shelter from the cold while we ate our lunch. We didn't spot you when we arrived. Have you been here all the time?"

The man ignored Nigel's question. "You see the cloud? That's how they travel. They can leave the cloud, but only to go a few yards, then they have to get back inside. The cloud can take them from one place to another. When they want to, that is. If they don't want to go, they stay put. If there's enough food about, they aren't going anywhere. Sheep's blood is plentiful and nutritious."

"They?" queried Maurice. "How many are there? And what are they anyway?"

The man obviously wasn't in a question-answering mode. "They are invisible when the air is dry. When it becomes wet they can be seen. The one you were watching disappeared because he went back to the cloud."

"I didn't see him go back," said Maurice, "but I was more concerned with Rod, trying to keep him safe."

"Hmph. It'll take more than you to do that."

"So what do we need to do?" asked Rod. "How do we get out of here? All we want to do is get back to our bikes and go home."

"What do you need to do. That's a good question. I can't think of a good answer for you. Not that I have an interest in you getting home. Your best bet, although it isn't an attractive option, is to stay here until the cloud goes away." He laughed. The friends felt very uncomfortable and glanced at each other then back at the man.

"Is there anything we can do to persuade them to go away?" Nigel asked. The man laughed again and shook his head.

"I think we should make our way downstairs and make a dash for it next time a sheep comes along. Will you help

154

us with that?" asked Maurice. The man shook his head again and grinned at them.

Rod had been standing by the window watching the cloud. "Look!" he said. "The cloud – it's starting to move!" Nigel and Maurice joined him at the window. The cloud moved very slowly away from the corner of the field.

"Oh, no!" exclaimed Nigel. "It's coming this way!" The cloud moved very slowly, but it was definitely moving toward the house. It stopped at the doorway. "We're trapped!"

"Will you help us?" said Maurice, hoping to appeal to the man's better nature.

"They won't leave the cloud to come up the stairs. They won't have the energy. But why should I help you? You come into my house without asking and make yourselves at home in my bedroom. What have I done to deserve this invasion?"

"We're sorry about that. We didn't realise anyone lived here, and when we came in we didn't see you," said Maurice. "Just a minute, we didn't see you. Were you here all the time?" The man nodded and smiled. "We didn't see you – are you one of them?" The man nodded again. "Come on, lads, let's get out of here before he kills us and drinks our blood!" They ran to the top of the stairs, then stopped dead in their tracks. Coming up the stairs, slowly but deliberately, was a swirling cloud. They looked back at the man, who laughed and moved toward them.

You'll Like It Here!

Chapter 1

The car came slowly up the gravel drive and parked near the front door.

"Look, Mum," said Tina. "It looks very nice. It has a very good reputation, and there'll be people of your own age."

"Hmph!" said Celia, her arms folded, from the back seat.

"Try not to see it as a negative thing," said Clive. "They have specialist staff who'll look after you much better than we can. They'll be on hand to make sure you don't forget your tablets and if you fall over they'll have you back on your feet straight away instead of you lying on the kitchen floor through the night, waiting for us to appear."

"Yes, Mum. When you fell the other week, well, if it had been winter you could have died from hypnotheria"

"Hyperthermia, dear," interrupted Clive.

"Yes, whatever he just said, before we came the next morning. That is, if we turned up. Suppose the car wouldn't start. We'd have thought 'Oh, she'll be alright until tomorrow.', and you would be there on the floor, dead, because that little kitchen, well I know it's a warm house, but that kitchen is like a fridge. And you were just wearing that thin nightdress. I know it's nice, I'm on the lookout for one myself, but only for the summer because it is very thin. Just think how you would have felt. You would be lying there thinking 'It can't possibly get any colder' but it could, and it would, and, well, what a way to go! It's no good looking nice if you're not there to appreciate it."

"Anyway," said Clive before Tina could start another sentence. "Here we are. Let's get out and have a look." He got out and went to the other side to help Celia out of the car and across the gravel to the door. They were greeted by a middle-aged woman in a dark blue skirt and jacket with a white business-like blouse beneath, and sensible black shoes. She smiled obsequiously and leant forward with an outstretched hand.

"Good afternoon," she said. "You must be Mr and Mrs Walker, and is this Mrs Colindale?" Clive nodded and shook her hand.

"Yes, that's right," he replied while she shook hands with Tina and Celia.

"Welcome to Oaklands. I'm Miss Pocklington. We spoke on the telephone. I do hope you find we meet your requirements. We have a reputation for not only being very friendly, but technically excellent and extremely good value for money." She glanced down at the clipboard she was holding. "I see you aren't funded by the local authority."

"Yes, that's right. Her husband left her adequately provided," Clive answered before Tina could speak. "But we'll talk about that later. No point in dealing with that if she doesn't like the place." Clive pressed on past Miss Pocklington into an open airy foyer with a pretty young woman behind the reception desk. She held out her hand. Clive took it and smiled.

"Good afternoon," she said, smiling warmly. "I'm Phoebe." They all shook her hand, then followed Miss Pocklington into what was obviously the residents' lounge.

"This is Jeremy and Alice," said Miss Pocklington introducing them to an elderly couple sitting together in comfortable armchairs. "They're our oldest residents in more ways than one. They are our oldest in years, and have been here longer than anyone."

"Longer than all the staff too," said Jeremy, with a wink to Celia. "Do stay. It's really nice here. We have a laugh. You'll like it here."

"Especially when the staff aren't watching," butted in Alice with a cheeky grin.

"Yes," Jeremy went on. "Especially. Life can be fun if you let it be. Of course, they come round with our medicines, nasty stuff, but it's better than the alternative. And we do have such larks. You wouldn't believe the things we get up to."

"But he mustn't tell when the staff are listening, must you Jeremy."

"Oh, no. Nearly forgot myself there." He tapped the side of his nose with his forefinger. "Mum's the word." He sat back in the chair and smiled.

"Come along," said Miss Pocklington. "I'll show you one of the suites." She walked along the corridor with an affected gait, a bit like a model on the catwalk. They followed, Clive trying not to laugh.

"They seem a jolly pair," said Tina.

"Yes, they are the group leaders for games and activities and so on. We have staff who are professional organisers, but those two always seem to have the final word somehow. But they give the place a happy air so I don't try to stop them. All the other residents like them." She led them into a room which was spacious and nicely decorated. It had a single bed with a bedside cabinet, a dressing table with drawers, a wardrobe, a table and an armchair. There was a modern television attached to the

161

wall positioned so that it could be watched from the bed or from the armchair. In the corner was the door into the bathroom, which had a hand-basin, a bath with a chair lift and a shower over it, a toilet and a small cupboard for towels etc. On the bedside cabinet was a telephone and the remote control for the TV. "We encourage our residents to bring small ornaments and family photographs, but we discourage bringing their own furniture, as it makes the room seem overcrowded. One of the drawers is lockable for keeping valuables safe, not that petty crime is common, but it's a confidence issue for some of our residents." She turned to Celia. "Do you like this room?" she said loudly.

"I'm not deaf," replied Celia, loudly. "Nor am I stupid. I can run rings around these two, you know, if it weren't for the transport issues."

"Mum never learned to drive," Tina whispered to Miss Pocklington. "Women didn't in those days."

"Oh, there needn't be any transport issues here. We organise an outing once a week, which you are free to go on or free to stay behind, and if you need to do a special shopping trip one of our staff will take you to a nearby town." She turned to leave the room. "Follow me and I'll show you the dining room. You can eat in your own room if you want, but most prefer the dining room, unless they're unwell, of course, but illness isn't something that's a problem here. Touch wood." She touched the door frame as she left the room. They followed her along the corridor to a spacious dining room with tables set for four, and a good view of the garden from the big windows. After they had taken in the view she led them back to the lounge. "Would you like to sit here and chat to the other residents to help make up your mind?" she said. Celia plonked herself into

162

an armchair by Jeremy and Alice while Tina and Clive went into Miss Pocklington's office to talk business. When they returned Celia struggled to her feet and addressed them.

"Ok, when can I move in?" she asked. Tina and Clive were speechless. "Well? Is the money side of things ok?" They nodded.

"Mum, are you sure? It sounds as though you've made a very big decision very quickly. Do you want to sleep on it?"

"No, my mind is made up. These people are my kind of people. This is where I belong. If the money's ok."

"Well, yes," said Clive, with an air of surprise. He turned to Miss Pocklington. "Do we get discount for a quick decision?" She shook her head.

"I'm afraid not, but nice try. If Mrs Colindale's mind is made up, we can get the ball rolling this afternoon and you'll hear from our legal team tomorrow." Tina led her back to the car while Clive went into the office to sign some forms. A few minutes later he joined them in the car.

"Well, that seems fine. I think it's a nice place."

"Never mind the place. It's the people. They're my kind of people, and they've still got their marbles, those two anyway. And I think we'll have a lot of fun together. It's going to be like being a teenager again." She leaned back and close her eyes with a smile on her face. Tina and Clive glanced at each other. Clive shrugged his shoulders and drove off.

Chapter 2

Six weeks later Tina and Clive brought Celia to her new home. They moved her in with as much of her clothing as they could fit into the drawers and wardrobe, kept some at home, and gave the rest to the charity shop. She had a few family photos and ornaments in the room, and a few books she liked to dip into now and again, and things like her needlework basket and knitting bag. She gave the impression she wasn't particularly bothered, but was more interested in meeting her new friends, so after a while Tina and Clive left. Tina was upset that Celia seemed to be turning her back on them, but Clive reminded that to Celia it seemed that they were turning their backs on her. She settled in very quickly, and as soon as they were gone made her way to the lounge to have a cup of tea and a chinwag with Alice and Jeremy. They introduced her to some of the others, and it was soon time for lunch so there were invitations from many to sit with them so they could meet the 'new girl'. By the end of her first week she knew the first names of all the other residents and most of the staff and decided she had definitely landed on her feet. Alice and Jeremy seemed to be 'senior residents' and anyone with a problem went to them first before going to Miss Pocklington, or 'Poxy' as they referred to her behind her back. She asked Alice and Jeremy about the staff.

"Well, Poxy isn't as strict as she appears. She tries to be, but we can wrap her round our little fingers," said Alice with a mischievous grin."

"Yes, agreed Jeremy. "Sometimes she gives the impression she has a bit too much of a liking for the sherry. Phoebe, on the other hand, she's the one who runs the place on a day-to-day basis. Doesn't do any management, of course, but she sees what needs doing and gets it done. And she is absolutely gorgeous. All the men stop what they're doing when she walks past and have a good look."

"Yes," said Alice. "She just needs to smile sweetly and wiggle her hips and the men are like putty in her hands. She never has any problems with getting them to do things."

Jeremy looked around, and when there was no-one near their table he leant forward and spoke to Celia. "I say, old girl, would you like a little something to make you live longer?" Celia wasn't sure what to make of this.

"What do you mean? I'm not expecting to pop my clogs for a good few years yet."

"Not talking about years – decades!" said Alice in an urgent whisper. "How old do you think we are?"

"Well, I'm not very good at ages, but I would say you're both in your early eighties." Alice put her hand over her mouth and giggled quietly.

"That's what most folk say, but I'm a hundred and twenty-eight, and Jeremy's a hundred and thirty." Celia's mouth hung open.

"Really? You're not pulling my leg? But you look so young, and you seem so fit and healthy!"

"That's because we take our 'special medicine'. We look younger and fitter than we did when we first arrived here forty years ago. We think of it as 'vitamin supplements', but none of the staff know about it, because taking anything without telling them is strictly forbidden."

"So why aren't you on TV for being the oldest people in town?"

"We want to keep it quiet. No-one knows how old we are, because we lie about our age."

"Yes," said Jeremy with a concerned look on his face. "No one must find out about our special medicine, because of its ingredients."

"What do you mean?" asked Celia.

"Let's say some of them aren't exactly 'fair trade' and leave it at that. Do you want some?"

"Well, I'm not sure. Is it illegal? How much does it cost?"

"It's on the border of the law. But it costs nothing. More than half the people in here are on it, and all you have to do is help with its manufacture every few months. And there are other things we do, but we'll tell you about them when you need to know." Alice nudged him with her elbow.

"Don't go saying too much at the moment. Celia obviously isn't interested."

"Oh, yes I am," said Celia. "Yes, count me in."

"Okay. I'll pop round to your room with the medicine at about two thirty tomorrow morning."

"Two thirty? That's the middle of the night! I'll be asleep then."

"Just leave your room door unlocked and we'll wake you up. Look out, here's June coming." She raised her voice. "Yes, I always have difficulty knitting through the back of the loop." June was middle aged, short and fat, and had a bit of a sour expression.

"Don't ask me," she said without smiling. "I can't knit at all. Don't see the point of making extra clothes. You lot all have more clothes than you can wear anyway." She cleared the coffee cups away. "Lunch in half an hour. Be making your way through to the dining room." She turned and left with the tray of cups and saucers having given the table an inadequate wipe with a damp cloth. Jeremy levered himself onto his feet with his walking stick then held out his arm for Alice.

"Your medicine isn't doing you all that much good, judging by the way you got up," said Celia, rising without difficulty. Jeremy looked round to see if there were any staff in the room, and seeing none, danced a little jig.

"It's just an act so as not to arouse suspicion," he said with a grin. Celia nodded knowingly and they made their way to the dining room, following the others.

Two thirty came, and Celia's door handle turned slowly. The door opened and Alice and Jeremy came in. Alice woke Celia, who was sleeping soundly. She switched on a little torch and held it while Jeremy poured from a little bottle into a little measuring jug and from there into a tumbler. He passed it to Alice who passed it to Celia.

"Drink this now, so we can wash the tumbler before we leave," she said. Celia did as instructed then handed the tumbler back to Alice who washed and dried it in the bathroom. They bade her goodnight and left.

At eight o'clock Celia joined them at breakfast in the dining room. Looking round she noticed how most of the residents were bright and chirpy and thought this might be the work of the potion. She smiled at the thought of having this to look forward to. Once the staff had finished serving she asked Alice about her next dose.

"Not until next week," Alice replied. "Need to build up gradually. Once a week for about three weeks, then two or three times for another few weeks, then every night."

"And will you deliver in every night? Or will you trust me?"

"We will trust you when you are taking it every night," said Jeremy cautiously. "But you have to promise to keep the bottle locked away and always wash the tumbler afterwards. There's nothing on the bottle to trace it back to us, but we can't be too careful. If they found it in your room you might be in danger of being put out, and we've no idea what happens when someone stops taking it." Alice nodded and held a finger to her lips as a staff member approached.

Tina and Clive visited dutifully every week at first and commented on the friendly atmosphere of the place. After a few months Celia said they didn't have to come if they didn't want to. They had been finding it a bit tedious, sitting in the lounge with coffee, but with nothing to really talk about. They both thought she was looking better and put it down to being in a nice place with people of her own age. Their visits dropped to once a month, but they still didn't find anything to talk about.

One morning Alice was sat at the breakfast table looking concerned.

"What's up?" asked Jeremy as he joined her at the table.

"Poxy has changed the password. I can't get in." she said in an angry whisper. She didn't realise Celia was right behind her.

"Can't get in where?" she asked. The other two froze when they realised they had been overheard.

"It's about our age," answered Jeremy in hushed tones. "Every now and then Alice has to change the records so that they don't realise how old we really are."

"That's enough, Jeremy," said Alice holding up her hand. "Celia wouldn't be interested in that."

"Oh yes, I would," said Celia. "Because if this stuff does what you say I'll be in that boat one day. Come on, what's going on?" Jeremy and Celia glanced at each other, then Alice nodded.

"Once in a while Alice goes into the office and does things to the computer so that everyone thinks we are ninety something. That's all, but Poxy has changed the password and now Alice can't do it."

"So why don't you just ask Poxy for the new password?" Jeremy and Alice rolled their eyes.

"Because she doesn't know we do it," explained Alice, exasperated. Jeremy flapped a hand at her to calm her down.

"No, she hasn't a clue about it. Alice does it in the middle of the night."

"Oh, I see. So how do you get into the office?"

"We made a copy of the door key."

"Well, how did you get the old password? Can't you do it again?" Jeremy's eyes lit up.

"By George, I think she's got it! Remember when we got her high and talked it out of her? Yes, I forgot about that. Yes, we can do that again. It wasn't difficult."

"Wasn't difficult? We very nearly got caught. That's why we agreed we wouldn't do it again, you great oaf. You can be a plank at times, Jeremy. I had already thought of that but dismissed it as a non-starter. Just think of the consequences if got caught!" Jeremy looked her square in the face.

"So do you have a better idea?"

Chapter 3

Alice knocked on Miss Pocklington's door. Jeremy stood behind her holding a tray bearing three cups of coffee.

"Come in," came the voice from within. They went in and Jeremy carefully placed the tray on the desk.

"Miss Pocklington," he began. He cleared his throat and started again. "Miss Pocklington, there's something we would like to have a word about." Poxy put a hand up to her forehead.

"Oh, dear," she said. "Last time you two brought me coffee I had an absolutely splitting headache by the time you left. What is it?"

"Well," began Alice. We have been asked by some of the inmates, sorry, I mean residents, to have a word with you, because they all know you respect our views and take us seriously, do drink your coffee before it gets cold dear, and we are always willing to er," she paused to take a sip of her coffee – the others followed suit. "Well, er, to represent their views in a dignified and considered manner and in a way that both respects your position but gives a way forward which can lead to a harmonious outcome whereby all parties are satisfied, to a certain extent, and we can still remain friends." She took another sip of coffee.

"For goodness sake, Alice, get on with it," said Poxy.

"I say," butted in Jeremy. "This coffee's rather good, don't you think? Eh?" He drained his cup.

"Yes, it is," agreed Poxy, taking another drink. "But please get to the point."

"It's about the heating," continued Alice, pausing for another drink of coffee. "Some would like it on an hour earlier in the morning, and to compensate so as not to run up too much of a gas bill, perhaps it could go off an hour earlier after breakfast because after breakfast we are full up with warm drinks; tea, coffee,"

"Yes," butted in Jeremy. "Excellent coffee like this. Do drink up before it gets cold or you'll not appreciate it fully." He smiled as he pretended to drink from his empty cup. Poxy and Alice drained their cups and put them down. Jeremy smiled sweetly at Poxy. Alice continued.

"Yes, quite, Jeremy. Excellent coffee just like this, and so being full of hot food and warm drinks they don't need it quite as much at that point in the day. So do you think you can accommodate their wishes? We understand if you refuse because it would put extra work on the staff and we wouldn't want that, but it would make such a difference to the early risers among us."

"The early bird catches the worm, you know," added Jeremy.

"So I am led to believe," said Poxy with a look of resignation. "Yes, I suppose we can manage that. When do you want it to begin?" She yawned as she said this. Alice and Jeremy glanced at each other.

"What about the end of this month?" suggested Alice. "Thirty-first of September?" Poxy looked from one to the other.

"Yes, that'll be fine. Now was there anything else?"

"Well, said Jeremy with a wink to Alice. "Now you mention it, there is. Your tits are looking particularly lovely today, Poxy old girl." Poxy glanced down, then looked up and smiled at Jeremy.

"Why, thank you, Jeremy. It's very nice of you to say so." Jeremy rose to his feet and leaned across the desk.

"Poxy, old thing, may I kiss you? You look absolutely ravishing."

"Oh," Poxy was flustered. "Oh, I don't know. Oh, all right then. Shall I come over there?" she added getting to her feet.

"Yes, that would be best, so that we don't damage the computer. Speaking of which, what's the new password?"

"You don't want to know *that*," she said with a girlish giggle. He wrapped his arms around her.

"Yes, I do," he replied. "It's a hobby of mine. I make a study of passwords. It gives me an insight into people's minds. And why did you change it? Wasn't the old one good enough?"

"It's er, it's, let me see. It's 1968jaws. Is it? Yes, that's right. 1968jaws, the year of my birth and the name of my goldfish. The auditor chap said we should change it often. It hadn't changed for fifteen years and he wasn't very pleased. So 1968jaws in little letters. There. Now, what about that kiss?" Alice sat in Poxy's seat and keyed it in, then gave a thumbs up sign to Jeremy.

"May as well do it while we're here," he whispered. "How long do you need?"

"Twenty minutes will do. I gave her enough to occupy her little mind for at least half an hour. But we want her more or less sober by the time we leave in case someone else comes in."

"Come here, you most gorgeous of all gorgeous ladies, and kiss me like you've never kissed before." He tightened his embrace and she slapped her lips onto his and they had what can only be described as a long snog. About fifteen minutes later she pulled away from him.

173

"Oh, I've never been kissed like that before. Do it again!" she panted. They sealed lips again while Alice struggled not to laugh and got on with her work. The next time they broke Jeremy was concerned the effects might be wearing off, so he put his arm around her waist and steered her over to the window. He pointed at some flowers while she rested her head on his shoulder.

"Look at those beautiful flowers, Poxy. They're almost as beautiful as you." She put her hand up to her forehead and turned to face him. Suddenly she looked angry and pulled back.

"Just what is going on here? What do you think you're doing? You hand is touching me. Stop it at once or I'll call the police. This is sexual assault."

"Calm down, Miss Pocklington. I wouldn't assault anyone. No, we were looking out of the window, admiring the flowers, when your legs went from underneath you and I grabbed you to stop you falling to the floor and hurting yourself, didn't I, Alice?"

"Of course. We didn't want you to be injured, and I was on my way round the desk to support you at the other side." Poxy looked a little flustered.

"Oh, I see. Thank you both. I was concerned because I don't go in for sexual behaviour. I really am sorry for accusing you of misbehaving. I realise now I've been stupid, but I do feel a bit squiffy. It's probably the heat in here. I am feeling very warm. Yes, thank you both for looking after me. I think I'd better sit down. Now, what was it you wanted?"

"Oh, we've covered that already," said Alice. "It was just about the timing of the heating in the mornings. We'll go now, if you're okay, and let you rest a bit."

174

"Yes, I'm fine now, just a bit unsteady on my legs, but I'll be okay." They left the room and spoke to Phoebe on the way out.

"Miss Pocklington's a bit under the weather, dear. Would you get her a glass of water, please?"

"Of course," replied Phoebe, with a wink. "She often has one of her heads when you two have been in. I don't know what you get up to in there but it certainly takes it out of her." They walked away. As soon as they were out of earshot Alice turned to Jeremy and grinned.

"'Your tits are looking lovely'. What tosh. Her tits are rubbish. Mine are better than hers and they're twice as old and have fed six babies."

"But it did the trick. She hates the word 'tits'. Phoebe told me some years ago. Apparently they were having training on coping with difficult residents and that little coarse woman, what was her name?"

"You mean Tracey?"

"Yes, that's the one. Tracey. Well at one point Tracey said something like 'and if all else fails, get your tits out'. Poxy went wild. She said 'They are not tits. They are breasts, bosoms, boobies, or even mammaries, but they are never, I repeat, NEVER 'tits' in my company, and you shouldn't be 'getting them out' either.' So I knew she was under when she didn't react to the word or to having them admired." They both giggled.

"Yes, I can just imagine her being a bit put out. What happened to Tracey anyway?"

"Oh, she was sacked shortly after that for using inappropriate language. She said 'arse' in public, or something." They giggled again and returned to the lounge.

"Well, that's one problem solved. Onward and upward."

"Is June on duty this evening?" Alice nodded. "Well she might be the answer to the next problem. No one likes her."

"Yes, she is a bit miserable."

"A bit? No, she wouldn't be missed."

Chapter 4

At about two in the morning Celia was preparing her 'medicine'. She had been reading a book for a while so that she could avoid taking it when someone was likely to drop by. She measured the correct amount, added some cold water, and downed it in one, then washed the tumbler and the little measuring jug, dried them and was about to put them away when she heard a commotion out in the corridor. He opened the door a fraction and peeped out. One of the rooms on the other side had its red light blinking and two carers were running along to it. She wasn't sure, but it looked like Alice's room. They went in, and in a minute or so Celia heard comforting chat, so she shut the door and went back to her equipment and was putting them in her lockable drawer when she just happened to glance through the gap in the curtains. There was a man out on the lawn carrying something heavy on his shoulder. He walked along the path almost to the far corner then he suddenly disappeared. Celia opened the curtains just a fraction more to get a better view, and minutes later the man reappeared. It looked very much like Jeremy. He stood still and looked around, as though making sure he wasn't being observed so Celia shrank back into the room just in case, then he came back at a trot and vanished from view. Celia climbed into bed but didn't sleep much, partly because she didn't need as much because of the medicine, and partly because her mind was occupied by Alice's sudden alarm and Jeremy's nocturnal excursion.

The next morning as Celia was going down to breakfast she saw Alice a few yards ahead and hurried along to catch her up.

"Are you okay?" she asked.

"Yes, fine, thanks," Alice replied.

"Was that your alarm went off at about two?" Alice looked flustered for a moment but composed herself quickly.

"Yes, I was unwell through the night but I'm okay now."

"Nothing serious then?"

"No, stomach pains, that's all."

"Stomach pains?"

"Yes. A bit like period pains." Celia grabbed her arm and stopped walking.

"Period pains? Just a minute, is this stuff reversing our aging? Are we going to become fertile again? Does this mean I shouldn't have unprotected sex?" Alice turned to face her and smiled.

"And who are you having sex with?"

"Well, no one, actually, but I have felt the urge sometimes."

"No, don't worry. It isn't an issue. Our eggs went a long time ago and they aren't coming back."

"Thank goodness for that. But I thought one of the purposes of the medicine was to stop us being unwell."

"Yes, it is. I'll explain later when I've had a chat with Jeremy."

"Jeremy? He was out on the lawn last night moving something heavy while you were calling for help. Oh, I see. He was up to no good and you were causing a diversion. Is that it?" Alice nodded reluctantly.

178

"Yes, you could put it like that. Since I've been taking the medicine I haven't had a day of illness, not even a headache, and neither have you. I just needed to make sure none of the staff looked out of the back windows. But you were awake."

"So what's going on? What was he doing? I want to know."

"You'd better ask him that. Here he comes now." Jeremy joined them looking his usual jolly self, but his face dropped when he saw Alice's expression.

"What's up?" he asked nervously.

"She saw you last night," admitted Alice.

"Saw me? Last night? No. It can't have been me. I was fast asleep at two o'clock." He put his hand over his mouth when he realised what he had said. "Yes, it was me. I was just putting some rubbish out." He walked away from them, but they followed him into the dining room, and sat down at their usual table.

"No use trying to hide it, Jeremy. I saw you skulking about on the back lawn hiding something at two o'clock and I saw Alice's little diversion at about the same time. I wasn't born yesterday, you know, and I want to know what is going on." Jeremy and Alice glanced at each other.

"Well, if you must know, some of the ingredients, well, they are a little unconventional so it's best if folk don't know."

"Unconventional? What do you mean?"

"Well, not to put too fine a point on it, illegal, and we might be in serious trouble if we were caught with them. So I hope you understand why it had to be done when there aren't any prying eyes. Can we change the subject now, please?" Celia nodded.

179

"Okay, for now. I'll think about what you said." Alice was looking angry and raised a wagging finger.

"Look, do you want to spoil everything for everybody? Keep your nose out," she hissed. Jeremy gently grabbed Alice's arm and pushed it down to the table.

"No need for unpleasantries, dear," he said calmly as though nothing were wrong. "I'm sure Celia doesn't want to, er, rock the boat." He smiled a hostile smile at her before returning to his bacon and eggs. As soon as he had eaten he got up and left hurriedly. This wasn't like him; he always liked to sit around for a natter over two or three cups of coffee.

Celia went to get up but Alice held her back. "He'll tell you when the time is right." No one saw Jeremy for the rest of the morning, and at lunchtime he dashed in for a quick bight to eat looking very hot and sweaty then dashed out again. Celia made to get up but Alice held her back again.

Chapter 5

Jeremy made his way to the yard behind the kitchens. A young man came out of the kitchen door.

"Hello, Jeremy, what brings you round here?"

"Hello, Ben. Cigarette?" Jeremy offered a strange looking packet. Ben took one and lit it. He took a drag and started coughing.

"Hey, that's a bit strong, isn't it."

Jeremy winked. "Special stuff." He tapped the side of his nose. "The stuff that isn't cheap on the streets, if you know what I mean." Ben grinned and made a 'thumbs up' sign. "My son brings them back from Turkey." They stood in silence for a little while. Ben's eyes started to glaze over. "You know who I am, don't you?" asked Jeremy. Ben squinted at him and stroked his chin.

"Yes, sort of. I know who you are. You're, er, you're, em, you're that bloke. I know who you are but can't remember your name. I'm sure you have one, but I can't think what it is." Jeremy stepped forward and patted Ben's shoulder, then held out a black bin liner. This is for you. The delivery man left it in the herb garden by mistake."

"Herb garden? Didn't know we had a herb garden."

"No, we don't. Here. I'll get the other one." Ben looked in the bag while Jeremy brought the other.

"What is it?"

"Looks like pork to me," said Jeremy. "And good quality stuff. But the trouble is, he left it in the sun, so if I were you I'd get it cooked before it goes off. It will be just right for soup or stew or a curry, but it wants cooking straight away because it's been left in the sun. You understand what I'm saying?" Ben nodded.

"Yes, I'll do some dishes this afternoon and freeze them before they go off."

"Good lad. And no need to tell anyone. Just do it and it can be our little secret." Ben picked up the two bags and hauled them into the kitchen. Jeremy popped his head round the door. "Remember, our little secret."

"Our secret. That's right."

The next day most of the residents were going on an organised trip to a stately home.

"Are you coming along, Celia dear?" asked Jeremy in his usual jovial manner.

"No," she replied. "It's just round the corner from where I used to live. In the summer my daughter used to take me there to try to relieve the boredom, but it didn't work. I would have been less bored if I'd stayed at home and gone to sleep watching Countdown. But I suppose they tried. Don't expect anything wonderful. The things there are nice, but nothing special."

"Oh, I know," said Jeremy. "I've been before, several times, but it's a day out, isn't it?"

Celia turned to Alice. "What does he see in it? I didn't think it was his sort of thing. Nor yours, come to think of it."

"Oh, you've a lot to learn about our Jeremy," she said with a mischievous smile. "He likes to be with the ladies. And in places like that the carers can't keep an eye on him all the time. That's why I'm going – to make sure he doesn't get thrown out for lewd behaviour, like he did once before."

"Lewd behaviour?"

"Yes, on one occasion he and, let me think, was it Elsie? Yes, I think it might have been Elsie. They were asked to leave because they had gone behind a curtain and were all but having sex. But they made too much noise and one of the guides came upon them and made a fuss. They had to go and sit in the café for the rest of the day where someone could keep an eye on them." She smiled.

"Don't you mind, then?"

"Mind? Mind what?"

"Him chasing after other women."

"Good heavens no! Jeremy and I are not an item. We're just good friends, although we have been known to, er, you know, practice parenting when we've had a drop too much to drink." She put a hand up to her mouth to hide a giggle.

"Oh, I see," said Celia, not knowing where to look. The residents got onto the coach, all but Celia and two others who wanted to watch some important programme on TV. They went back into the lounge and chatted over coffee for a while, then Celia said she needed to go for a walk. And that's exactly what she did. After making sure no one was watching she took a gentle stroll around the back lawn, stopping just before she got to the corner. She checked she wasn't being observed, then pushed at the privet hedge, moving along slowly, until it gave way. She almost fell through the gap into a small garden with a decent sized wooden shed in one corner. Steadying herself, she looked round. There were little raised beds, most of which contained what she recognised as herbs, and a few flowers she had never seen before. She walked around slowly, making a mental note of what she saw. Some were straight forward culinary herbs, some were medicinal, if you believed the folklore, and the others, well they could be anything. She went up to the shed and tried the door but it was locked. Searching round under flowerpots and under paving slabs didn't reveal a key, so she tried looking through the windows. They hadn't been cleaned, inside or out, for quite some time, so she couldn't see much. But she did recognise one or two items from school chemistry lessons – test tubes in racks, tripods, pestle and mortar etc., but couldn't see enough to be able to tell what might happen. She decided there wasn't any more to be discovered, so she made her way back to the main building, making sure she wasn't seen going through the gap in the hedge, and rested in her room with a good book.

Chapter 6

The trip to the stately home had gone without incident, and all had had a good day out. They got back in time for dinner, which was a lovely pork curry. The three friends sat together, as usual, and chatted about the trip. Celia concluded she hadn't missed anything, and was happy with her discovery, for now. One day soon, when circumstances were right, she would question Jeremy. She wasn't sure how much Alice knew, as Jeremy was definitely the brains behind it. Her day came sooner than she expected. They were sat at their usual table having breakfast when Jeremy leaned across to her.

"Are you doing anything special this morning, Celia?" he asked surreptitiously. She looked up from her cereal to see him staring intently at her.

"Are you making an improper advance, Jeremy?" she asked with a mischievous grin. He was taken aback. Alice almost choked on her porridge.

"Oh, no. Not that I wouldn't. I mean, you are beautiful and charming. Perhaps later in the day, or tomorrow. No, I was thinking about something else. Something more practical and productive."

She feigned disappointment. "Oh. Never mind. What is it?"

"Well, remember when we first gave you the medicine we said your payment would be to help with the manufacturing?" She nodded. "Well, today it's your turn to help. It won't take more than a couple of hours today and a couple of hours tomorrow. It isn't difficult or dangerous. I'll do the complicated bits. Okay?"

"Okay. Where and when?"

"Meet me here at, er," he looked at his watch. "Meet me here in half an hour."

"Okay."

They met at the appointed time and went out to the back lawn. They walked gently, arm in arm, until they reached the gap in the hedge. They stopped and Jeremy looked about, and seeing no one, dragged Celia through the gap. She pretended to be completely taken by surprised and almost fell over, grabbing his arm to remain upright. She looked around with feigned incredulity at the herb garden, then her eyes lighted on the shed.

"Is that where we do it?" she asked. He nodded and took a key from his pocket. He unlocked the door and opened it then stood back for her to go in. There was dust everywhere, as though it hadn't been cleaned for a very long time. She fastened her cardigan, not because she was cold, but to stop it trailing on the dusty benches.

"Sorry about the mess," he said. "When I'm in here cleaning isn't uppermost in my mind." He picked up a rag and made an attempt at dusting the bench but only succeeded in throwing clouds of dust up into the air. Celia went outside until it settled. "That didn't really work, did it?" he said with a chuckle. "You stay there for a minute." He went back inside and emerged a few minutes later with a piece of paper and a trug, which he handed to Celia. "Here's your shopping list," he said. "You'll find everything on the list here in the garden." He disappeared back inside and she set about collecting. Some were flowers which she broke off; some were roots or tubers which she dug up with a little trowel she found in the corner of one of the raised beds. After about twenty

186

minutes she had collected everything on the list and went back to the shed. She couldn't open the door but heard a shout from within. "Just a minute!" he called and opened the door. She went in with the trug and noticed a strange smell. She recognised it but couldn't put a name to it. Jeremy took the trug, thanking her, and set to work grinding up the contents.

"What are you doing?" she asked.

"Making soup," he replied with a grin. "See those bottles over there? While I'm doing this can you wash them please? Then stand them on the rack to dry." He indicated with a nod of the head to a cardboard box containing twenty or so brown glass bottles. "There's water in the blue bowl. Don't worry about washing-up liquid. Just give them a good rinse. She did as instructed, recognising them as the medicine bottles she was given once a fortnight. By the time she had finished Jeremy had completed the grinding and was measuring quantities of powder with some old-fashioned scales, the type you might see in the apothecary shop in a museum. He added some boiling water from the kettle, after measuring it in a jug, then gave it a good stir. "That's it for today," he said abruptly. "That needs to fester for a good few hours and then we can do the next bit tomorrow. Let's get back before we're missed." He bundled her out of the shed and quickly locked it then they made their way back through the hole in the hedge, making sure they weren't observed.

They strolled into the lounge and sat down with Alice for a cup of coffee. Alice smiled at them knowingly but didn't mention their absence. Half an hour later it was time for lunch, and they sat together, as usual, but none of them said much. After lunch Celia went back to her room and sat with her book on her lap. She tried to read, because it was just getting to the exciting bit, but struggled to concentrate. What was that smell? She recognised it but couldn't pin it down. And what had Jeremy been up to while she was in the garden collecting ingredients? She had her next session the next day at the same time, so she might learn more then, but what was that smell? She put the book down and turned on the TV to watch the news. What was that smell?

Next morning she met Jeremy by the door half an hour after breakfast. They strolled along arm in arm then, with a glance around, disappeared through the gap in the hedge. Jeremy opened the door and they went in. The smell was stronger now, but Celia still couldn't put a name to it. Jeremy inspected the potion in the big pan and gave it a stir, then dipped his finger in it and tasted it. He grinned with satisfaction and turned to Celia.

"That's just right," he said with a big smile. "All we have to do now is strain it and bottle it." He took another pan and a sieve down from a high shelf and put them on the bench next to the potions. "I need your help to lift this," he said. "It's a bit too heavy for one person." Fortunately, the pan had a handle at each side, so together they lifted it and poured it into the sieve over the other pan. It didn't take long to drain through, then Jeremy produced two ladles and two funnels, and they set about filling the bottles. An hour later they were finished. Jeremy emptied the contents of the sieve into a plastic bag while Celia washed the pans and funnels, then the sieve when Jeremy had finished. While she was waiting for the sieve she spotted a little box in the corner, a bit like a cool box. Everything else she had either used or washed. Everything but this box. While Jeremy was

188

reaching up to put the pans back on the high shelf she went across to it and opened the lid. She recoiled at the stench and stepped back just as Jeremy slammed it shut. He looked angry. Very angry. She recognised the smell as the strange odour, but now it was much stronger, and unpleasant, as though whatever it was had gone off.

"Don't you ever open that box again!" Jeremy shouted. "Did you see what was in it?" Celia shook her head. She couldn't speak because she was trying not to retch from the obnoxious smell. She had never seen Jeremy like this. She had seen him angry when she had touched on something sensitive, but this was anger at a new level. She was scared. His eyes glared at her and spittle flew from the corners of his mouth as he spoke. "Are you sure you didn't see?"

"No, no. The smell was too overpowering. I had to shut my eyes." She burst into tears and sat down on the chair by the bench.

"Good," said Jeremy, putting his arm around her shoulders. "It's the most secret of all the ingredients, and it's better for you if you don't know. I'm sorry, dear, I didn't mean to frighten you. It's just that we can't be too careful."

"What do you mean?"

"If word got out, well, that would be the end. And as I said before, we don't know what happens when you stop taking it. I know you wouldn't tell anyone deliberately, because you know what's at stake, but you might accidentally let slip when your family are here. You know, when they say, 'You're looking very well, Mum' as they do."

"Oh, my lot never say things like that. I don't think they really notice."

"Okay. Dry your eyes and we'll go back. I'm sorry for frightening you." He kissed her tenderly on the forehead and they left the shed and walked back to the building, arm in arm. But Celia *had* seen what was in the box. It was a head. It was a human head. It was the head of June, the miserable care assistant. She realised what the smell was; it was the smell of raw offal.

Chapter 7

Celia went straight to her room, undressed and had a shower. She dressed and lay down on the bed. What should she do? Should she tell Poxy? Should she tell Tina and Clive next time they visited? Should she call the police? An occasional tear ran down her face. She got up and paced round the room wringing her hands. June was universally unpopular, but that wasn't a good enough reason to kill her. Would Poxy believe her? She felt sure Jeremy and Alice had such a grip on Poxy that she wouldn't be taken seriously. Tina and Clive would probably think it was early signs of dementia, as would the police. Who could she tell? Would telling be the right thing to do? If the medicine stopped, what would happen to them? She had only been taking it for four months or so, so she might not be affected very much, but some of the others had been taking it for years, apparently, and they might suffer horrific withdrawal symptoms. But murder is murder. And if the police asked, she could put an exact date on it; it was the day before the trip to the stately home. She mulled it over for an hour or so, then went downstairs to join the others for lunch. Lunch wasn't really very appetising under the circumstances, and she just pushed the food around the plate, like the Queen does, so as not to attract attention. She soon left the dining room and went back to her room and lay on the bed. She must have dropped off to sleep, as it was five o'clock next time she looked at her watch. But she didn't feel at all rested, so she splashed some water over her face and tidied her hair before going back downstairs to the lounge, where she poured herself a coffee and sat at a table in the corner. Alice joined her.

191

"Are you okay, Celia?" she asked.

Celia nodded. "Just a bit tired," she replied. "I've had something on my mind and haven't slept well recently."

Alice patted her hand. "Don't fret," she said. "Jeremy can give you something to help you sleep; all you have to do is ask." Celia nodded again and sipped her coffee. It was soon time for dinner, and she sat with Alice and Jeremy as usual, but didn't join in with the conversation. Jeremy seemed his jovial self and showed no sign of noticing Celia's lethargy. She decided she would ask Jeremy for help sleeping, but would wait until there wasn't anyone around, and left the table as soon as she had finished eating.

"I think she's about to blab," said Alice under her breath to Jeremy as soon as Celia was out of earshot.

"We'd better keep an eye on her," Jeremy replied.

The next day Celia woke after tossing and turning all night and decided she must do something about it. Telling someone was the only thing she could think of, but who should she tell? And how would she tell them? 'By the way, Miss Pocklington, did you know someone is killing people and feeding them to the other inmates?' didn't seem the best way to get help. But she must or she might never sleep again. After breakfast she wandered along to reception and noticed Phoebe wasn't at the desk. Celia took a deep breath, drew herself up to her full height, and knocked on Miss Pocklington's door.

"Come in," came the voice from within. Celia opened the door to find Phoebe sat at Poxy's desk.

"Oh, sorry, I was expecting to see Miss Pocklington," she said apologetically.

"Was there something I could help with?" asked Phoebe smiling sweetly. "Miss Pocklington isn't here at the moment and might be away for a few days so I'm looking after the place in her absence. Come in and have a seat. Coffee?" Celia nodded and sat down. Phoebe went to the door, looked out, and beckoned to someone. "Could you get two coffees, please? And if anyone comes looking for me tell them I'm in here talking to one of the residents." She returned to the desk and sat down in a business-like fashion and took up a pen and a notepad. "Now then, how can I help?"

Celia fidgeted, looking down at her hands. She suddenly raised her head and spoke. "Phoebe, I have something very important to tell you, and I won't be surprised if you think I'm losing my marbles, but I'm not. This thing I'm about to tell you really is happening right under your nose, and I think the authorities need to be told."

"Authorities? Do you mean the care home inspectors?"

"No, I mean the police. What is going on is criminal activity by some of the residents."

"Oh, dear! You'd better tell me everything. Start from the beginning."

Celia took a deep breath and slowly but steadily told Phoebe all about the special medicine, her introduction to it, how she had got involved with its manufacture, and June's head in the cool box. She sat back in the chair. "Do you think I'm mad?"

"No, Celia. I don't think you're mad at all. In fact, I've heard much the same story from other people. Staff, residents, next-of-kin, all much the same."

Celia was taken aback. "So someone's told you this before? I can't believe it. What's been done about it?"

Phoebe leaned forward in the chair. "Nothing," she said in a loud whisper. "Nothing – how do you think we keep our reputation? It isn't easy to stop old people dying, you know. Miss Pocklington, well, she has a vague idea that there's more than just good luck to it, but she isn't bright enough to work it out, with a little help from the sherry bottle when her conscience pricks a bit too much. It keeps her in a job and when she wants a pay rise she just drops the statistics on the table in front of the board." Phoebe smiled.

"So you're in on it too!" Celia was appalled. "And I thought I could talk to you about it!"

"Well, you can, but it won't do you any good." There was a knock at the door. "Come in," she called. In came Alice carrying a tray with four mugs of coffee, followed by Jeremy who closed and locked the door while Alice put the tray down on the desk. "Hello, Mum," said Phoebe.

"Mum?" exclaimed Celia. "Mum? This young woman is your daughter?"

Phoebe smiled again. "Not so young, actually. I'm ninety-six; older than you. Ninety-seven next birthday, but unfortunately you'll not be here for the party."

Communication
Meetings

Chapter 1

Number thirteen Foxglove Close was a big house. It had originally been designed as two semi-detached houses, but before work commenced Joe Macmillan got planning permission to make it one detached house instead, and had the plans redrawn. Joe had initially made his money betting on the horses, then gambling in casinos, and in later years, speculating on the stock market. He wanted a bigger than average house because he was a big man, his wife, Georgina, was a big woman, and they had six big children. Eventually the children grew up and left home, and Joe and Geraldine downsized to a four bedroomed detached bungalow, making a considerable profit on the sale, to the point where Joe didn't even need to do the stock market. But he still played it, just for fun.

The big pantechnicon rolled into the street shortly after nine in the morning and what seemed like an army of men, some arriving separately, unloaded it. Lionel and Sophie Donaldson had arrived about half an hour earlier with the keys, and directed the men to various rooms, Sophie fussing over boxes containing fragile items, Lionel instructing the men on the positioning of the larger items of furniture. By six thirty everything was in, and the men departed, tired, but with handsome *pourboires*. Lionel and Sophie put the bed together and sorted out the bedding before collapsing into the armchairs in the parlour.

Sophie looked at her watch and glanced across to her husband. "Fish and chips?" she asked. He nodded.

"And mushy peas. Do we know where the pickled onions and red sauce are?"

"I'll find them while you're out." He returned half an hour later with a bag of food and looked for a table to put it on.

"Every table is full of stuff!" he said in dismay.

"Never mind that," said Sophie. "I can't find the crockery or the cutlery. I've got two soufflé dishes and a dozen plastic picnic spoons. The red sauce is here, and the onions."

"That'll do for me," he answered, unwrapping the food on top of a small stack of packing cases. "We haven't eaten since breakfast. I can feel myself fading away."

They enjoyed the first meal in their new home, listening to the radio as the TV had things piled up in front of it. After the meal they sat on the floor, holding hands and grinning for a little while, then went upstairs and searched for their toiletries. An hour later they were fast asleep in bed.

The next morning, they got up and found some cereals, cereals bowls and milk, but were still limited to the plastic spoons, when there was a knock on the door. Sophie went to answer it, dressed only in pyjamas and slippers. It was an elderly lady, probably in her late eighties, with neat grey hair, dressed in smart clothes appropriate to her age.

"Hello, I'm Lydia," she said. "I've brought you a beef casserole to help over the first day or so, as I'm sure you won't have time to cook properly."

Sophie smiled warmly. "Oh, thank you," she said. "I'm Sophie. We'll be having a garden party next week to get to know people. Will you and your husband be able to come?"

"Oh, yes, that would be lovely," answered Lydia, before suddenly becoming flustered. "Oh, I mean no. Sorry, yes. Here take this." She handed over the casserole dish, burst into tears, and ran off. Sophie carried the dish into the house and put it down quickly, then ran back to the door, but Lydia had already disappeared. She went back to the kitchen and sat down at the table and poked about in her cereal with the spoon, looking somewhat disconsolate.

"What's up, dear?" asked Lionel.

Sophie shook her head slowly. "I've managed to upset the first neighbour we met, but I'm not sure how. I'm sure something dark has happened to her recently."

"Well, you would know. Perhaps you'll get a chance to find out next week." He carried on with breakfast then got dressed and set about moving boxes to various rooms. They both opened boxes, starting in the kitchen, and soon found the crockery and cutlery, and had a good laugh about their previous night's meal. In about two hours they had all the essential items sorted out and set about doing the others in a more leisurely fashion. Later the same day they had visits from Olive, Diane, Harriet and Patricia, and had amassed a beef casserole, a corned beef pie, a plate of assorted sandwiches, a Victoria sponge and a pork curry. All the ladies seemed friendly, and none came beyond the front porch, realising the couple were very busy.

Chapter 2

The following weekend was the house-warming garden party. The weather was dry and warm, and the sun shone brightly into the Donaldson's back garden. Lionel had printed little invitations, inviting the entire street, which amounted to fifteen houses, and telling them it was 'drinks and nibbles' so have lunch beforehand, but not too much. Sophie had made some 'nibbles' and bought others, and they were laid out with paper plates on a picnic table in the garden near the kitchen door. Lionel had organised cans of beer, lager and stout, wine boxes and cartons of fruit juices, which were on a similar table in another part of the garden, with plastic tumblers. Various dining chairs, folding garden chairs and a couple of deck chairs were arranged in a semicircle, with a couple of tartan rugs on the grass for the younger ones. One o'clock came, and no one showed up. Lionel went round to the front of the house and saw one neighbour making his way along the path. He held out a hand.

"Hello," the man said. "I'm Gordon. Number six." They shook hands warmly. Gordon leaned on his walking stick and handed over a bottle of wine for which Lionel thanked him. "Expecting many?" he asked.

"Well, we've invited the whole street, and the folk at number one are the only ones to decline."

"Yes, they're friendly enough, but don't often join in things like parties. In fact, everyone here is friendly." He looked round to make sure no-one could overhear then said in a hushed voice, "Piece of advice; don't lend Tony anything. And I mean *anything*, specially money, or you'll have a devil of a job getting it back. Don't get me wrong, nice enough chap, but rather flexible when it comes to recognising ownership, if you know what I mean." He tapped the side of his nose and gave a meaningful wink.

"Ah, okay, thanks for the tip," replied Lionel with a grin. "By the way, who's the little old lady? She brought us a rather good beef casserole the other day but fled in tears. Sophie hasn't a clue what it was she'd said to upset her."

"Sounds like Lydia. Yes, her husband died about three months ago, and she hasn't got used to the idea of being single. Keeps saying 'we' when what she really means is 'I' then gets upset when she realises. That's probably what it was. Lovely old girl. Darn good cook. No children, no pets, they meant the world to each other, so it's hit her very hard. Very hard indeed." Just then another man hove into view.

"Tony. Number seven. Good to meet you." They shook hands.

"Come on into the garden. That's where the food and drink are, and chairs. Is standing too long affecting your leg, Gordon?" Gordon seemed to have a bit of difficulty setting off, but he waved Lionel away with a smile.

"I'm better sat down, but don't worry about it." Lionel ushered them through and they introduced themselves to Sophie while he returned to the front to look for others. It was as though a bus had just pulled in. Almost all the other guests arrived together and introduced themselves with smiles and laughs, some bringing food, some bringing drink. Sophie and Lionel had fun trying to remember everyone's name and caused a few laughs by getting them wrong. A few hours later the people began to drift away until only Harriet and Richard remained, making themselves useful gathering plates and tumblers into a black sack while Sophie and Lionel put the remaining food and drink back into cupboards and the fridge. Richard helped Lionel put the chairs away.

"Good party," said Richard. "They're a friendly bunch in this street, even though one or two are a bit odd."

"Odd?" replied Lionel. "Odd in what way?"

"Well, Jean and Kenneth in number one won't come to any social events, even though they are both really nice people and happy to chat in the front garden and always willing to help out. Tony will borrow anything; lawn mower, pressure washer, hedge trimmer, but always forgets to give it back. I don't think he does it deliberately, but when you go for it he can never find it. Thoroughly nice chap, but don't lend him anything. They're all perfectly nice people."

"Yes, Gordon mentioned Tony's ownership problem."

"Gordon is a man to know. He keeps an eye on everything – a sort of unofficial Neighbourhood Watch. If you want to know anything, ask Gordon."

Sophie and Harriet emerged from the house. Sophie had a hand on her forehead and looked weary.

"What's up, dear?" asked Lionel.

"Oh, nothing. It's just I seem to have accidentally invited half the street to a communication meeting tomorrow evening. Still, it will use up some of the leftovers from this."

"Ah! That explains it," said Harriet. "Lydia was talking about something – sounded like a séance to me, but I wasn't close enough to hear properly. Yes, she was telling just about everybody."

Richard looked puzzled. Lionel grinned. "Don't worry, dear. You'll cope. I'll be at your side to help." He turned to

Richard. "Sophie is a medium, and we hold communication meetings. Don't like the word 'séance' because it conjures up images of Madam Arcarti."

"Poor Lydia is troubled about her dead husband and I said I would try to help. I was just thinking of her – not the whole street."

"We'll stay at home then," volunteered Richard.

"No, please come along. You strike me as sensible. We might need people like you there."

"Really?" said Richard.

"Yes," replied Sophie. "Some people get upset when they hear things they don't want to, and on the odd occasion there have been fisticuffs."

"Well, if you want us here, we'll be here," said Harriet. "Just give us the nod if you want us to step in."

"Thanks awfully but keep an eye on Lionel for the nod. I'll be out of it." She smiled as they took their leave.

Chapter 3

The next evening at about six o'clock people began to arrive. Lionel had arranged chairs and beanbags in a semicircle, with a central armchair for Sophie. He had a stool positioned on her right within touching distance. The seats soon filled up, and one or two people came in but went away when they saw how many there were. "We'll come back another time," they said. When they were settled Lionel stood up and explained the rules.

"Sophie will go into a trance and contact her spirit guide. While she is in the trance there must be no shouting out or other loud noises. You may ask her questions; she will hear your question even if she doesn't reply immediately. She might not know who has asked the question, but the spirit guide, a young girl from Victorian times called Elspeth, she will know. You might not get the answer you want or expect. Indeed, you might not get an answer at all, or your answer might be delayed by days or weeks, and not necessarily when you are expecting it. If I think things are getting out of hand, I will stop the meeting and ask you all to leave. Is that clear?" They all nodded. Peter raised his hand. Lionel indicated to him to speak.

"Shouldn't the room be dark with candles and incense and stuff?"

Lionel smiled and shook his head. "No, that's only in the films. It isn't necessary." He stepped back and took his seat on Sophie's right. "Sophie will call upon Elspeth. If Elspeth isn't available, nothing will happen and that will be the end, but if that's how it turns out you can stay afterwards for drinks and snacks. Now please remain quiet until Sophie is fully in her trance."

Sophie closed her eyes and raised her head. She remained motionless for about five minutes, although it seemed a lot longer to the others. She opened her eyes, staring straight ahead, and spoke gently. "Elspeth, I'm here waiting for you." There was silence for a few minutes, then Sophie closed her eyes and a child's voice was heard. It seemed to be coming from Sophie, whose mouth was open, but her lips weren't moving.

"I am here, lady."

"One of our company has a question for you," said Lionel, and he indicated to Lydia to ask her question.

"Hello, Elspeth," she said nervously. "Is my Henry with you? Is he in heaven?"

"I can talk to him."

"Is he happy? Please tell him I miss him terribly and wish he was still here with me." There was a pause.

"Henry is comfortable. He understands that you love him and miss him." Tears came to Lydia's eyes; someone handed her a tissue.

"Does he wish he were back here?"

"Henry is comfortable. He knows you miss him. He sees you."

"What does that mean? How does he see me?"

"He watches over you." Lydia was flustered and didn't know what to say at first.

"Thank you, Elspeth. You have been kind."

"It is my duty to help if I can." Sophie closed her mouth.

Lionel looked round the room. "Does anyone else have a question for Elspeth?" Everyone looked round, but no one spoke until Tony put his hand up tentatively. Lionel indicated to him to speak.

"Not sure if this is appropriate," he began, "but which horse will win the one o'clock at Goodwood tomorrow?" A disapproving murmur went round the room; some rolled their eyes. Lionel held his hand up for silence.

"The Happy Wanderer," came the reply in Elspeth's voice from Sophie's unmoving mouth.

Pauline raised her hand. Lionel indicated to her to speak.

"If he can be flippant, so can I. I'm desperate to lose weight and have tried every diet under the sun. Will I ever lose weight?" More eye rolling from the others, as Pauline wasn't fat by any stretch of the imagination. Popular opinion was that if she lost any more weight, she would look ill; some thought she already did. There was silence for a moment, then Sophie's lips parted.

"You will lose weight before this time next year," came Elspeth's voice.

Pauline smiled. "How much will I lose?"

"As much as ..." There was a pause. "As much as ..." Another pause. "As much as a small sack of grain." Pauline didn't know what to make of this but decided to ask later. No one else had a question ready, so Lionel was about to close proceedings when there came a noise from Sophie like a cough, but her open mouth still didn't move. Lionel turned to look at her. Her mouth closed then opened again and Elspeth's voice said, "I have a message."

"Who is the message for?" asked Lionel.

"I can't say," said Elspeth's voice sounding confused, or perhaps upset, it was difficult to tell. "The message is from Maria." Several people glanced around to see if the name registered, but there was no visible reaction from anyone.

Lionel spoke after a brief silence. "Who is Maria's message for?"

"I can't say," came the answer again.

"I understand, Elspeth. Tell us Maria's message."

Sophie's eyes sprung open and she stared, quite intensely, straight ahead. The person immediately in front of her was Peter, who flinched in a startled way. Sophie wasn't so much looking at him as through him, but there wasn't anyone behind him. "Maria says she wants to be with him for the rest of eternity."

"Him? Who is that?"

"I can't say." There was another silence, longer this time.

"Will she get her wish?" Lionel asked gently.

"Yes, she will."

"When will she get her wish?"

"Soon."

"How soon?"

"Very soon?"

"Who is the message for?"

"A person in this room.

"Which one?"

"I can't say. I cannot stay. I must go. I am being called back."

Sophie closed her mouth and her head slumped forward, her chin falling onto her chest. She looked as though she was about to fall forward so Lionel got up and caught her by the shoulders and gently pushed her back into the armchair. She opened her eyes and looked round the room.

"Did she come?" she asked. Many people nodded. "Thank you, Elspeth," she said breathily, then laid back and closed her eyes.

"That's the communication finished," Lionel announced. "You are welcome to stay for drinks and snacks, but let Sophie rest a little while before you ask her too many questions."

"Would you like me to see to the food and drinks?" asked Harriet.

"Oh, yes, please. It's all prepared in the kitchen – just needs uncovering and bringing through to the dining table in the next room." Harriet set about bringing the food through, assisted by Pauline.

Monica grabbed Peter's hand and dragged him away. "Come on," she said crossly. "We're going."

Peter looked disappointed. "Aren't we staying to socialise?" he asked.

"Not after the way I've been humiliated tonight we're not." They disappeared through the front door. After about half an hour Sophie felt able to get up and walk round. Lydia thanked her repeatedly for about ten minutes, hugging her and leaning her head on Sophie's shoulder. Sophie eventually managed to prise her away and explained that she didn't know anything that had happened, much to Lydia's disappointment, and munched on a slice of cake while the others filled her in on the details.

"You see, when Elspeth's here, I am not actually in the room," she explained.

"So where are you?" asked Harriet.

"Good question. I'm not anywhere, I think. It's as though that period of time, be it half an hour or an hour or whatever, didn't take place. Lionel always fills me in on the details afterwards in case anyone stops me in the street to ask about it." She was asked many questions, most of which she couldn't answer, and started to look a bit weary.

Lionel stepped in. "Give her a bit of space, please. She's just been through a traumatic procedure. Talk to her about the weather or something. Something not taxing."

Those around her apologised and brought her food and drink, looking at her in admiration and puzzlement in equal proportions. In the far corner of the sitting room Richard and Gordon were sitting enjoying cake and wine.

"What did you make of that, old bean?" asked Gordon.

"Not sure," replied Richard. "She certainly pleased old Lydia, poor old thing, and Pauline. Not sure Tony should have asked for a tip, but that's Tony."

"Yes, I thought he was a bit crass. Now think about what she said. Did she really please Lydia? Think about the actual words. 'He's comfortable; he understands you miss him'. She didn't actually answer Lydia's question. She didn't say if he was in heaven or hell, if you believe those things, which I'm sure Lydia does, and she didn't mention loving her or missing her at all. What does 'he's comfortable' mean? It's like when you're in hospital and they don't want to tell your family anything."

Richard thought for a moment. "Yes," he said. "See what you mean. And what about Pauline? 'Lose weight by this time next year' was quite definite, but how heavy is a 'small bag of grain'? Does she mean a two-pound bag you might get from Sainsbury's, or a small sack you might get at the farmers' market to feed the animals? Could mean anything."

"Did they have Sainsbury's in those days?"

"What?"

"Well, Lionel said she was a girl from Victorian times, so perhaps if she was from far enough back you'd get your grain from the farm."

"If you lived in the country, yes, but if you were a townie you'd get it from some grocery shop or other, even if it wasn't Sainsbury's"

"Yes, you've got a point there. Anyway, did you see Peter and Monica zoom off at incredible speed? "

I think he wanted to stay but she wasn't having any of it."

"Not at all surprised. Isn't Maria the name of his floosie?"

"Floosie? What's that?"

"Sorry, old bean. I'm a good bit older than you. That's what they called them when I was young. Floosie. A young woman of great beauty but small brain. Usually kept for sexual purposes in a little flat above a shop somewhere in a dodgy part of town where the chap isn't known." He paused for a nibble of cake and a swig of wine.

"Oh, I see. I did think he had one, but I didn't know for certain, and didn't know her name."

"Well, Monica obviously does and wants to keep it under wraps. She didn't want any prying questions, even though it wasn't obvious Sophie was looking at him. I thought she was looking at the chap standing behind him."

"But there wasn't a chap standing behind him, was there?"

"Not that I could see, but we don't know. I always thought these things were fake. You know, just made up to prise hard earned cash from people's hands, but there was no fee to get in, and if she *was* looking at Peter, well that does it for me. I'm sure the floosie *is* called Maria." He

210

paused for another swig of wine. "Anyway, if The Happy Wanderer is running in the one o'clock at Goodwood, and if it wins, I'm convinced."

Richard took his smart phone from his pocket and tapped a few words into it. "Yes, The Happy Wanderer. Rank outsider, so I doubt even Tony would entertain that. But if it *is* fake, how did she know? Unless Tony's in on it. And the other thing, all the time Elspeth was speaking Sophie's lips never moved. Her mouth was open, but her lips never moved. And Sophie has quite a deep voice for a woman and Elspeth's voice was quite light."

"Got to admit, I've never been to a séance like it."

"Oh, you're an old hand, are you?"

"Hell, no. This is the first I've been to, but when I was a boy Aunt Agnes used to go to them all the time. She would call in on the way home and tell mother all about it, who was contacted, who was about to die, and they were all like you see in films: fat old dear in diaphanous clothes in a darkened room with candles and incense and fingers touching on the table and all that guff. Nothing like this."

By now most people had started to drift off. Harriet and Richard cleared the food and plates away and did the washing up, then Harriet made tea for Sophie and Lionel before going. When they had the house to themselves Lionel sat back and laughed.

"What's funny?" asked Sophie.

"You should have seen the expression on Monica's face when you mentioned Maria."

"Just remember, *I* didn't mention Maria; it was Elspeth, and I didn't see anything. You know what it's like for me."

"Yes, sorry, darling. I bet there's a rabbit away there somewhere. And another thing – I thought Elspeth only fulfilled need, not greed."

"What did she say?"

"She gave Tony a tip for tomorrow's horses."

"Hmm, that's unusual. I always thought it was need based too. Perhaps there *is* a need there somewhere. I'll try to speak to her later in the week – I'm too tired to do it now."

"Okay. You looked absolutely trashed. Shall we go to bed?"

"Yes, I am worn out. Good idea. I'll leave you to lock the place up."

"See you soon."

Chapter 4

The following day Tony had popped out of the office to get a sandwich for lunch. He just happened to pass the betting shop and checked his watch. Twelve thirty. He went in and scanned the screens. There it was – The Happy Wanderer, one o'clock at Goodwood. This must be more than a coincidence. Long odds. Very long odds. Worth a small wager. Or perhaps a big wager. He placed his bet and went off in search of an attractive sandwich before heading back to work. He spent a nervous afternoon wondering about his 'investment'. He daren't look on the internet, as he had already been warned about it more than once. Next time would be the last. As soon as he decently could get away he walked quickly down to the town centre and made his way to the betting shop, more in hope than expectation, but The Happy Wanderer had come in. First place, very much against the odds, and made him five hundred pounds richer. He stuffed it in his wallet and made his way back to the car park with a happy smile on his face.

Later in the week Tony was sat in front of the TV with a glass of whisky in his hand after a particularly gruelling day at work, when there was a knock at the door. It was Kenneth and Jean from number one. They tilted their heads to the side together and said "Hello!" in unison in that annoying sing-song way they had of speaking.

"Oh, hello," he replied, then stood leaning on the door post looking bored.

"We're collecting again," said Kenneth.

"Yes," said Jean. "The council has given us a building."

213

"When we say 'us' we don't actually mean us. It's for the Churches Together group, to make a refuge for the homeless. But they've just given us the building, so we are collecting to decorate it and kit it out with furniture."

"Just basic furniture, you understand, not luxury items."

"No, basic furniture, so we're collecting to make this possible, because there are a lot of homeless people in our little town and we want to help them."

Jean thrust the collecting box forward and rattled it, smiling. Tony folded his arms and continued to look bored.

"Look," he said. "Why don't these scroungers go out and get jobs? That way they could decorate it themselves, or perhaps they wouldn't even be homeless in the first place. I'm fed up with folk asking me to give my hard-earned cash to help those who sit on their bums all day instead of working. Scrooge had the right idea when he said, 'Are there no workhouses?' Tell these lazy blighters to get up at a decent hour and go to work instead of staying in bed all morning. No, I'm not giving you a penny." He slammed the door and went back to his whisky.

Jean and Kenneth looked at each other in disbelief. Tony wasn't known for his generosity, but he had never behaved like that before. "I hope the Lord can forgive him, because I certainly can't," said Kenneth sadly.

"Yes," said Jean. "He is one of God's creatures, but he isn't acting like one. It isn't as though he's hard up. I imagine he would be on a good salary where he works." They moved on to the next house, where the people were more generous.

A few weeks later Pauline was out shopping with her friend, Amanda. They had had a most enjoyable morning buying clothes and handbags, chatting over tea and cakes, well, Amanda had cakes; Pauline just had tea because she was watching her figure. No one else was watching it, least of all her husband, because there wasn't much to watch. She was thin to the point of looking ill. She insisted she didn't have a health problem such as anorexia or anything like that, because she was perfectly in control of her appetite; she wanted to eat but resisted, because she didn't want to put the extra pounds on. Thin was beautiful in her eyes. The thinner she could be, the more beautiful she became. Her husband, Ralph, loved her dearly and tried to persuade her to eat 'sensibly' for her own good. But no. Thin was beautiful. "You don't want to be married to a great dumpling, do you?" she would say. Actually, he wanted to be able to put his arms round her without being scared of breaking something. Her mother didn't help. Once upon a time Pauline had been normal, average size, average weight, curves in the right places but none of them excessive, but her mother kept going on about her weight. "Why don't you look like your cousin?" mother would say. The cousin in question was painfully thin due to some hormone imbalance and didn't look at all healthy, mainly because she wasn't. But Pauline got it into her head that thin was beautiful, the thinner the better. She wasn't very tall either, so had to buy some of her clothes in children's shops, but she didn't mind that. This made it hard work for Amanda, who remembered her from the 'normal' days. But she was a good friend and went along with her just to keep her happy. After the tea and Amanda's cake they did more shopping, until Pauline was tired. They sat down on a seat in the shopping centre.

"It's no wonder you're tired," Amanda complained. "You've got no energy because you haven't eaten anything. What did you have for breakfast?"

"I didn't have breakfast. Too many calories."

"So, what did you eat before we came out?"

"Nothing."

"So, you haven't had anything all day, other than that cup of tea?"

"That's right. That's how to stay thin. The little girl at the séance said I would lose weight before this time next year. About the weight of a small sack of grain, she said, so I'm looking forward to that." Amanda rolled her eyes and got to her feet. "We can't go yet – I'm still tired."

"Look, walking burns up calories, so get up and move, or I'm going to die of boredom sitting here. Come on. I haven't got all day." They did more shopping, then it was lunch time. The café on the corner did light lunches, so they went in. Amanda had a normal meal. Pauline had a salad and left most of it. When Amanda had had enough, they went home. She dropped Pauline off at the corner of the street with her bag of shopping and waved as she drove off. Pauline waved back and turned round to go home. She turned round a bit too quickly and suddenly felt faint. She dropped her shopping and staggered out into the road just as a large motorcycle came round the corner. He swerved to miss her and mounted the pavement just as she fell back onto the path. The bike ran over her legs and she screamed in agony. Amanda saw all this through the rear mirror and stopped immediately to call an ambulance. After seeing Pauline off in the ambulance, she drove up into the street only to discover that Ralph wasn't at home. She scribbled a note on a scrap of paper, pushed it through the letterbox, and drove off to the hospital.

Four hours later Ralph arrived at the hospital; Pauline was still in surgery, so he went over to Amanda. She got up and hugged him. "Oh, I'm sorry, Ralph. I just dropped her at the street end. If I'd taken her all the way home this wouldn't have happened. It's all my fault."

"No, Amanda, I'm sure it wasn't your fault, but what's happened? I got a phone call at work to say she was in hospital, but they wouldn't say why, other than 'she's had an accident' so I got here as quickly as I could."

"Oh, she's in the operating theatre now. She's still alive, but a motorbike ran over her legs. She looked in a bad way. But I don't think the man on the motorbike was at fault. She seemed to pass out and fall into the road and he tried to avoid her, but she went down in front of him and he hit her. The police spoke to me very briefly and said they wanted to speak to me again later. Oh, look, here's one coming now."

A police officer strode up to them. "Good afternoon, sir. Are you Mr Carpenter?"

Ralph nodded. "Yes, I am. Can you tell me what's happened to my wife? The staff here can't, or won't, tell me anything until she comes out of theatre."

"We've interviewed the man riding the motorcycle, who says he hit her because he swerved to avoid her, but we'll interview him again later when he has calmed down a bit. He's in shock at the moment. Mrs Pickford here has given us a brief explanation, but we'll interview her again later on, perhaps tomorrow. I'm here to see the extent of

Mrs Carpenter's injuries. Usually we just phone up but I was here interviewing someone about another case, so I thought I'd call by."

Just then a man in a green gown came into the waiting room and approached them. "Are you Mr Carpenter?" he asked Ralph. Ralph nodded and the doctor indicated a side room with half a dozen seats. They went in, and he invited the police officer in too. "I'm Mr Upton, the surgeon. I've just finished operating on Mrs Carpenter. My team are just finishing closing her up. You'll be able to talk to her in about an hour."

"Thanks," said Ralph. "What's the score? I mean, I don't know anything. I don't know if the accident is life threatening or anything."

"I see. Well, she's alive and will make a good recovery, but the accident has had life-changing consequences. She's going to be in bed for a few weeks, then in a wheelchair for a while. We've had to amputate her left leg as it was damaged beyond repair. All other injuries are fully recoverable, and she'll be back to normal eventually, and can be fitted with an artificial limb in about a year's time, but that isn't my department so don't quote me on that. She has very little muscle mass, and if her legs had been 'normal' for someone of her age, well, we might have been able to save it. As it was there was no muscle to protect it, so when the wheel hit it, it was just like snapping a piece of firewood. My advice is to go home and have something to eat then come back in a couple of hours. You can see her in five minutes if you want, but she'll still be unconscious; it's up to you. Do you want me to find someone to take you to the recovery room?"

Ralph and Amanda looked at each other. Ralph nodded. "Yes, please," he said. "I want to see her."

"Okay, take a seat." They sat and waited until a nurse came along and led them away. The police officer didn't see any point in going along, so he took his leave, promising to come back tomorrow. Ralph and Angela were shocked at what they saw. Pauline was covered in scratches and bruises, which looked much worse than they actually were, but her left leg was little more than a stump from just a few inches below her hip.

"She did say she wanted to lose weight," said Amanda," but this is a bit of an extreme way to do it." Ralph burst into tears.

Chapter 5

Peter was ready to leave the office and picked up the telephone. He dialled home, and when Monica answered he told her he needed to stay behind to do some work for head office.

"When do you think you might be home?" she asked.

"Can't really say," he replied. "Head office are desperate for these numbers. I had it all ready, then the boss came in and said he'd been given misleading info by operations and we'll all have to start again. Not just me – the whole team. Can't see it being done much before eleven."

"But your dinner's in the oven. It'll be ruined. I've spent the last two hours making something really nice and now it'll have to go in the bin."

"Sorry, sweetheart. You eat what you can. I'll send out for a pizza or something. I'll put it on expenses."

Monica hadn't actually made anything. Wednesday evening was a popular day for 'working late'. She knew what he would be up to, and didn't waste her time and energy, but strung him along, making sure he bought her a new pair of shoes at the weekend to make up for it, or a new handbag, or some expensive clothes or jewellery. She phoned out for a take-away and when it arrived settled down for an evening in front of the TV with a bottle of wine.

Peter stayed in the office until everyone else had gone and had time to get well away from the car park, then visited the toilet to smarten up his hair and tie before trotting down the stairs with a spring in his step and a tune on his lips. Maria would be ready for him and he didn't want to keep her waiting. He wanted enough time to have a roll in the hay before going out to a nice restaurant and get home just after eleven. He hadn't realised Monica knew anything until the other night at the séance, even though his affair had been going on for about six months. She didn't mention it on the way home, and he didn't either. Neither of them brought the subject up so he thought perhaps it was something else. He thought Gordon might know, or at least suspect something, as they had met unexpectedly at a restaurant on the other side of town. He pretended to be someone else, putting on a fake Italian accent and keeping away from the well-lit part of the room, but he knew Gordon wouldn't mention it anyway because he didn't particularly like Monica. He drove to Maria's little flat and went inside. After a sensuous kiss and gropey hug he threw his jacket onto the sofa and began to undress.

"No, no, no," she said. "No sex tonight, darling. Wrong time of the month *and* my sister's coming round as soon as she finishes work. Just had a big row with her hubby and needs to stay here for a week or so. Put your clothes back on and we'll have a meal, then perhaps a snog in the car on the way home, like we used to do in the old days." She winked as she felt his bottom.

"Okay, sweetie," he said as he returned the grope and smiled. "We'll make up for it next week."

"We certainly will. Julia will be working evenings next week." They had a quick snog on the landing then made their way downstairs to the car. The weather had taken a turn for the worse. They arrived at their favourite restaurant and ran inside. Even though it was only a few yards from the car to the door they were both drenched by the time they got in. The receptionist took their coats and hung them up then seated them at their usual table in the corner. They had a romantic dinner with cocktails before the meal and a bottle of wine with it. Then he had a large glass of port afterwards. He knew he shouldn't because he had to drive across town to get home and the police were everywhere after about ten, but well, once in a while wouldn't hurt. When they left the place the rain had stopped and the breeze was quite warm, but the roads were still wet. He decided on a short cut and was chatting away quite merrily when we spotted a police car just coming out of the next junction. He slammed the brakes on and took the next side road, but it was too late. The police car was following him. He put his foot down – he knew these side streets like the back of his hand – but he couldn't shake the police car off. Blue lights. This was it. The game was up. How would he explain this? As far as Monica's concerned, he is at the office with a grotty pizza. No, only one thing for it. Foot down and take every back street he knew. Suddenly there's a lorry parked in front of him. He slammed the brakes as hard as he could, but at that speed it was too late. His car disintegrated into the front of the lorry. And so did Peter and Maria. The newspapers made it sound so romantic – 'young lovers together for ever' was on the front page of the local paper.

The postman was delivering a letter to Tony just as he left the house. He shoved it into his jacket pocket as he was already going to be late, and that was the last thing he wanted. The boss was on his case. The quality of his work was fine, but his timekeeping, which hadn't been good to start with, was now deplorable and seemed to be getting worse as the weeks went by. Three times this week already

222

he had set off and had to turn back for something he had forgotten. This made him late even though he had started getting up early and leaving the house early. In the old days his wife would wake him up and make him tea and toast while he dressed, as she left half an hour later, but she walked out when she learned the extent of his gambling debts. Her dad had bailed them out three times to the tune of twenty-five thousand pounds in the last six months, but the more help they got, the more it seemed that Tony couldn't learn from his mistakes. His father had always told him that gambling was a mug's game and the punter never wins, but Tony was convinced the big win was just round the corner and it would end his problems. Now he was on his own and had the mortgage to pay without her salary. It had been difficult with two incomes, but now with just his, it left literally nothing to buy food. As soon as he sat at his desk he opened the envelope. The bank wanted to see him, and it didn't sound friendly. He telephoned them, but the man who had signed the letter refused to discuss it over the phone. He managed to find a mutually convenient time for an appointment two weeks later.

Tony did his best to look smart but not too affluent and had all the papers he thought he might need in his briefcase. He went in and sat down at the little table. Mr Wallace came into the room looking very stern and sat opposite him. He took some papers from a folder and put them on the table. He looked down at them and shook his head.

"Mr Sanderson, this isn't the first time we've been in this situation, is it?"

"No, Mr Wallace."

"But it is the last. We refuse to continue in this vein. I have tried to be understanding, but head office are tightening up on customers who they see as irresponsible. I am instructed to begin proceedings to repossess hour house."

"What? You're taking my house?"

"While you have a mortgage agreement it is only your house if you stick to the terms of that agreement. It is a legally binding contract. We need to take it back now while its value is still greater than the outstanding debt, or you will be in a much worse situation."

"But, but, can you actually do that?"

Mr Wallace pointed to a paragraph on one of the documents. "Yes, we can. And we will. In fact, we must in fairness to our investors and our other borrowers." He put another document in front of Tony and handed him a pen. "I need you to sign this. This is to say that I have explained the situation to you and you have understood it. We will begin the procedure next week. I also need you to advise your solicitor to expect to hear from our solicitor in the very near future."

"So this is it. I've given you my business for all these years and now you're making me homeless."

Mr Wallace shook his head. "No, Mr Sanderson, you're making yourself homeless. If you'd made your payments on time, as per the agreement, we wouldn't be sitting here now. When you realised that your situation was getting difficult you should have come in to see us straight away, instead of ignoring it. As for being homeless, there is rented accommodation in the town, and if the worst comes to the worst, I believe there is a hostel for homeless people, supported by the local churches. We'll review your current account once your mortgage situation has been finalised.

Good day, Mr Sanderson." He stood up and offered Tony his hand. Tony walked out and slammed the door.

Chapter 6

A few weeks later Gordon walked across the road and knocked on the door of number twelve. Harriet answered it and was surprised to see Gordon.

"Hello, Gordon, come in. It isn't very often we get a visit from you. You're looking a bit grim. Is something up?"

"Good question, old girl. Is Richard in? I want to see both of you. Do you mind if I sit down?"

"Oh, of course, have a seat. Richard's in the garden. I'll go and get him. Cup of tea?"

"Yes, please."

Harriet came back a few minutes later, followed by Richard who was drying his hands. They perched on the edge of the sofa.

"What's up, Gordon? You don't look very happy," said Richard while Harriet brought a plate of biscuits.

"It's our friends just along from here," he replied picking up a biscuit. "Lionel and Sophie." He shifted uneasily in the chair. "I'm concerned they're somehow getting themselves into hot water, so I thought I might run my thoughts past you two, as you get on so well with them." Harriet and Richard glanced at each other.

"Okay, yes," began Richard slowly, "we get on pretty well with them. What do you think is the problem?"

"Remember that evening shortly after they arrived?"

"The communication party? Yes. What about it?"

"Do you remember who was mentioned by the little girl – the spirit guide?"

"Ah, yes. I see," said Harriet. "Tony is homeless, Pauline has lost a leg, Peter is dead, although he wasn't actually mentioned but some of us knew it was him she meant. Yes, but what about Lydia? She was the main reason for the party, and she seems okay. Better than she used to be, actually."

"That's why I haven't mentioned it before. The other three had bad things happen within a few weeks. Lydia seems happy as a sandboy, even to the point of walking about six inches above the ground. But people at the other end of the street are a bit disquieted. Some of them are saying they want Lionel and Sophie to move away."

"Oh, surely not!" said Richard. "Pauline's leg was a tragic accident, but Peter and Tony, well, their downfalls were their own fault. I mean, I wouldn't wish it on anyone, but if they had behaved themselves, well, things would have turned out differently. And as you said, Lydia is happy as a pig in poo."

No, Richard," Harriet objected. "Don't talk about poor Lydia like that. She would be affronted if she knew."

"Yes, I'm sorry, but you know what I mean."

"Yes," said Gordon. "But most of them don't know Lydia all that well and haven't seen much of her since Henry died. They're just seeing the bad stuff. Anyway, what do you think? Is there anything we can do? You two know them better than I do." He turned to Harriet. "Could you have a chat with Sophie? And perhaps with Lydia too – see what is making her tick at the moment. Make sure she is genuinely happy. Woman to woman, you might get more out of them than Richard or me."

"Well, I got to know poor Lydia quite well when Henry died. She came over to talk to me quite often, seeing as I work from home most of the time – sometimes I was the only one at this end of the street through the day."

227

The next morning Harriet phoned Lydia and invited her in for coffee and a chat. Lydia came across straight away. Harriet made a pot of coffee and put a plate of biscuits on the table in the sitting room.

"Thanks for coming, Lydia," Harriet said. "We haven't had a chat for quite a while. Are you okay?"

Lydia nodded with a smile. "Yes, I'm feeling much happier, ever since that séance thing with Sophie. I've got what I wanted."

"Oh, what's that?"

"Henry." Lydia looked round, even though they were the only people in the house. "I've got my Henry back." She put her hand over her mouth while she gave a little giggle. "That's all I wanted. Sophie's little girl is wonderful."

"Well, I'm not sure I understand," said Harriet. "How is he back?"

Lydia blushed and put her hands up to her face. "He visits me through the night," she said.

"Through the night?"

"Yes, when I lie in bed, he's there beside me. The first time it happened I put the light on, and he disappeared straight away. I cried myself to sleep. Then the next night I didn't touch the light, even though I wanted to. I put my arm across and held his hand. And we do that every night. Sometimes I lean over and hug him. Sometimes he leans over and hugs me. Sometimes we kiss. Sometimes we, er, well, I'm not sure I should mention it, but sometimes we do, er, we do what young couples do when they first get married. You know, the baby-making thing."

Harriet looked shocked. She was in the act of lifting her cup and paused with it in mid-air. Her voice dropped to a whisper. "Do you mean s-e-x?" Lydia blushed again and covered her mouth. She nodded and smiled and looked away. Harriet didn't know which way to look. "Well, er, what can I say? I mean, it's a dream, isn't it?" Lydia shook her head. "But, well, Henry's been dead for almost a year now. Hasn't he?" Lydia nodded. "Well, I'm really pleased for you, that you're enjoying life, and happy with Henry, but oh, Lydia, you need to come to terms with this. It isn't Henry. I don't mean it's someone else," Lydia looked shocked and opened her mouth to speak. Harriet continued. "It must be a dream. A lovely dream, but it must be a dream."

"No, Harriet. This is no dream. It happens every night. Have you had the same dream every night for a month? No, this is really Henry. Sometimes we just hug and kiss. Sometimes we do 'the other thing', but he comes to me every night in my bed. In *our* bed that we shared for almost sixty years. Don't tell me it's a dream. You don't know. You haven't been there. I know my Henry." Lydia folded her arms crossly.

Harriet wasn't sure which direction she should take this conversation. "But you're asleep when it happens, Lydia. How do you know you're not dreaming?"

"I've seen the dent his head makes in the pillow. It's there every morning. And then there's this." Lydia undid the top two buttons of her blouse and pulled it open at one side, revealing a love bight on her neck. "Is this a dream?" she asked, with a self-satisfied smile.

Harriet put the cup down and sat back in the chair. "Well, you've got me there," she said. Lydia fastened the buttons and sat back, picking up a biscuit and her coffee cup. "Can we change the topic of conversation for a bit?"

They talked about the comings and goings of the neighbourhood for a few moments, then Lydia got up and declared it was time she went.

"Thanks for the coffee," she said, smiling. "And thanks for listening. And thanks for understanding." She gave Harriet a big hug, then went home with a spring in her step.

"Thanks for understanding," Harriet murmured to herself as she stood at the front door and watched Lydia cross the road. "Not sure I did." As soon as Lydia was back in her house Harriet phoned Richard. "Darling, we need to talk about Lydia. I'll call Gordon and tell him to come across as soon as he sees your car."

"What is it, honey?"

"Can't tell you over the phone. You'll think I'm mad. See you tonight." She phoned Gordon, who promised to come over, pretending he was returning something in case Lydia saw him. He came over as planned and after a brief chat they agreed Harriet would visit Sophie and take it from there.

Chapter 7

Sophie usually arrived home about an hour before Lionel, so Harriet watched for her and popped out to catch her as she was getting out of the car.

"Sophie, dear," she said. "Hope you don't mind, but I could do with a little chat. Are you able to pop in for a coffee?"

"Yes, of course," Sophie replied. "Tonight's dinner is all prepared – just needs heating up. Plenty of time for that. I'd love a coffee and a chinwag. I'll just put my stuff in the house first."

Five minutes later Sophie arrived. Coffee and biscuits were already on the little table in the sitting room and Harriet was sat there trying to look unconcerned. "Have a seat. Good day?"

Sophie nodded. "About normal," she replied. "What's up?"

Harriet forced a smile, which obviously wasn't genuine. "There are two things I want to mention," she began slowly. "One is Lydia. Ever since your séance,"

Sophie stopped her. "You know we don't call it that," she objected.

"Okay, sorry. Ever since the er, communication meeting in your house Lydia has been seeing Henry, her dead husband. 'Seeing' isn't the right word but I don't know how to describe it. Henry has been 'visiting' her." Harriet went on to relay the facts as Lydia had described them and Sophie's mouth dropped further and further open.

"Let me get this straight – she's having sex with a ghost?"

Harriet nodded. "I tried to tell her it was a dream, but when she showed me the love bite, well, what could I say? I mean, she couldn't inflict that on herself, could she? It's about here." She pointed to her neck just above the collar bone. "I can't work out how to do it by myself. It must have been done by someone else, and Lydia isn't the type to go 'putting it about'. She's about ninety, for goodness' sake!" Sophie shook her head. "So, well, I'm not an expert in these things. Is it possible Henry *has* come back?"

Sophie put her cup down on the table and sat back, looking into the distance for a moment. "I honestly haven't a clue," she said eventually. "Are you free later on this evening? I might try getting in touch with Elspeth, and it might make it easier for Lionel if you are here."

"I am, yes. Could Richard and Gordon come along too?"

"Yes, but no one else. I'll put the dinner on to heat up now so we can have it as soon as Lionel gets in. Oh, you said there were two things you wanted to mention. What's the other thing?"

"Ah, yes. Gordon came over the other day and said there was disquiet at the other end of the close about what happened to Tony and Peter and Pauline. Some people want you and Lionel to leave. Obviously, we don't, but we wanted you to be aware of it, and see if Elspeth could do anything to put things right."

Sophie was shocked. "Those things were nothing to do with us! If Peter had kept his bits in his pants he would still be with us. And people tell me Tony had a gambling problem long before we came here, and he gambled money he should have been spending on other things. As for Pauline, she's mentally deranged. They can't blame us!"

232

"I know that, but they're seeing you as the bringer of disaster to the close."

Sophie glanced at her watch. "Will you and Richard have finished eating by about eight thirty?" Harriet nodded. "Okay, come over then, and bring Gordon. And have something to make notes on, just in case it gets complicated."

"We'll be there. We are your friends, even if the others aren't."

At eight thirty Harriet, Richard and Gordon arrived. They had tea and biscuits while Harriet recounted her conversation with Lydia and Gordon related the feeling of the other end of the close, then Lionel rearranged a few chairs.

"I'm not going to do a normal communication with Elspeth," Sophie explained. "I'll try to stay in the room while I talk to her, but I want you to take notes in case I drift away." Lionel closed the curtains in case there were any prying eyes about, and they settled down in their chairs. Sophie sat bolt upright and closed her eyes. "Elspeth, Elspeth, can you hear me?" Silence. "Elspeth, are you there?" More silence. She opened her eyes and looked round. "It's no good. I'll have to go into a normal trance. Lionel will be your mouthpiece. Make plenty of notes because I won't have a clue what's what." She relaxed into the armchair and closed her eyes. She took a few long, slow deep breaths, then she spoke. "Elspeth, I am here waiting for you." Her eyes sprung open.

"I'm here lady. I'm listening to you."

Lionel spoke. "Can you hear me, Elspeth?" Silence. He repeated his question. More silence. "Sophie, can you speak?"

"Yes, Lionel, I can speak. She can't hear you. I'll talk to her. Elspeth, things have been happening here. Do you know about them?"

"Yes, lady. I know. But I didn't make them happen. I wouldn't do that. I can't do that."

"Do you know of any other bad things that will happen here?"

"Oh, lady, yes. People hate you and want to kill you, but they won't."

"Why won't they?"

"Oh, lady, I can't tell you that. But it isn't good. Oh, lady, those people with you, they are good people. They will try to stop the others. Listen to what they say." More silence.

"Elspeth, are you still here?"

"Yes, lady, but they're trying to pull me back. There are things I need to tell you but they're pulling me back."

"What things, Elspeth? What are you trying to tell me?"

"No, lady, they won't let me." There was a scream from nowhere and Sophie lurched out of her chair onto the floor. Lionel and Harriet rushed to help her up and sat her back in the armchair. She was totally disoriented and her eyes flickered open and shut many times. She opened her mouth and a voice was heard – not her voice, but a man's voice, a very deep voice, almost a growl.

"You are doing things you ought not to be doing. You are making a link between your world and ours. You must stop this. Now! You will be punished. Elspeth will be punished for helping you." They could hear Elspeth sobbing, but no more words came. Sophie closed her mouth and collapsed onto the floor again. Lionel picked her up and laid her on the sofa while Harriet brought a glass of water. She was totally unconscious. Lionel opened one of her eyelids and there was no semblance of normality. He checked her pulse and breathing, and both seemed normal.

"This has never happened before," he said with a worried tone of voice. "I'm not sure what to do next." He glanced round the others anxiously. They were silent but worried.

After a moment Gordon spoke. "From what I remember from my days as a First Aider, we can't do much other than check her pulse and breathing, which you've done. We should put her in the recovery position. Then we need to decide do we phone for an ambulance, and what do we tell them?"

"Yes, good idea. I remember the recovery position," said Richard, and he had just started to move her when her eyes flickered open.

"Oh, hello," she said. "What am I doing here? Let me get up." She raised herself into a sitting position and accepted the glass of water Harriet offered her. She looked tired, but apart from that seemed okay. When she had gathered herself together Richard told her what had happened, reading from his notes. "Oh, dear," she began.

"Don't worry," said Harriet. "You seem to be fine now."

"No, I'm concerned about poor Elspeth. What will they do to her?"

"Well, you're not doing any more today," said Lionel. "That can wait for another time. You're exhausted." The others looked confused.

"I need to know if there's anything I can do to help her," said Sophie with a rising level of anxiety in her voice.

"Look here, old girl," said Gordon. "You've had a bit of an experience here today. Do as Lionel says and leave it for today. Anyway, who are 'they'?"

Elspeth seemed flustered. "The others. The other spirits. They can punish her if she upsets them. She is just a little girl and they will be nasty to her. If they think she has told us too much, well, I don't know what they will do, but it won't be nice."

"Sophie, dear," said Harriet. "We realise that you want to help Elspeth, but we don't understand any of this, and as Lionel says, you're exhausted, so get some rest. Shall I pop round tomorrow to see how you are?"

Sophie nodded. "Yes, bless you."

Richard cleared the cups away while Harriet helped Lionel get Sophie upstairs to the bedroom. After they had gone Lionel undressed her and put her into bed. She was asleep on no time.

Chapter 8

At the other end of the close a few neighbours were chatting outside Patricia's house.

"Yes, I agree," said Diane. "They do seem like nice people, but we all saw what happened to Tony and Pauline and Peter. Do you want to be next?"

"But Peter and Tony were architects of their own downfall. Those things would probably have happened if the Donaldsons *hadn't* moved in," said Patricia. "And we all know Pauline has a screw loose."

"It's alright you saying things would *probably* have happened," said Olive, "but the thing is, those situations have been ongoing for a while, and they *didn't* happen, until now. Nothing happened until the séance thing, which I wasn't at, and I'm glad I wasn't there, or something might have happened to me too."

"Oh, I see," said Diane, arms folded. "Have you got some dark secret? Are you seeing your fancy man when you tell Adam you're working late? Or are you spending your life savings at the bingo?"

"I don't have a fancy man. Chance would be a fine thing. If Adam were to take the hick and leave, well, I'd be clapping my hands. But that's beside the point. And I haven't got any savings either. All that went on getting the car fixed. Look out! Start talking about something nice. Here's Jean heading this way. Hello, Jean!" She waved at Jean, who waved back.

"Hello, girls," said Jean cheerfully. "Are we discussing the price of carrots, or are we plotting the overthrow of Ena Sharples?"

237

"Ena Sharples? She's been dead for years, Jean," said Patricia while they all laughed. "Try to keep up."

"Oh, I don't know," Jean said, shaking her head. "I try to stay up to date so that I don't look stupid when I talk to you lot, but it doesn't always work."

"Don't worry, darling," said Olive. "No, we were talking about what's happened down your end of the close. Those two doing their seances and stuff. They probably do witchcraft when our backs are turned. We were debating who might be next."

Jean looked shocked. "Oh, no, you mustn't joke about things like that! They need our prayers, not our blame. Kenneth and I pray for them every night. Well, to be honest, we pray for everyone in the street, but especially for them."

"Do you even pray for me?" asked Olive, laughing.

"Of course," said Jean with a serious expression.

"Anyway," said Diane. "What are we going to do about them? I don't want them living in my street bringing bad luck to anyone who puts a foot out of place."

"I don't believe in luck," said Jean, "and if you don't put a foot out of place you've nothing to worry about." The others rolled their eyes. "Well, I'm not perfect, nor is my Kenneth, but if we do put a foot out of place it's by accident. When we do wrong, which we do sometimes, we pray for forgiveness."

"Well I don't want them here either," said Olive. "We've got to do something or one of us will end up dead. Perhaps more than just one."

"I've told you what to do," said Jean. "Pray for them." She turned and walked away.

"Now there's an idea," said Diane in a whisper. "You're a Catholic, aren't you, Olive?"

Olive nodded. "Where's this going?" she asked.

"Well, why don't you have a word with the Holy Father, get him to exorcise the place. That would drive them out, wouldn't it?"

"Do they still do that sort of thing?" asked Patricia. "I thought that was medieval claptrap."

"Course they do," answered Diane. "Do it all the time in America and eastern Europe. You don't watch the right TV channels or you'd know all about it. Yes, you have a word with Father and see what he says."

The following week Father Michael came to visit Olive. She offered him tea, which he graciously accepted.

"You see, it's like this, Father," she began. "This couple have moved in at the other end, and since then bad things have happened." She told him about Tony and Peter and Pauline.

"I understand why you're anxious," he said. "I wouldn't want people doing these dark arts near me. Sadly, the country's going to the dogs and they're allowed to do them. The state has no respect for the church, not like it used to. Now if you had a word with the bishop or the cardinal even they wouldn't take our side. 'Enlightened' is what they call it now. But I understand your point of view." He sipped at his tea and took another biscuit from the plate.

"So can you help us, Father?"

"Well, yes. And no. I can't do an exorcism. I'm not sure that would be the right thing to do anyway. Getting permission takes years, and I don't think it would be granted for this. The people who suffered, Tony and Peter, did wrong. I feel sorry for Pauline – she seems almost the innocent victim. But no, an exorcism isn't appropriate. What I can do for you, however, what I can do is to bless the house and those who live there, and pray for them."

"Would that do the trick? Blessing their house?"

"Oh, no! You don't understand. I can't bless *their* house without their permission. But I can bless *your* house and family. And I can pray for you too. Now how does that sound? Is that the sort of thing you think might help?"

"Could you bless Diane and Patricia's houses too?"

"Well, let me see, are they good Catholics?"

"Not exactly. I don't think either have been to church of any sort recently, apart for hatches, matches and despatches."

"I'll thank you not to be flippant about holy rites, Olive. Well I can do their houses too, but there would be a small fee. And for your house there wouldn't be a fee, but I might expect to see you at mass a bit more often."

"Okay, Father. I would like to have my house blessed, and me and my hubby, if that's okay. I'll have a chat with the others and see what they say."

The father took a little note book out of his pocket and flicked through it. "Would next Saturday be okay, about ten o'clock?"

"Yes, Father that'll be fine. Can Diane and Patricia be in here when you do it?"

"Of course they can. It might help them see the advantages of being Catholic." With that he picked up his little briefcase and left, collecting another biscuit on his way out.

Harriet popped in next day to see how Sophie was, and she was feeling much better, so much so that she decided to try to contact Elspeth even though Lionel was out.

"I'm not sure about this, Sophie," said Harriet. I'd much rather you waited until Lionel was here. He would know what to do if anything went wrong."

"I appreciate your concern, but I want to contact the poor little thing as soon as possible. You're here and you'll be able to help if things go awry."

"But I wouldn't know what to do!"

"Just rely on your instincts. I'll sit in my armchair, as usual, and I want you to sit right next to me, so that you can hold my hand. Yes, that's right. If you hear Elspeth talking and I'm not answering, you need to talk instead, but don't ask her any leading questions. Just keep it vague and let her do the talking."

"Oh, I'm not sure about this. I wish Lionel were here."

"But he isn't. Just relax and we'll get started. Elspeth, can you hear me? Are you there, Elspeth?" Silence. They waited about ten minutes and nothing happened. "Elspeth, dear, are you able to talk? Can you hear me? Can you give me a sign that you're still able to listen?" Another silence of more than ten minutes. Sophie was getting visibly distressed.

"Oh, dear, are you okay, Sophie? You look upset. Is there anything I can do?" asked Harriet.

"Oh, Harriet, I think I've lost her. My little friend isn't there. Oh, what have I done?" She burst into tears and Harriet did her best to comfort her and dry her eyes. "This is my fault. When we had the first meeting I put too much onto her. I should have insisted we stop after Lydia. But I didn't know what was going on until afterwards. Lionel should have realised. We never have lots of questions like that. We always restrict it to one enquirer, two at the most, and then only if the questions are easy. Lydia should have been enough. And now Elspeth has gone. Perhaps she's been taken away or punished, or even destroyed. Oh, Elspeth, I'm sorry darling. I've let you down. What can I do to make amends? Is there anything? I want to bring you back. You're my friend and now you're gone." Sophie sat in silence again, and the silence continued. She let go of Harriet's hand and sat back in the armchair and sobbed her heart out. Harriet knelt in front of her and wiped her tears with tissues and tried to calm her down. When Lionel returned an hour later she hadn't moved from the chair, and was still in tears.

"Sophie, dear," said Lionel. "Whatever is wrong?" Harriet explained what had happened. "Oh, Sophie, you know you shouldn't try this when I'm not here." He picked her out of the chair and put his arms round her. "Thanks for your help, Harriet. I'll take it from here."

"Are you sure? Do you want a cup of tea or anything?"

"No, she'll be okay when she's had a rest. Pop back in a couple of hours if you want, but there's nothing more you can do at the moment. Thanks, Harriet. You're a good friend."

Chapter 9

On Saturday morning Father Michael arrived at Olive's house at ten o'clock on the dot. Diane and Patricia were already there, and they sat drinking tea while he explained what was going to happen. The first thing would be a short act of worship, which started with a prayer and included two readings from the Bible and the Lord's Prayer, then he would go outside and bless the front door, then come back in and bless the living room. It would end with another prayer and a short silence, then he would go. "Other priests do it diffcrently," he explained. "We each have our own preferred method, but the result is the same. But I must admit, sitting here soaking up the atmosphere, I don't think you have anything to worry about. There aren't any feelings of evil or dark forces or anything here. As there's nothing of concern I won't bless the individual rooms; that's only appropriate if it's a very big house, or if you've had manifestations. But I'll do the blessing anyway just to be on the safe side, put your minds at rest, and protect you for the future." He opened his little briefcase and took out a Bible, a crucifix, and some other small items and arranged them neatly on the dining table and began. It proceeded just as he had described, then he shook hands with the ladies and left. They sat down and watched him disappear out of the street, then Patricia turned to Diane.

"Did you get that?"

Diane smiled and nodded. She took her mobile phone from her pocket and played back the beginning of the blessing ceremony. "Yes, here it is."

"Don't play the whole thing!" said Olive. "We don't want to end up 'unblessing' the house!"

"Yes, said Patricia. "See what you mean. When are we going to do it?"

"About three today would be best, I think," said Diane. "The street's usually quiet then so we won't get interrupted, and if anyone comes along, we're just having a chinwag."

"In the middle of the street?" asked Olive.

"Well," said Diane. "My Adam reckons we can talk anywhere. 'You lot can talk under water without a mask' is what he says." They all laughed.

At three o'clock they met outside Sophie and Lionel's house. No one appeared to be at home, but they decided that wouldn't matter. They stood in a row directly in front of the house, Diane in the middle, and she took her mobile phone from her pocket. She looked at the other two, and said "Okay, are we ready?" They nodded and she pressed the 'play' button. It played the entire blessing from Father Michael, and when it finished she pressed 'stop' and put it back in her pocket. "I don't mind if they leave or stay," she said to the others as they walked back up the street. "As long as this black magic stuff stops. They are quite nice people."

"Yes," agreed Patricia. "They are quite nice."

"I'm not sure about this," said Olive. "Are we doing the right thing? We're using Father Michael's blessing without his permission or knowledge. Suppose he finds out. What then? Suppose something goes wrong – it'll be our fault."

"Ner, what could go wrong?" said Diane dismissively. "Anyway, there's nobody about so if something *does* happen they can't pin it on us."

"That's right," said Patricia. "Let's have a cup of tea."

244

"Actually, I think I've got a bottle of wine in the cupboard. We can have that. Adam won't be back from the match for a while," said Olive.

"Good idea," said Diane. "Then we can have a cup of tea as well." They all laughed.

Later that afternoon there was a muffled bang. More of a dull thud really, but difficult to describe. It seemed to come from Lionel and Sophie's house, but there was no one round to hear it. The house shuddered and whisps of smoke began to rise up from the bottom of the walls. After an hour it was a fire, and Lydia saw it out of her front window. She ran out and hammered on Harriet and Richard's door. When Harriet answered it, she saw the fire immediately and phoned the fire brigade. They only took twenty minutes to arrive, but in that time it had become an inferno and most of the neighbours were out in the street watching. Richard arrived home and had to leave his car on the main road. After ten minutes two more fire appliances arrived and they got the blaze under control, but not before the upper floor had crashed down, crushing everything beneath it.

"I do hope they're not in there," said Lydia, hanging on to Harriet's arm.

"No," said Harriet. "They went off this morning and said they wouldn't be back 'til late. Visiting her sister for a birthday or something. I've got Sophie's mobile number – I'll give them a ring when it's a bit quieter. I wouldn't be able to make myself heard in this noise."

"You can come into my house to make the call," offered Lydia.

"Good idea." They went inside and Lydia made coffee while Richard stood at the front window. Harriet went to the back of the house, because it was still quite noisy at the front. Lydia was bringing the coffee mugs through on a tray when she tripped on something. She put her hand out to save herself but managed to spill coffee down the front of her skirt.

"Damn!" she said. "This is a new skirt. First time I've worn it." Harriet took the dripping tray from her. "I'll just pop upstairs to get changed." She had only been gone less than a minute when Richard and Harriet heard an earsplitting scream from upstairs. Lydia came running down, screaming, with a terrified expression. She just screamed and screamed and didn't stop until she passed out. Harriet and Richard caught her before she hit the floor and put her on the sofa. Harriet tried to rouse her while Richard went upstairs to see what had caused the problem.

"Harriet!" he called urgently. "Come up here. I don't believe what I've just seen! And be prepared for a shock." Harriet made sure Lydia wouldn't fall off the sofa and ran up the stairs. There in the double bed in the front bedroom lay a skeleton, fire-blackened, and with wisps of smoke rising from it. He took his mobile phone out and called the police.

A few days later DCI Scott went down to the mortuary in the basement. "Hello, Doc," he said.

"Hello, Greg," he replied. "Which one are you here about today?"

"The one from Mrs Steel's bedroom, mainly. That one over there, I assume." He pointed at a blackened skeleton on one of the tables.

Doc stroked his chin. "Yes, that's a strange one, that one. I can identify him from his dental records. It's actually Henry Steel, Mrs Steel's late husband."

"Yes, he's obviously late, but why do you say it like that?"

"Well, he was on this very table almost a year ago. He had a heart attack while he was driving and ploughed into a concrete bridge support. He died instantly, but it was the heart attack rather than the crash."

"So why was he in here?"

"Usual checks for substances in the blood stream to see if there were contributory factors to his losing control. Clean as a whistle apart from prescribed meds. What's puzzling me is why he is here now. How did he end up in his own bed a year after his cremation? That's something you don't see very often – a man being cremated twice."

"That was going to be my next question. If he died a year ago how did he end up back in his own bed?"

"I'll leave that question to your lads. As far as I'm concerned, the cause of death was fire. That's why he is blackened. He still had wisps of smoke coming off him when they brought him in."

"Thanks for giving me a jigsaw with most of the pieces missing!" Doc laughed. "And what about the other two? Mr and Mrs Donaldson – did they die when the house came down or were they already dead?"

"Not that simple, Greg. They aren't Mr and Mrs Donaldson. Dental records show they are actually Joseph Macmillan and Georgina Macmillan who lived there seven or eight months ago." Greg scratched his head and looked at the two bodies while Doc put his jacket on. "Another puzzler for your lads. I'm off to get some lunch. Coming?"

He paused, deep in thought for a moment, before answering. "No, thanks. These two cases are making me doubt my own sanity. Let me know if you have any bright ideas."

Lydia spent the rest of her days in a mental hospital. Sophie and Lionel were never seen again.

Visiting Grandma

Prologue

O, nasty virus, why have you
Come here to devastate our land?
You take the weak folk, strong folk too
And smite them with your pow'rful hand.

O, nasty virus, go away!
We do not want you on our shore.
We do not want you here to stay
To hang about for ever more.

O, nasty virus, we are strong
And all your germs we will destroy
And this will be our joyous song
'We did our wits and skills employ'

But, nasty virus, if we fail
And you for evermore live here
We will succumb to your regale
And struggle on in mortal fear.

So, nasty virus, do not live
Among us bringing misery
But some compassion to us give
So we can live in liberty.

Chapter 1

The radio alarm crackled into life. "It's seven o'clock on Monday, the eighteenth of March, 2095, and here is the news." Ria hit the snooze button and lay there looking up at the ceiling for a few minutes. She smiled. No work today – a few days' holiday to visit Mum and Dad; Dad's sixtieth birthday on Tuesday. She got up and washed her hands thoroughly, cleaned her teeth, then made breakfast. A cooked breakfast today because she wasn't in a hurry. Baked beans, mushrooms and tomatoes – lovely. She showered and dressed and packed a few things into a holdall; only staying a week, need to be back at the weekend for work. Ready to go. Oops! Dad's card and present - mustn't forget them. She retrieved these from the bottom of her wardrobe, picked up her bag and handbag (and present, of course) and went downstairs to the garage. There was no one about, as most people had already set off for work. No one to see her go. Hope no one thinks she is ill and tries to break the door down. No, if they thought that they would leave well alone until the flat started to smell, then they'd get the council to do something. The roads were quite quiet, and her trip across London only took twenty minutes. She arrived at her parents' house and pressed the button by the gate. Mum opened the front door looking anxious.

"Sorry, darling, I can't let you in. We think Daddy has the virus; we sent for the doctor yesterday afternoon – he's due today," she called from the front doorstep.

"Oh, dear!" said Ria. "Shall I wait?"

"No, I need you to do something. We had a surprise lined up for you, but we can't do it now. We intended to take you up to see Grandma tomorrow. I need you to go up and let her know we're not coming. If I write she won't get the letter until Friday at the earliest. It's an opportunity for you two to get to know each other. She hasn't seen you since you were about two."

"I don't actually remember her at all. Yes, it would be nice. I think. But spending time with someone you don't know is a bit strange."

"No, she's lovely. You'll get on like a house on fire. I'll get you her address." Mum disappeared back into the house while Ria put Dad's card and present into the security box by the gate. Mum reappeared with a little book in her hand. "Have you got your book and pencil ready?" she asked. Ria scrabbled about in her handbag and found them. "Okay. It's number eight, Nidd Crescent, Town 11, Area HG. Have you got your map book in the car?"

"Of course I have," Ria replied. "It stays in the car."

"Well, it's just off the main road through the town. Turn right about ten yards past the shop."

"Which shop?"

"There only is one shop. And that's another thing, don't tell anyone you're from London, don't admit to anything, and you will be surprised at a few things, but don't let it show. We haven't been out of London for a while, and things might have changed, so I won't tell you in case they don't happen." She smiled enigmatically. "Bye, darling, love to Grandma."

"You've got me worried now," she answered. "I don't know what to expect now. I thought it would be like London, but smaller."

"Nothing you can't cope with, just how amazing it is the way things are different from London, but be careful what you say, and above all, don't show surprise. Act as though everything is normal." She came to the gate and took Dad's card and present out of the security box after Ria had taken a few steps back, then went inside and shut the door. Ria got into the car and found the page in the map book. She located the street quite quickly but gazed at it while she thought about Mum's remarks. Mum was like that. She would get your interest by telling you half a story. She would say something like, 'But of course, you don't know who Cynthia is related to,' and walk away, then when you asked about it she would say, 'No, you don't need to know,' and walk away again. But she didn't usually do it over anything serious. No, Mum wouldn't do anything to get her into trouble, so it's probably just her idea of a joke. She left the book open on the seat and set off. She'd never been outside London before, so it would be quite an adventure. She looked at the energy gauge – only a quarter full. Not enough to get to that page of the map book, but there would be plenty of places to fill up. It was late morning, so she would top up when she stopped for a bite of lunch.

It was a nice sunny day, warm but not hot, and she was enjoying the journey. This was the furthest she had driven, and never before outside London. It seemed strange compared with her usual trips. Not much traffic, not many pedestrians, no traffic lights or crossings. Perhaps this is what Mum meant. Lunchtime had been and gone, and no sign of anywhere for a snack, let alone a meal. She pulled into a lay-by and ate a cereal bar. That was the one she always kept in the car for emergencies. Well, it was an emergency – her concentration was starting to fade, partly because of hunger, and partly because she had never driven for more than forty-five minutes before, and this trip was two hours already. Then back on the road. She was amused at the idea of the town having only one shop. It must be a very big shop. It would be really convenient to be able to get everything in one shop, if you didn't want a great variety. Yes, life in the country must be very different from London. If only there were more places to buy lunch. She could tell the temperature was falling as she got further north. She wasn't even halfway there and it was decidedly cooler, and she was hungry, and there was a hint of fog setting in. Area HG is a long way off at thirty miles per hour. Her little car could do fifty, but the law said thirty. She couldn't remember why – Dad explained it once when she was learning to drive – but the reasons sounded good at the time. Anyway, the energy was getting low, so if she didn't find somewhere in the next thirty minutes or so she had a problem. The fog was getting worse, so she slowed down. Panic over! Up ahead she could see a fuel station on the left. The fog was getting really thick by now, so she couldn't see if they did food, but most did these days. In London, anyway. She pulled in and parked beside the charging machine and got out, taking her handbag with her. She could relax for half an hour while the car was being topped up. A middle-aged man in a checked shirt came over but stopped at the required distance.

"Hello," she said cheerfully. "I need some energy; can you do me eight units please? More if you can manage it." The man smiled, but shook his head.

"Sorry, miss," he said. "I can't do anything at the moment. The power's off." He pointed up at the lights over the forecourt, none of which showed any life. "It doesn't usually go off this soon. I'm not expecting it back on until six in the morning." Her face dropped.

"Oh no!" she exclaimed. "I'm on my way to HG and I'm almost out. Is there anywhere else nearby with power?" The man stifled a laugh.

"You're not from round here, are you?" he said. "When the power goes off here it goes off everywhere for miles around. Tell you what I can do, though. My wife does rooms for people that get stuck, like you. I know for a fact they're all empty, so we can put you up for the night." Relief spread over Ria's face.

"Oh, thank you!" she said. "Do you do food, too?"

"We don't usually, but I'll have a word and see what we can do." She took her bag from the boot and was about to follow him in when she stopped and turned to look back at the car.

"Where should I park the car?" she asked. He glanced at his watch.

"Leave it there. We'll not get any more customers today. And it'll be ready for tomorrow morning. I'll be able to let you have ten units, but no more. I'll start filling as soon as the power comes back so you can get away." She followed him into the back of the filling station and met his wife. She put her right hand over her heart and bowed slightly. The other woman did the same.

"This young woman needs a room for the night. She's out of fuel."

"I'm Roxanne," the woman said. "Yes, we can put you in room number four. Come on and I'll show you where it is." She led the way and Ria followed at a distance. It was upstairs in a dark corridor. "It's at the far end. We can't be too safe, can we? And I overheard Tyson saying you want something to eat. I've got some fruit, but I'm afraid I can't do any vegetables with the power being off. Will that be okay?" Ria nodded and smiled.

"That would be wonderful. I'll just put my stuff in the room then I'll come down." Roxanne's face took on a worried look.

"Sorry, miss, but no, I can't permit that. Our room isn't big enough for you to keep far enough away. I'll bring it up and leave it outside your door."

"Of course, sorry, I didn't think. You can't tell how big the rooms are from the front. I just assumed with you doing Bed and Breakfast ..."

Roxanne cut her short. "Oh no, miss, we don't do Bed and Breakfast. We just do Bed. Can't be too careful. Sorry."

"Oh, don't apologise; I agree. We can't be too careful." Ria went to the end of the long dark corridor to find the key in the door. She went in and unpacked a few essentials. The light was fading, so she sat in the dark and waited. After a few minutes there was a knock at the door. She went to open it but stopped with her hand on the handle. "Are you still there?" she asked.

"Just a minute, miss. I've brought you a candle and some matches, too. Give me a couple of minutes to get away."

"Okay, thanks." Ria gave her five minutes, just in case, then opened the door. On the tray were the candle and matches, as promised, and a bowl of fruit; an apple, a pear, half a dozen grapes, and a banana which had seen better days. She brought it into the room and lit the candle. The room was about the same size as her bedroom back at the flat, with a single bed, a little table, and a chair. In the corner was a small washroom with a hand-basin, toilet and shower. There was a mirror on the wall and hooks on the back of the door. She sat at the table and devoured the fruit. She had been starting to feel unwell, but now felt much brighter. The candle was nowhere near bright enough to read by, so she changed into her nightdress and settled into bed for an early night, feeling tired from the unaccustomed journey. The bed was comfortable despite its uneven appearance and she soon dropped off to sleep, even though it was only seven o'clock.

At half past eleven Ria was woken up by a noise. She couldn't tell where it was coming from, but it was loud. Very loud. And there were bright lights shining through the flimsy curtain at the window. Very bright. So bright that it was almost like daylight inside the room. She checked her watch. Yes, it was eleven at night, and not in the morning. The noise was coming from outside the window. At least that was something to be grateful for – it wasn't in the corridor, whatever it was. She slipped out of bed and went over to the window. Should she move the curtain to see? What if they, or it, saw her and ... and what? If they were after her, lifting the curtain would make no difference. And if they weren't after her she wouldn't attract their attention. Or would she? She pulled the corner aside and peeped out. There were bright lights moving in the sky, and some sort of commotion on the ground. She couldn't see if they were people or animals. Or aliens from outer space, considering the lights. Aliens were always being talked about on the news, and she hadn't believed in them up to now, but perhaps it was all true. She knelt there, watching but not seeing much. Eventually it all died down. The commotion stopped, the people or animals or aliens went away, and the lights went out. She went back to bed, but didn't sleep well, hoping it wouldn't happen again.

Chapter 2

The next morning Ria got up and washed her hands. She cleaned her teeth, showered and dressed, and packed her belongings away. After checking the room to make sure she hadn't left anything she went downstairs. Tyson was on the forecourt seeing to her car. Roxanne appeared from the back room and greeted her.

"Did you sleep well?" she asked.

"I did at first, thanks," Ria replied. "But at about eleven o'clock there was a lot of noise outside. I couldn't see what was going on, but it lasted well over half an hour. After that I couldn't settle."

"That would be breakouts," Roxanne explained. "They happen two or three times a week round here."

"I see," said Ria, remembering what Mum had said. "We don't get them where I live." She supposed there must be a prison nearby or something. "Anyway, thanks for letting me stay the night. How much do I owe you? And do you have something I can buy to snack on for the journey?" Roxanne brought out a box of cereal bars, little packets of biscuits, and some very small chocolate bars. Ria selected three or four and handed over the money. Roxanne put the money in the till then washed her hands in the little sink set into the counter. At that moment Tyson came in.

"Your car's ready," he said. "I've put the charge onto your account. I put ten units in but it only shows eight units on the account – I'd be in trouble if I put more in."

"Oh, thank you," said Ria. "How much do I owe you for the other two?"

"Call it three," he said with a smile. "You're obviously not from round here, and we're not in the habit

261

of cheating strangers." She got more money out of her purse and handed it towards him.

"No, I don't do money," he said, putting his hands behind his back. "Give it to Roxanne." Roxanne gratefully accepted the money, then washed her hands again after putting it in the till. "Can't be too careful," he said. Ria thanked them both and drove off. The rest of the journey was uneventful. The weather was cool but dry; the traffic was light. Eventually she arrived at Town 11. It didn't look much like a town, but, well, Mum did say things were different outside London. She slowed down and looked out for the shop. The shop was a small general dealer. Food and household essentials were obviously its main line of business. Mum's directions were spot on. Ten yards after the shop was a road, Nidd Crescent. She turned into it and stopped outside number eight. She got out and retrieved her bag and handbag and pressed the button on the gate. The door of the house opened and an old lady peered out.

"Hello!" she called, with a cheery wave. "Mrs Windlestone?"

"Yes," the woman replied. "Who are you?"

"I'm your Granddaughter, Ria. Hello, Grandma." The old woman's face lit up.

"Ria! I haven't seen you for, well, I'm not sure exactly but it must be more than twenty years. I wasn't expecting you. I was expecting your Mum and Dad for his birthday. Come in." She pressed a button by the door and the gate swung open. Ria went along to the door, where they greeted one another with a big hug.

"Shouldn't have done that yet," said Grandma. "Are you alright? Not got anything?" Ria shook her head, looking guilty.

"You're right, we shouldn't have. But no, I haven't got anything, and I was just tested last week." They went inside.

"Best wash our hands," said Grandma. "Just in case." Ria put her bags down in the hall and went to the washroom and washed her hands thoroughly. When she returned to the hall Grandma led her into the parlour. "Here, have a seat. I'll make us a pot of tea." Ria's eyes opened wide in surprise.

"Tea! Wow! Luxury! I haven't had tea since my twenty-first birthday!"

"Calm down," said Grandma, smiling. "It isn't that much of a luxury in this house."

"Well it is in mine. It's so expensive." Grandma shook her head and went through the door into the kitchen. She put the kettle on, rinsed the teapot and went back into the parlour and sat back in the armchair.

"I wouldn't say it's cheap round here, but I can afford it. The problem is there are so many other things you can't get, so the money builds up. My old dad used to say, 'Spend it while you can 'cos you can't take it with you, and you're a long time dead' and he was right. I try to spend it but there's so much stuff the shops don't have. Of course, they always seem to have the stuff you don't want. Now then, how come you're here and your Mum and Dad aren't? Not that I'm complaining about you turning up, but I was expecting them. Before you answer that, there's the kettle." She went back into the kitchen to make the tea and returned a moment later.

"Well, Mum had planned to bring me up here as well, but didn't tell me. You know what she's like for surprises. All I knew was that I was going to their place for a few days for Dad's birthday, but when I got there Mum met me at the door and said they think he might have the virus." Grandma looked alarmed and put her finger to her lips.

"Sh! Don't mention that thing!" she said urgently. "If you talks about it, you gets it!" Ria looked alarmed.

"Surely you don't believe that, do you?" she said in surprise.

"Not exactly, but a lot of folk round here do. Some of them believe that you can get it anyway, but if you talk about it it's more likely to kill you." Ria shook her head.

"No, I don't believe such old wives' tales. Sorry, I shouldn't have said that, but I don't believe most of the strange rumours about it."

"No need to apologise. I am an old wife. Well, I was. I'm an old widow now, but folks that believe these things, well, most of them *are* old wives, and if you try to tell them it's twaddle you just get a load of abuse. Back in a minute." Back to the kitchen, then she returned with two mugs of tea, which she put down on the hearth. Ria leant forward to pick hers up but Grandma stopped her. "Too hot at the moment. Give it a minute or two. You really aren't used to tea, are you?"

Ria looked embarrassed. "No, s'pose not. Anyway, Dad's fit and healthy, so if he has got it, he'll probably recover okay. So that's why I'm here. Mum said if she wrote you probably wouldn't get her letter before Friday and might be thinking something was wrong if we didn't turn up, and you might have got extra food in by then."

"Food! That's a good point. Look at the time! I bet you haven't eaten since breakfast. Bring your tea and we can chat while I make us some dinner." She went into the kitchen and Ria followed and perched on a stool in the corner. She looked round in amazement. The only thing she recognised was the microwave. Grandma set to peeling and chopping vegetables, then arranged them in an enamel dish with some oil and black pepper and put it into the oven which had been warming up. Ria asked about the electric cooker, the washing machine, and the fridge, none of which she had in her little flat.

"So how do you wash and dry your clothes?" Grandma asked.

"I rub some soap into them in the shower, then rinse them and hang them up in the shower to dry, and a few hours later they are ready to wear again."

"Don't you iron them?"

"What? Iron them? I don't know what you mean." Grandma produced an electric iron from a cupboard and demonstrated an ironing motion and showed a creased skirt from the washing basket waiting to be ironed.

"Flatten them with this so they aren't all creased up."

"Oh, my clothes don't crease. I've never seen clothes crumpled like that before," she said, looking upon the skirt with curiosity. Grandma laughed.

"Perhaps there's something to be said for drying them in the shower. Come upstairs and I'll show you your room while we're waiting for that to cook." Grandma led the way and Ria followed into a bright and cheerful little room with two single beds, a bedside cabinet, a chest of drawers and a small wardrobe. There was a bit of a musty smell, but she opened the window and put a bowl of newly opened pot pourri on the chest. "That'll be okay by bedtime. Give me a hand with these sheets." She got the bedding from the bottom drawer of the chest and they had the bed made in a few minutes. "There, it's smelling better already. Remind me to come up and shut that window about tea time or it will get too cold. How long are you staying?"

"I'd better leave on Saturday at the latest. Friday would be better, because I have to be back at work on Sunday. I'd like to stay longer, but not this time. Now I know where you live I could come up again in the summer. If you don't mind, that is."

"Mind? Of course I don't mind. I've spent twenty-odd years wondering how you turned out. Your mother wrote, but it's not the same as seeing you in the flesh. You can come here whenever you want." They smiled and hugged. Downstairs mouth-watering aromas were drifting through the house from the kitchen. "It'll be ready soon. You sit yourself down at the table there." Grandma brought in place mats and cutlery which Ria set out. Dinner consisted of roast and boiled vegetables, followed by fruit. Ria hadn't eaten so well for years and tucked in with enthusiasm. Grandma asked her about her life in London. "What do you do at work?"

"Well, it's quite boring really. I collect papers from the next office then mark them off on people's cards in the filing cabinet, then I file them away. I don't know what it achieves, but if I get one wrong there is a terrible fuss, so it must be important for something."

"Oh, when I first started work, admittedly a long time ago, we had machines to do that. The machine read the sheet and recorded it on the person's record. Computers they called them. Computers did lots of stuff, but they stopped using them shortly after the 'you know what' came along because they used too much electricity. Everything used a lot of electricity in those days. They wouldn't

266

manage now with the restrictions we have." Ria looked puzzled.

"Restrictions? I don't know what you mean."

"Don't you? Hmm. I'll explain that later. But I want to know more about you for now. What do you do in your spare time?"

"I read a lot and go for walks in the park if there aren't too many people around, and I have a few close friends and we sit and have a chat in the park, sitting well apart of course, but only when the weather is nice. And I do crossword puzzles, and sudokus, and listen to the radio a bit, especially in winter. I tried learning to play the flute once, but it was too difficult so I gave that up. If they offer extra hours at work I'm usually the first to volunteer, because the extra money comes in useful."

"It sounds as though you don't spend much, so what do you do with the extra money?"

"Well, clothes are always wearing out, and I buy quite a lot of books, and there are general bills, rent, keeping the car on the road, you know, normal stuff."

"Speaking of the car, I need a little favour, if you don't mind me asking."

"Of course not. What is it?"

"I need to visit someone. You can stay in the car. It's just to buy something. I usually walk, but it's a long way for my old legs."

"No problem. When do you want to go?"

"Straight after dinner, if that's okay." Ria nodded her agreement as she had a mouthful of delicious vegetables. Just as they were finishing the washing up the doorbell went. "That'll be Keith," said Grandma, and went outside. She came back with a bag of shopping and put it on the

267

floor, then went to her purse and took out some notes. She called to the visitor, "Did you say fifty-three, Keith?"

"Fifty-three point six," he replied.

"I haven't got the right money, so I'll give you sixty and we can square up tomorrow. Here's the list for tomorrow." She returned to the front gate and put the money in the box. Keith took it out as soon as she had gone back inside.

"Keith? Delivery man?" asked Ria.

"No, he's my friend from next-door-but-one. He does my shopping and things like that. I do his washing because his washing machine broke down and they can't get the parts because it's too old, and he can't afford a new one."

"Oh, I see. So is he doing more shopping tomorrow?"

"Yes, he does shopping most days. He's a lovely man but he doesn't have much money so I sometimes give him too much. He's retired, and when his wife was alive they managed alright, only just, but they managed, but after she died they stopped her pension and he's struggled ever since."

"So why do you need more shopping tomorrow? I thought there was only one shop in the town." Grandma got a disinfectant wipe out of the box on the shelf.

"Here's why." She took the list out of the bag and read down it, taking things out of the bag as she came across them and wiping the packets thoroughly before putting them on the table. "No sugar, no plain flour, no bread, no tomatoes, no parsnips. That's why."

"Oh, I see. And will they have them tomorrow?"

"Tomatoes and parsnips he says definitely, if he gets there early enough. Sugar and plain flour are anybody's guess, and as for bread, well. They hope to have them in, but nothing's certain these days." Ria looked puzzled.

"Do they often run out of things? I mean, they're quite basic items, nothing exotic."

"All the time. They always have the exotic stuff. It's the basics they can't get. Can you get them in London?"

"Oh, yes, my local shop never runs out of anything, although they sometimes restrict how much we can have. But a bag of sugar lasts me a year or so, and I never buy flour because I never cook anything. Wouldn't know how to for one thing, and my flat isn't big enough to have one of these cooker things. It must be wonderful to be able to make your own stuff."

"Changing the subject, would now be a good time to visit my friend before we settle down?"

"Yes, I'll get my keys." Grandma's friend didn't live far away, but there was a quite steep hill, so Ria understood why the car was an attractive option. She waited in the car while Grandma went into the house. Five minutes later she was back in the car clutching a little paper bag.

"It's my medication," she explained. "She makes it herself, otherwise I would have to order it three weeks in advance to get it on time. And it puts a bit of money into her pocket and we usually have a little chat while I'm waiting for my poor legs to recover, but she never has anything interesting to say." Ria was too polite to ask what it was for, and she did wonder how safe home-made medicines might be, but she did understand the value of a chat. As soon as they got home Grandma put the bag away in the cupboard without opening it and washed her hands. "Now, young lady, another cup of tea?" Ria smiled.

"Yes, please. I'm not used to this; it's usually water in my house, apart from fruit juice at breakfast." Grandma made the tea and brought it through with a plate of biscuits. "So tell me, Grandma, what was life like when you were young?" Grandma slurped on her hot tea, and an expression came across her face, one of memories, some happy, some sad.

"When I was a little girl, about four or five, we had all manner of things you wouldn't dream of, and we did things you wouldn't dream of either. All the children played together in the school yard, all the grown-ups went to a big house at the end of the street for drinking together, people visited each other's houses all the time, in the hot weather we all went to the seaside and sat together on the beach, oh, so different from today." Ria's eyes opened wide at the thought of such prohibited behaviour. "And we had machines. I was very small when they stopped them, so I only have a vague memory. We had a box in the corner of the room and you could see people singing and dancing and reading the news, just like on the radio, but with pictures. TV they called it, I think. We had a thing called a telephone and you could talk to people miles away with it. Well, then the virus came. It was pretty grim at first, because they brought in all sorts of new laws, a bit like today's rules, about not going to places together, not getting close to people, all the places where they went to eat together closed and half the shops shut as well. The TV thing was stopped because it used too much electricity, and the telephone thing stopped because it carried too many germs. Other things were done away with too, for similar reasons, but I was a little girl and didn't understand. Anyway, after a few years everyone got used to it. And some of these things

270

like flour and sugar were difficult to get for the first few years. And toilet paper. I remember having to use cut up newspaper for quite a while, until they stopped people buying too much." Ria laughed.

"What's newspaper?" she asked.

"It was a bit like a book, except bigger and thinner and without a back. And we got a new one every day, so there was always plenty about, but it could be a bit rough on your bum. They stopped making them because they used up -" but she didn't get the chance to finish.

"Too much electricity," interrupted Ria with a grin. Grandma smiled.

"You're getting the hang of it, girl." She had another slurp of her tea. "Let's sit in the garden for a while before it gets too cold." They took a couple of small stools and sat on the lawn. Ria was amazed at the variety of flowers, and totally puzzled by the vegetables. "I grow a few bits and pieces, but when they're out of season there aren't any. When I was a girl we could get anything all year round, but not now. Since the 'you know what' we don't buy much foreign stuff." Eventually Grandma glanced at her watch and announced it would soon be tea time. They went inside and she got a bowl out of the fridge. Removing the cover, she put it in the microwave. Three minutes, then a stir, then two minutes, and another stir, then the soup was ready. She dished it out and brought a few small pieces of bread.

"Bread!" exclaimed Ria. "First tea, and now bread! Wait 'til I get home and tell my friends. They will be totally jealous." Grandma smiled.

"By the time we've finished this it will be just in time for another cup of tea before the power goes off." Ria looked horrified.

"Power goes off? What do you mean?" Now it was Grandma's turn to look horrified.

"The electricity stops at seven o'clock. Don't they do that in London?" Ria shook her head in astonishment.

"No, we have electricity twenty-four hours a day. And I was thinking you had it easy up here!"

"If that got out there would be riots. It goes off at seven o'clock at this time of year, eight in the winter and six in the summer. No wonder there's a shortage. You lot down there are using it all up."

Ria sipped her soup, thinking. "That explains a lot," she said slowly. "That's why the man at the charging station knew the power would be back on at six. That's why they had no power after dark. It wasn't a power cut – it was the normal shutdown. And that's why Mum said 'don't act surprised and don't admit to being from London'." Grandma nodded wisely. "But what are the 'breakouts'? I've never heard of such things."

"That'll be people out of the house when they shouldn't be. An hour after the power goes off everyone is supposed to be at home, but some folk can't stick to rules if their lives depended on it. It's to reduce crime, because criminals love the dark. Yes, I knew things were different, but I didn't know how different. Time is getting on. I'll make the tea now and by the time we've finished our soup it will be ready." They finished eating, did the washing-up, and settled down in front of the fire with their mugs of tea, listening to the radio. Grandma glanced up at the clock. Seven o'clock. Click – everything went off and they were left in the warm glow of the fire, chatting about Ria's parents, and aunts and uncles she'd never met, and life in the Old Days. At ten o'clock Grandma went to the cupboard and brought out two old candle-holders, a bit like saucers with handles, two short stumpy candles, and two little boxes of matches. They talked a bit more, then they went up to bed with their little candles to light the way. Ria changed into her nightwear and climbed into bed. She blew out the candle and went straight to sleep.

Chapter 3

Ria awoke feeling refreshed. For a moment she wasn't sure where she was, looking round the unfamiliar room, then it all came back to her. She washed and dressed and went downstairs to find Grandma busy in the kitchen.

"Do you like porridge?" Grandma asked without turning round.

"Good morning, Grandma," Ria said. "I don't know, never had it before, but I'm willing to give it a try, if that's what you normally have."

"Yes, I have porridge every day. Keeps you regular. I would like to offer you toast but I haven't got any. Bread, I mean; think of it as raw toast. We used the last of it last night. Perhaps tomorrow – we'll see what Keith can get at the shop." Ria smiled. Toast was another luxury she didn't have at home.

"Anything I can do to help?" she asked. Grandma shook her head.

"No, dear, you sit down. You're my guest."

"Yes," Ria replied. "But I'm also family. You don't have to wait on me hand and foot."

"Yes, but you can't cook," Grandma laughed. "Go and set the table. The place mats are in the table drawer and the spoons are in here. Then sit in there and look pleasant." She pointed at the cutlery drawer in the kitchen dresser. Ria did as she was told. Grandma dished out the porridge, then took a little bottle from one of the drawers in the kitchen. After making sure Ria couldn't see, she put one drop of the liquid into her own porridge and four into Ria's and stirred vigorously to mix it in well before taking the bowls through to the front room. She gently placed them on the table with a smile and sat opposite Ria. "Tuck in, dear, eat it before it gets cold." They ate in silence. It didn't take long, then Ria got up and cleared the table. Grandma joined her in the kitchen and they did the washing-up together.

"What are you doing today?" Ria asked. "Do you need any help with anything? Taking out in the car, for instance?"

"No, dear. I'm doing Keith's washing today. You can help with that if you want, but it's only to set away then wait for it to finish. Then when it's dry you can have a go at ironing!" Her face split into a grin with a wicked glint in her eye. "If you think you're capable."

Ria smiled. "Yes, I'll give it a go."

"Come on, then, let's get started, then we can sit and chat while the machine does its work." Grandma retrieved Keith's laundry from a bag in the far corner of the kitchen and unpacked it into the washing machine. She showed Ria where and how to put the washing powder and conditioner in and pressed the 'start' button. They returned to the front room and had just sat down when the doorbell went. Grandma went to the door and looked outside. Keith stood by the gate, so she went to talk to him. His trip to the shop had been more fruitful than yesterday and she came back with a big bag of shopping. She gave him some money, and off he went. Ria went into the kitchen and helped clean the items while Grandma put them away. They sat down with a mug of tea.

"What do you do for the rest of the week?" Ria asked.

"Well, I do washing for one or two others, but usually only once a month, when their electricity is running short; Keith is the only one I do every week."

"Running short? How does that work?"

"Life up here is obviously a lot different to in London. Are you telling me your electricity isn't monitored?"

"We have meters, but I think that's mainly for working out the bill. I don't think they bother about how much we use."

Grandma shook her head in disbelief. "We have electricity quotas and if you go over your allowance, when it goes off at night it doesn't come back on the next morning until the end of the month."

Ria looked shocked. "So how do they manage?" Grandma pointed at the fire.

"That's why we have fires. You can keep warm and boil a kettle and make soup and porridge and toast even if you can't do ought else. I can't believe you can do what you like with the electric in London."

"Ah, but we aren't allowed fires in our flats. I know Mum and Dad have one in their house but I thought that was just a touch of luxury. Never realised it had a practical use."

"You're not very good at the practical side of life, are you."

Ria looked embarrassed. "No, s'pose not." She sipped at her tea. "But I can learn a lot from you and amaze my friends when I go back," she said with enthusiasm.

Grandma smiled a knowing smile. "I'll make dinner now, unless you want to do it."

"Ooh, yes! That'll be another new skill. I've only ever used the microwave. I have a toaster, but it doesn't get an outing very often because I rarely have bread."

"Good. Then by the time we've eaten, the washing machine will be just about finished, and it will be ready for ironing just after tea," she said after a glance at the clock.

Ria set about peeling and chopping the vegetables, under Grandma's supervision, and almost burned her hands, not realising that the cooker door and shelves were hot. They sat down in front of the fire with mugs of tea.

"How else has life changed since you were a girl, Grandma?" Ria asked. "What did you eat in the old days?" Grandma smiled a wicked smile.

"You'll not believe some of the stuff we ate," she said. "We had meat in those days."

"Meat? What's that?"

"You've never heard of meat? This is going to take some explaining. Have you ever been to a farm?" Ria shook her head. "Well, on farms today they grow cereals and vegetables and fruit, but in the old days they used to grow meat, too." Ria nodded her head.

"Yes, I saw some farms on the way here; fields full of green things and yellow things."

"Well, try to imagine something a bit like a person, like you or me, but a different shape, and with four legs instead of two." She paused to give this idea a chance to sink in. Ria pondered for a while, then her face lit up.

"Oh, you mean animals, like in the zoo!" she said, then sat back in the chair and laughed. "I thought it was going to be something complicated!" Grandma was appalled.

"In the zoo? You know about zoos?"

"Yes, of course. I've been to London Zoo a few times, in Regent's Park. Didn't you know about it?" Grandma wasn't pleased.

"Of course I knew about it. But they closed down all the zoos when I was a teenager. Too expensive to run, they said. The animals use up valuable food which could be used for starving people, they said. It's a luxury we can't afford, they said. I loved going to the zoo, but that had to stop. Obviously not in London!" Ria touched Grandma's forearm.

"Oh, that's really sad. Perhaps you can come and visit me sometime, and I'll take you to the zoo. We can stay all day!"

"Anyway, as I was saying, in the old days we used to grow animals on farms and eat them."

Ria was horrified. "Eat the animals? That's disgusting! I'm pleased they stopped that. It must have been horrible being made to eat animals."

"Oh, no. Not *made* to eat them, just *allowed* to eat them. They tasted lovely; well, most of them did. But that all stopped because it cost too much to feed them so one day they announced that when the current lot were all gone that would be it; no more meat."

Ria was flabbergasted. "Well, I don't know what to say about that, other than it's a good thing they stopped it." Just then the washing machine beeped to signal it had finished. They went into the kitchen and hung Keith's clothes on a clothes horse to dry, then set about preparing the soup for tea. After tea Grandma set the ironing board up and showed Ria how to iron the clothes.

"This isn't easy, but I can see it's worth it. These shirts look much nicer than my stuff does when it's just been hung in the shower."

"You're doing a good job," smiled Grandma. "But you're taking too long over it." She glanced at the clock on the wall. "You've been at that for over an hour; it would take me about twenty minutes." She smiled and patted Ria on the shoulder. "But don't be despondent – all you need is practice." Ria smiled.

"Yes, but my flat isn't big enough for an ironing board, so I won't get much." They returned to the chairs by the fire.

"It's lovely having you here," Grandma said. "Just lovely having someone to talk to."

"But you've got Keith, and your friend round the corner."

"Not really. Elsie never has anything new to say; she just repeats what she said last time. And Keith doesn't talk at all about anything, except his washing and the shopping. No, having you here is like a ray of sunshine." Grandma popped into the kitchen and managed to slip a couple of drops of her special liquid into Ria's tea without being noticed.

* * *

Two weeks later

Ria came downstairs rubbing her eyes and yawning.

"Good morning, Grandma," she said sleepily. "I'm feeling really tired, and I have a bit of a headache. It must be from that long drive yesterday."

"Yes, very probably," said Grandma, slipping a few drops of liquid into Ria's porridge. "Sit yourself down at the table and have some breakfast; it'll make you feel better." Ria did as instructed. Grandma brought the porridge in and was just about to sit down when a letter dropped through the letter box. She picked it up and opened it as she sat down.

Dear Mum, hope you are okay. Did you enjoy Ria's visit? Unfortunately, I have some sad news. Donald died yesterday. The virus was too strong for him. Father Michael will say a Mass for him and he has sent me some prayers to say. I don't think I will ever see you again, because I have it now. I'm not sad about that because it means I will soon be with my lovely Donald, and we'll be together forever. Ria didn't call in to see us, which is just as well really. She probably has a lot of catching up to do at work. All my love, your loving daughter, Maxine.

A tear rolled down her cheek. Ria noticed her sad expression and asked, "What's up, Grandma? You look sad."

"Oh, yes. Some people I know – one of them has died and the other will soon." She quickly folded the letter and put it in her pocket as Ria came round the table to comfort her. Grandma got up and they hugged for a while, then they sat down again.

"I know now probably isn't a good time to talk about it, but I really need to go back on Friday. If the journey is going to give me this sort of headache, I'll need a day to recover. I'm only away for a week, but I bet there's loads to do back at the office. No one does my job when I'm away. Horrible lot." She kissed Grandma tenderly on the cheek and returned to her seat. She held Grandma's hand while she finished her porridge.

"Oh, I understand. You're being her is a real comfort to me. I don't want you to leave, but you have your life and friends back in London." They finished breakfast and did the washing up. Ria sat in the chair by the fire while

Grandma tidied up in the kitchen. The doorbell went. Ria looked out of the window.

"Grandma, there's a man at the gate," she called. Grandma came bustling through and looked out.

"Oh, it's just Keith," she said casually. She went to the gate and talked to Keith.

"Keith," Ria said to herself. "I know that name from somewhere, but not sure where."

Other books by this author

Rookery Villa and other strange tales

A collection of stories showing the impact ghosts and witches can have on normal people's lives. What can possibly go wrong when you're away on holiday? Then again, what can possibly go wrong when you stay at home?

Rookery Villa – Fiona and her family lose their home and go to stay with her mother until they find somewhere. But her childhood home has memories.

Holiday Breakdown – Two young couples from London are on holiday when their car breaks down in North Yorkshire. A jovial old lady offers them shelter until they get it repaired, and a little longer.

The Big House – Lizzie invites her best friend, Maddie, to spend a week with Aunty in her country mansion. Aunty turns out to be a bit stranger than Maddie expected.

PW (in brackets) – Four young women on a camping holiday come across the ruins of an ancient church. The church – and the nearby village – have dark pasts that come to the surface.

Available from Amazon

Printed in Great Britain
by Amazon

57109624R00163